Dead in Devon

By Stephanie Austin

Dead in Devon
Dead on Dartmoor

a&b

Dead in Devon

STEPHANIE AUSTIN

Allison & Busby Limited
11 Wardour Mews
London W1F 8AN
allisonandbusby.com

First published in Great Britain by Allison & Busby in 2019.
This paperback edition published by Allison & Busby in 2019.

A CIP catalogue record for this book is available from
the British Library.

10 9 8 7 6 5 4 3 2 1

ISBN 978-0-7490-2417-8

Typeset in 10.5/15.5 pt Sabon LT Pro by
Allison & Busby Ltd.

The paper used for this Allison & Busby publication
has been produced from trees that have been legally sourced
from well-managed and credibly certified forests.

Printed and bound by
CPI Group (UK) Ltd, Croydon, CR0 4YY

For Martin

AUTHOR'S NOTE

The town of Ashburton is real, and people living there will recognise streets, shops, pubs, cafes and other places of good cheer mentioned in this book, but there are a few foggy areas around the town where fact and my imagination merge, places that will not be found on any map. For taking these liberties, I apologise.

PROLOGUE

Murder is a messy business, especially for the person who has to clear up afterwards: in this case, me. I didn't commit the murder, you understand, I just found it. Him, I found him: poor Old Nick lying on the hearthrug, his skull smashed in and a lot of what should have been inside it spattered across the tiles of his fireplace.

I knew something was wrong when I arrived at his front door. It should have been tight shut, that door, leaving me staring at the scratched, black paintwork as I waited for Nick's shuffling footsteps to approach, heard the rattle as he drew back all the bolts and wondered, for the umpteenth time, why the silly old fool didn't save himself the bother and let me have a key. Very tight on security was Old Nick.

But the door moved at my touch, swung wide as I pushed it, leaving me staring down the corridor at the half-glass door that led to the back of the shop, and at the stairs rising to the flat above. I should have been following him up those stairs, listening to his laboured breathing as he climbed, hearing his radio playing in the kitchen, smelling his breakfast toast.

As I began to go up, I called out. There was no sound of running water from the bathroom on the landing, no movement from behind the frosted glass panel in the door. I tapped on the glass anyway and called his name. As I reached the turn of the stair I could see the main light was on in the living room, although it was daylight outside. I ran up the last few steps, calling out, thinking perhaps he'd had an accident, or a stroke, that he'd been lying there all night: which, as it turned out, he had.

'What were you doing there?' the detective inspector asked me later, as we sat across the table from one another, in a hastily requisitioned interview room at the back of an estate agent's.

'It's Tuesday. I work for Old . . . for . . . Mr Nickolai on a Tuesday,' I explained.

'What do you do?' He was a large, kindly-looking man, probably someone's favourite uncle, and was doing his best to set me at my ease. Not so his companion, the young detective constable sitting beside him. From her there emanated an air of silent contempt, almost hostility. Perhaps she was practising her bad cop; perhaps she just didn't like me. She was a striking-looking girl, ebony hair bobbed around a pale face and large, violet-blue eyes, but her mouth was disapproving and small, almost lipless, like the mark left by a fingernail in uncooked pastry.

'All sorts . . . furniture and things . . .' I answered, '. . . for Mr Nickolai.'

I wasn't at my most coherent.

'You're his cleaner?' The inspector's sandy eyebrows shot up in surprise.

'If you don't mind my saying, you seem too . . .' He left the sentence hanging but I knew what he was getting at.

'I'm working my way down in the world.'

My voice didn't sound my own. My throat ached with sobs, with silent screams.

I rolled the ragged ball of damp tissue up my hot cheek and sniffed, staring into the mug of walnut-brown tea growing cold on the table in front of me. I'd tried picking it up earlier, but my hand had shaken too much and I'd been forced to abandon the attempt.

'Now, Miss Browne . . . may I call you June . . . ?' The inspector asked gently.

'Juno,' I corrected him. 'My name is Juno.'

'Juno?' he repeated. 'Like the goddess?' The young detective constable gave the faintest smirk, a tiny tug of her little mouth. Perhaps she didn't think I was goddess material.

'Is that your van parked across the road, the old Astra?' The inspector went on, making a connection, '"Domestic Goddess" is written on the side. Is that yours?'

Mine. All mine. You can't really miss it. It's a bright, cheery yellow with black writing. *'Juno Browne, Domestic Goddess – Housework, Gardening, Home Help, Domestic Care, House-sitting, Pet-sitting, Dog-walking. No job too small*.' The paint job had cost me more than the vehicle.

'So, you clean Mr Nickolai's flat?' He returned to the murder in hand.

It was a bit more complicated than that. 'Not his flat, no . . . He employed me to help him with his stock . . . clean up things he might want to sell . . . take to auction . . . But recently, he decided to reopen the shop. I've been helping him get it ready, redecorating . . .'

'How long have you been working for him?'

'Um . . . about five months.'

'You got to know him pretty well?'

I nodded, forced to blow my nose. 'Yes, I think so.'

'Juno, do you know of any reason why anyone would have wanted to harm Mr Nickolai?'

I hesitated for a fraction too long and he leant forward intently.

'There were the Russians,' I breathed out at last.

'Russians?' he repeated, frowning.

I sniffed into the disintegrating tissue and nodded.

He cast a brief glance at his companion and then back at me. 'What Russians?'

CHAPTER ONE

It was the day before I met Nick, the day he phoned. It must have been back in May. I'd taken the Tribe out in the morning, as usual, and loaded them into the back of the van at the end of our run. They were exhausted after racing around up on Whiddon Scrubs, and there was much heavy panting and scratching going on.

I'd parked the van on the brow of the hill, the last place before the road drops down towards Ashburton, the last place I could be sure to pick up a phone signal. Down in the town it's patchy to say the least, and where I live it's non-existent. I slid behind the steering wheel and dropped the silent dog whistle into my shoulder bag. Somewhere in that cavernous void lurked my mobile phone and I rooted around until I found it. There were no messages. I glanced in the rear-view mirror. Behind the wire grille that separated us, Nookie the Huskie gazed at me with eyes of Arctic blue before she yawned, turned around a couple of times, and lay down with the others.

As I started up the engine, I lingered a moment over the view. It was still early, the sky pale and soft, dove grey above distant trees, where the tower of St Andrew's pierced the mist that floated in a veil over the valley. I turned the ignition, the radio blurted into life and Vivaldi spilt out all over the Devon countryside.

He interests me, Vivaldi. They used to call him The Red Priest. Perhaps other red-haired people just catch my attention. Anyway, all that strident strumming of violins was a bit intense for such an early hour, and I turned the radio off.

The old Astra rattled down the hill. We were among fields now. The whistling winds and gorse of the moor were far behind us, tatty sheep and shaggy ponies left nibbling by the roadside. In the wing mirror the sign recommending travellers to *Drive with Moor Care* disappeared as we rounded a bend. Our road dipped, vanishing between dense hedgerows frothy with white cow parsley, tiny pink stars of campion sparkling among dark ferns. This is one of the back roads into Ashburton, where trees mesh overhead in a tunnel of flickering green. It's pretty enough, but dwindles to a narrow twisting lane with few passing places, and as everyone who lives locally seems to drive a tractor or a four-by-four, and is either incapable of backing, or unprepared to give an inch on grounds of vehicular superiority, it can be a two-wheels-forward, four-wheels-back sort of journey.

That morning I was lucky, forced to pull in only once, stopping by a farm gate to let a tractor trundle by, and delivered the members of the Tribe to their respective homes without much delay. Sally, the arthritic Labrador was joyfully received by her equally arthritic owner, but Nookie had to be let into an empty house and fed. At least, after her run, she would sleep away the morning, and her lonely wait for her family to return would not be too long.

Ashburton is a nook-and-cranny sort of place, a solid stannary town of narrow streets and even narrower pavements, 'nestling' as the guidebooks like to say, among hills on Dartmoor's doorstep. In distance the town is a mere slip road away from the A38; in time, a century or more: a place where old cottages and ancient pubs stand wedged between elegant Edwardian town houses, a place of quaint corners, secret courtyards and long walled walks. It's a honeytrap for tourists and day trippers coming off the Expressway, the last place for a comfort stop before they head on up to the moor, the perfect setting for a cream tea or a pint of local ale, a leisurely browse among shops selling expensive gifts and artisan foods, shops selling nothing which is not rustic, artistic or picturesque. There are no fewer than sixteen antique shops, and that's not counting the flea market and the auctioneers, and most of these are packed within the framework of streets surrounding the broad junction where East Street becomes West Street, and North Street becomes St Lawrence's Lane.

The old town looks lovely, but it's a nightmare for the poor working woman trying to go about her business, getting stuck behind coaches in streets that were never intended for anything wider than a horse and cart, or trying to avoid knocking over knots of trippers, who stand about like waiting skittles in the middle of the road as they gawp at the delights around them. By the time I turned off North Street, my temper was not so much frayed as shredded. After walking the Tribe, I'd done two hours' house-cleaning for the odious Verbena Clarke, it was way past my lunchtime and I was starving hungry. You wouldn't like me when I'm hungry.

The lane in which I live is quieter than the main thoroughfare and a lot less picturesque. No Georgian houses in sugar-almond colours here, no thatches and hollyhocks, just a narrow cobbled street with what used to be a bookshop, now sadly boarded up, halfway down. The only other building of interest is *Sunflowers*, the vegetarian cafe owned by my landlords, Adam and Kate, set in what was once an old stable.

Beyond this, the pavement narrows to nothing, the cobbles peter out and the road degrades into a rough track pocked with potholes and gives up entirely in a dead-end patch of ground edged with a tangle of dusty bramble bushes and dominated by an old Victorian lamp post. Some people regard this as an excellent place to abandon shopping trolleys, tip old mattresses, dispose of defunct microwaves and the like. I use it to park the van. Not that anyone is likely to be mad enough to want to steal it, but parked there I can see it from the house, if I peer out of the window on the landing.

Adam and Kate inherited a cavernous Victorian property, which they have never had enough money to renovate. It's gloomy and damp, with creaking floorboards and rotten window frames, but there's little rental accommodation in Ashburton, the rent is cheap, and beggars can't be choosers. They're happy to have a tenant living above them who doesn't complain about the mouldy wall in her kitchen, the windows rattling, or the draught screaming like a banshee under the living-room door. To be fair, they've made several attempts to improve the place, but always run out of funds before these improvements can be completed. *Sunflowers* is not in a prime trading position and doesn't do as well as its excellent menu deserves.

When I got back that morning my landlords were still at the cafe, dealing with lunches, and the house was empty. I trotted up the steps from the garden gate, making a mental note that it was time I gave the shrubs in the front garden a good haircut.

I was on a promise to look after them that I hadn't honoured for some time.

I let myself in and went upstairs. Although the first floor is technically mine, I don't have a door that blocks it off entirely. The landing is shared territory because of access to the airing cupboard and the loft. I could see Kate had been upstairs today. A plastic box had been left on the table outside my living-room door, an offering from *Sunflowers*. 'Aubergine and Potato Curry' was scrawled on the label, the writing blurred by partial defrosting. I picked it up with a smile. Having landlords who own a cafe means there are always plenty of leftovers, and I'm not proud.

My flat consists of a living room, a small kitchen, one

bedroom with a brass bedstead and tiny original fireplace, and a bathroom with a dodgy boiler.

I unlocked the living room. Bill was sitting on the windowsill pretending to be a vase, his tail curled neatly round his feet. He likes the view from my living-room window, looking down into the mad tangle of the oddly shaped garden beneath, across to a crooked line of rooftops, and the green hills beyond. I stroked the short, black velvet between his ears and he started a deep, rasping purr, turning his head to gaze at me adoringly from one blazing, emerald eye. He'd lost the other as a kitten, in an encounter with an outraged chicken and his beautiful black nose was raked by long scratches. Bill's not my cat, you understand; he belongs to Adam and Kate downstairs. Whenever I leave my place I make sure he's locked out; and whenever I come home, he's back inside. Like a magician, it seems he can enter and exit at will; none of us can work out how he does it.

I made myself a mug of coffee, a peanut butter and banana sandwich and settled down in the armchair, kicking off my shoes and heaving my socked feet up on to the coffee table. I raked my fingers through the tangled mess of my curls and gave my head a rub.

Bill stretched his long body on the windowsill and wandered over to join me, leaping on my lap and flexing his claws into my thighs in appreciation. 'It's no good settling down,' I told him through a mouthful of sandwich, 'I don't expect I'll be here long.' I could see the red light flashing on the answerphone and reached over him awkwardly to press play.

I didn't recognise the voice. It was foreign and heavily accented, hesitant, awkward at talking to a machine. *I want speak to Miss Browne . . . er . . . Juno. This is Mr Nickolai . . . Nickolai Antiques. I want her come work for me.* He left a number. I dislodged a disgruntled Bill so I could reach for a pen to jot it down, and then phoned back.

'Mr, Nickolai?' I asked when the phone was picked up. 'Juno Browne. You called about a job?'

He gave a rich chuckle. 'You come today?'

'No, I'm sorry. I'm already booked for the rest of the day.' I'd received a distress call yesterday from Ricky and Morris and had promised the afternoon to them. I couldn't let them down.

My diary was open, ready on my lap. 'I'm pretty full up tomorrow,' I told him. 'But I could pop around about lunchtime, to discuss the job.'

'S'good. Tomorrow. Nickolai Antiques, you know where is?'

'Shadow Lane?'

He grunted in assent. 'Do not come shop door – flat door, round side.'

'I'll find it. About twelve o'clock, then?'

'See you twelve o'clock. I look forward.' He chuckled again. 'I never met goddess before.'

'Mr Nickolai, are you looking for a regular cleaner . . . ?' But he'd already rung off. 'Because I don't have any regular slots left,' I added lamely and put the receiver down.

CHAPTER TWO

When I first arrived in Ashburton I needed a job and somewhere to live. Ricky and Morris helped me find both and although I've built up a business of my own since then, I try to give them my time whenever they need me.

They run a theatrical costume hire business from their home in Druid Lane, a grand Georgian house standing in splendid isolation on a hill overlooking the town. It's the sort of house that you imagine in Jane Austen novels, an elegantly proportioned building, painted white, with long windows perfectly aligned on either side of an imposing front door, and set amongst wide, sweeping lawns.

Ricky inherited the place from an aunt. He and Morris met many years ago as chorus boys and decided to make use of Morris's tailoring background and Ricky's flair for design, and set up as theatrical costumiers, 'serving', as their website puts it, 'professional and amateur theatres up and down the country'. Nowadays, they keep claiming they're longing to retire. This, of course, is perfect bullshit. Suggest they begin the process by selling off any of their stock and they both have the vapours. Four of their six bedrooms are currently devoted to costumes and the attics are stuffed with hats, wigs and shoes.

Ricky must have spotted the van coming up the drive because the front door swung open as I approached. 'The goddess of Arsehole-in-the-Moor!' he declaimed, bowing low as I walked past him into the hall. 'Bless you for coming, my angel!' he added devoutly.

In his youth, Ricky had what might be described as Byronic good looks. Even now, somewhere in his seventies, his iron-grey curls fell becomingly, if not quite so thickly, over his noble brow. He had an aquiline nose, a strong jaw and looked as I imagine Mr Rochester might look, except, in his case, Jane Eyre would have been sadly disappointed on her wedding night.

'What's up?' I asked, eyeing the four wicker laundry hampers standing open in the lofty hall.

'Amateur company in Leicester are doing *Wizard of Oz* next week,' he explained rapidly, 'and their costumiers have let them down. They've asked us to help them out. So we have to get everything ready for the morning – the couriers are coming to fetch it all at nine.'

'Good job I've got the afternoon free.' I would normally have been cleaning for Mrs Berkeley-Smythe, but she was away on a cruise.

'*Maurice* is up in the workroom,' Ricky went on, 'you go on up. I'm just printing off the paperwork on the computer and I'll be with you.'

I negotiated my way around the laundry hampers, and climbed the curving staircase, unable to resist running my hand up the smooth, polished bannister. Morris was in the workroom, shaking out a jumble of fur fabric and muttering to himself.

If Ricky was Rochester, then Morris was Pickwick. If Ricky's features were carved in granite, Morris's were moulded in clay, all roundness. He peered over his little gold specs and grinned at me like an elderly baby. 'I swear this lion's got moth—Hello, Juno! Good of you to come.'

I bent down and planted a kiss on his soft cheek, 'My pleasure.' I could see the Wicked Witch of the West was already occupying an otherwise empty clothes rail, her black pointy hat hanging on elastic.

Ricky came up the stairs, puffing slightly, clutching a sheaf of actors' measurements that the Leicester theatre company had emailed through. '*Wizard of Oz* isn't a huge show,' he told me as he ran an eye over the lists. He raised an eyebrow. 'Their Dorothy's a bit of a porker! I doubt if that blue gingham will fit.'

'What would you like me to do?'

'Find the Scarecrow, and the Tin Man!' He thrust sheets of actors' measurements at me. 'And make sure the Tin Man's got all his bits!'

'If you don't mind, Juno,' Morris added, more politely.

For the next two hours the three of us hunted, sorted and packed, but the Tin Man had lost his funnel hat, we could only find one of Dorothy's ruby slippers, and we'd lost Glinda, the Good Witch of the North, altogether. We decided to stop for tea.

'You got any time tomorrow, darlin'?' Ricky lit one of his menthol cigarettes as we sat around the breakfast-room table, lifting his chin to aim his puff of smoke above our heads.

''Fraid not. Busy day tomorrow and I'm seeing a new client at lunchtime – well, he may turn into a new client . . . Mr Nickolai.'

'You don't mean Old Nick?' Ricky gaped at me.

'Is he still alive?' Morris frowned. 'He must be older than God.'

'Mr Nickolai,' I repeated. 'He runs an antique shop in Shadow Lane, although it always seems to be shut whenever I go by.'

'All his business gets done at the back door,' Ricky pulled a face suggestively. 'What's he want you for?'

'To clean his house, I imagine.'

Morris wagged a warning finger. 'You be careful, Juno.'

I was used to their theatrics but, in spite of myself, I had to ask. 'Why?'

'He's been inside, more than once.'

'For receiving stolen goods,' Ricky added in a stage whisper.

'Really?' I asked, in what I hoped was a pinch-of-salt type voice.

'And other stuff,' Morris added, nodding like an old woman.

'What other stuff?'

'Nickolai isn't his real name either.' Ricky flicked ash from his cigarette with a shoulder-shrugging elegance any Hollywood movie-queen would envy. 'It's short for . . . Nickoloviza . . . something longer.'

'He sounded vaguely Russian on the phone,' I admitted. 'Sort of middle European. What other stuff?' I asked again.

As I didn't get an answer, I strongly suspected this was just theatrical embellishment, until Morris mouthed the word 'blackmail' at me. 'You make sure he pays you properly.' He winced as he bit into a biscuit. 'He's been a right old chiseller in his time.'

'I haven't agreed to work for him yet,' I pointed out. 'I'm just meeting him tomorrow.' I glanced at the kitchen clock. 'What time's your concert?'

'Oh my God! Half past five already!' Ricky hastily stubbed out his cigarette. 'And we're not finished yet!'

'I'll finish putting the costumes together,' I volunteered, 'if you two want to rehearse.'

'We do need to run through a couple of things,' Morris admitted apologetically, hastily gathering up cups and clattering them in the sink. 'Can you cope, Juno?'

'Don't worry. You carry on.' The concert was a fundraiser for the local hospice. For years Ricky and Morris had performed as a double act. *Sauce and Slander*, they called themselves. They'd begin the evening with light operatic songs and witty repartee, gradually progress to biting satire and descend into scurrilous filth. They were very, very popular.

Ricky had already disappeared into the music room and commanding chords rang out from the grand piano. 'C'mon *Maurice*, get your fat arse in here!'

Morris grinned at me and bustled off to join him.

'*Take a pair of sparkling eyes*' – his mellifluous tones followed me as I climbed back up the stairs – '*take a tender little hand fringed with dainty fingerettes . . .*'

Gilbert and Sullivan is not my thing. I resisted the temptation to put my dainty fingerettes down the back of my throat and applied myself to playing hunt the ruby slipper. By the time Ricky and Morris had run through their material and got themselves ready, I'd found the missing items and had packed up most of the costumes. Each one was on a hanger, labelled with the name of the actor it was destined for, and sheathed in a thin polythene bag. Instead of lugging them all downstairs to the waiting hampers, I'd used the time-honoured method of dropping them over the bannisters on to the immaculate marble of the hall floor, then picked each one up, folding it and packing it neatly.

'Everything's labelled,' I told them, struggling to do up the leather straps of a hamper as they appeared, bow tied and cummerbunded, in the hallway. 'I've just got to put the address labels on the hampers for the courier tomorrow.' Fortunately, the hampers were on wheels. When I'd finished labelling, I could roll them up to the front door, ready for the morning. All Ricky and Morris had to do was push the hampers straight out to the waiting courier's van.

'Where did you find Glinda?' Morris asked.

'In with the *Cinderella* costumes. Remember last year, the lady who couldn't fit into Fairy Godmother? We gave her Glinda instead.'

'Juno, you're a marvel!' Ricky pressed a wad of notes into my palm, about twice my hourly rate. 'Don't argue!' he added, before I could protest.

'You don't need to pay me this much . . .' I began.

'What else can we do, if you won't let us adopt you?'

I gave a crack of laughter. They'd offered me a permanent job on several occasions, but much as I love 'em, I couldn't work with Ricky and Morris all the time. Half an hour in their company is usually enough to drive me insane. I glanced at my watch. 'You'd better get going. I can finish here and let myself out.'

Morris stood on tiptoe to kiss me. 'Just drop the latch. And you be careful with Mr Nickolai tomorrow,' he added. 'They don't call him Old Nick for nothing!'

I was ravenous by the time I got home, my hunger pangs made sharper by the cooking aromas that always hang around in the hallway downstairs waiting to mug me. At the sound of my arrival, Kate poked her head out of the kitchen door, her dark plait swinging over her shoulder. She has the hair I've always longed for: dark, sleek and straight, hair you can actually drag a comb through.

'Curry any good?' she asked, smiling.

'I'm about to find out.'

'Well, let me know what you think, it's a new recipe,' she said, and she and her plait disappeared.

Bill was sleeping in my chair when I got in the living room. As I swung my bag down from my shoulder, I heard Adam calling him downstairs. 'Sounds like your dinner time too,' I told him, scooping him up. 'You'd better go.'

By the time I opened the door, Adam was already standing outside it. 'Get your own cat, Juno,' he told me, taking a struggling Bill from my arms.

26

'My landlord won't let me.'

He nodded sadly. 'It must be tough.' Bill was wriggling in his grasp and he tucked him firmly under one arm and marched him downstairs.

The curry was worth the wait. After I'd eaten, I opened up my laptop in the vague hope that the hub might be working. The witterings on social media only serve to convince me that I'm living in the wrong century. I think the Middle Ages might have suited me better; I'm sure I could have coped with warfare, plague and pestilence better than the irritations of modern life. I scribbled belated happy birthdays on a couple of timelines, cooed dutifully over the latest baby pictures, and reminded a friend, who complained that I'm permanently unreachable because of Ashburton's erratic mobile signal, that I do still have a landline. All of my old friends from school or university seemed to be either having babies or living in vibrant cities, pursuing dazzling careers. I'm doing neither. Well, good luck to 'em. I care not, I like it where I am.

There was an email from my only surviving relative, my cousin Brian, a diplomat in South Korea, asking if I was still looking after other people's grannies and other people's pets and if I was OK for money. It was great to hear from him. I emailed back that I was fine.

Of course this was a lie. I've never got enough money. I know I only have to ask but I won't take advantage of Brian's generosity unless the wolf has got through the door and is actually sinking its fangs into my thigh.

I hauled myself off to bed; we dog-walkers have to get up early. Before I switched the light out, I consulted my diary for the next day. Owing to the haphazard way my business has developed I see some of my clients once a week, others once a fortnight, a few once a month and the rest only when they feel like it. Without my diary, I am lost. Tomorrow promised something new, it promised a meeting with Ashburton's master criminal: it promised Mr Nickolai.

CHAPTER THREE

At first glance *Nickolai Antiques* was not encouraging. For a start, it was definitely off-piste as far as the summer visitors are concerned. Their progress, once they've parked or been deposited in the very dinky car park behind the town hall and made use of the toilets nearby, will almost certainly take them on a pleasant meander from tea room to antique shop, to pub to museum to cafe, window-shopping in places selling local art and pottery, handcrafted jewellery and hand-blown glass, moorland honey and even moorland chocolate and gin, and return to their transport without needing to leave the tightly woven heart of the town.

Nickolai Antiques is tucked away around too many corners from all of this, out of sight in Shadow Lane, a narrow, cobbled street that rarely catches any sun and boasts nothing else of interest but a launderette and an undertaker. I peered in windows criss-crossed by security grilling, the glass so filthy and fogged up with condensation that I couldn't see inside, the surrounding cream paintwork filmed with a grey layer that hadn't been washed off in years. A cardboard sign on the door, scrawled in crayon, announced that the shop was closed. I couldn't imagine wanting to go inside anyway.

Down the side of the shop was a narrow alleyway between tall buildings, not one of Ashburton's famous walled walks, but a convenient nip-through running between Shadow Lane and Sun Street, and somewhere I had never, until that day, nipped myself.

About halfway down I found the door to the flat above. I pressed the bell, which responded with a sick rattle, and waited, staring at the scratched, black paintwork. Sometimes I have nightmares about standing in front of that door, pushing it with my fingertips, seeing it yawn open. But on that morning I just wondered what was taking so long. After a full minute there was a shuffling footstep, a drawing back of heavy bolts and Mr Nickolai opened the door.

I realised I knew him by sight – a shabby little man in a sagging grey cardigan. He was short, but thickset and powerful, as if he might once have been a wrestler.

I reckoned he was at least eighty, with wiry grey hair surrounding a balding crown and a drooping, sandy-coloured moustache. The hand he held out for me to shake was thick-fingered and strong, stained around the nails, not by nicotine, but something like wood stain or preservative.

He smelt very slightly of furniture polish, and the smell that old people living alone sometimes have, of neglect. But his handshake was vigorous and his blue eyes were bright, alive and wicked.

'Miss Browne.' His accent was strong.

'Juno, please.'

He smiled and white dentures gleamed below the bushy moustache.

'Come upstairs,' he beckoned. 'We talk.'

I followed him to the floor above, passing what I guessed was a bathroom on the landing, and turned up a few more steps into his living room. It was crammed with dark furniture, the floor a patchwork of faded, patterned rugs. A pretty Victorian fireplace with green tiles and a brass fender surrounded a more modern gas fire, the mantelshelf cluttered with ornaments and what looked like a month's unopened post. Chessmen were set out ready on a small table between two armchairs. The oldest television set I have ever seen stood in one corner, its twelve-inch screen heavily encased in wood.

Mr Nickolai followed the direction of my gaze. 'Not work,' he confirmed, dismissing it with a wave of his hand. 'I don't care. Crap on TV. I listen to radio.'

Sitting on a desk in the opposite corner was a laptop, looking as if it had landed from another planet and passed through several time zones along the way.

'Internet I like,' he told me. 'Online auction I watch, keep up with prices.'

'But you don't open your shop?'

'Shop?' He shrugged. 'Shop full of junk.'

He gestured at a table, which took up the centre of the room, its brown chenille cloth thickly spread with newspapers. Some kind of restoration work was going on.

A well-worn pair of rubber gloves, yellow fingers blackened like ripe bananas, lay amongst a collection of bottles and old jam jars. Scraps of leather, lumps of wire wool, and half a dozen old toothbrushes with frazzled bristles surrounded a gleaming wooden box with a beautiful inlaid lid.

'Boulle,' he said.

'Beg pardon?'

'Boulle,' he repeated, touching the lid of the box lovingly, 'is brass, ebony, tortoiseshell.' He pointed with his thick forefinger to the intricate parts of the design. 'Boulle work.' He gave me a searching, sideways glance. 'You are interested in such things?'

'Yes, I love old things. You're restoring it?'

'For special customer,' he answered, nodding mysteriously, and I remembered what Ricky had said, about his real customers coming to the back door. Then he added, 'You not touch. Things on this table, not touch.'

'Of course not,' I responded, with a slight bristle of indignation.

'You not understand.' He pointed to the bottles and jars. 'These things – poisons, acids, corrosives – I need for my work. Same under sink, chemicals, you not touch. You get hurt.'

'Oh, I see! Look, perhaps we should discuss exactly what you want me to—'

'Tea.' He silenced me with a wave of his hand. 'I make tea. Come.'

I followed him into the kitchen where an ancient, chipped enamel gas stove squatted on sturdy legs. There was an original Belfast sink, wooden draining board, and a Formica-topped table so outdated it could almost be considered retro.

'Sit, please.' He filled a kettle through its stubby spout and placed it on the gas burner, which he lit with a match. There was a woof of blue flame and he shook the match out, emptied tea leaves from an old china teapot into the sink and fetched a tin of evaporated milk from a sturdy old fridge in the corner.

'Can I do anything?' I asked, as much to cover the silence as anything. I watched him pour the thick, yellowish milk into two china mugs with misgiving. I wasn't looking forward to this tea.

'No, no,' he assured me. 'You sit. I am slow. I break hip at Christmas – in hospital six weeks.'

'Oh dear!' I responded dutifully. Could this really be the convicted criminal Ricky and Morris had told me about, this old man, shuffling about in his slippers, making me tea?

'When I come home, they send woman.' His face wrinkled in disgust. 'Social services.'

'An occupational therapist?' I suggested.

He nodded. 'She say to me, take up all your rugs. Rugs trip hazard. I tell her, is my rugs, piss off!' He chuckled and I laughed. He gave me a long appraising stare. 'What for you do this job? You beautiful girl, be model.'

I laughed. 'I don't think so.'

'Why not? You tall . . . red hair is beautiful, like autumn gone crazy.'

It's important to put things in perspective here. I am tall. I have long red hair, which curls riotously and which everyone, except me, seems to think is beautiful.

I would probably think it was beautiful too, if it grew on someone else. Admittedly, I have nice teeth. Apart from that I am not in any way remarkable. I learnt, as I grew up, that to be a tall redhead is no bad thing, but I am certainly not model-girl material. For one thing, I am too robust, and for another, I'd rather stick nails in my eyes.

To my relief the kettle, which had been warbling gently in the background, began a shrill whistle and Mr Nickolai was forced to turn his attention to making the tea, which he did, very methodically, warming the pot and spooning in four heaped spoonfuls of very black leaves before pouring in the water, and placing a knitted cosy over the pot.

'You work for those old queens up at Druid Lodge.' He slid a sly glance at me. 'Those Jew boys.'

'Yes,' I answered, taken aback. I tensed slightly, wondering what casual racism might be coming next.

'I see concert they give for charity' – he chuckled – 'very clever, very funny!'

I relaxed a little. 'Yes, they are.'

'You married?' he asked, blue eyes twinkling.

'You proposing?'

He shrugged. 'Maybe.'

'Mr Nickolai, I—'

'Nick. Call me Nick.'

'Well, Nick, what exactly do you want me to do?' I picked up my shoulder bag from the floor, grimacing a little at the weight, wondering what the hell I carry round that can weigh so much, and pulled out my diary. 'Cos I'm pretty busy at the moment. How often do you want me to come?' The place certainly needed a damn good clean. The table I was leaning on felt ominously sticky and the lino floor was black in the corners with years of ingrained filth. 'I haven't seen the rest of the flat, but it's obviously not large. I could probably blitz it in a—'

'Clean flat?' He frowned, puzzled. 'I not want you to clean flat.'

'Oh. Shopping?'

'No. I want shopping, I phone Mr Singh at corner shop, he bring it round.' He chuckled. 'We drink tea, play chess. When he get back to shop, Mrs Singh she shout at him for being gone too long.' He poured tea strong enough to trot a mouse across and pushed a mug towards me. 'You want sugar?'

'No!' I cried, a little too hastily, watching in horror as he spooned repeatedly into his own mug. 'Tell me, cos I'm curious,' I pointed at an ancient washing machine with mangle attached. 'Does that thing still work?'

He nodded. 'Yes, it work, but is easier to use launderette, three doors down.'

'Ah! So, what is it you want me to do?'

'I show you. In minute. Drink tea.'

The interior of the shop was dark and smelt of the past, of ancient dust and polish like the smell of an old church. Something of the same silence too, all the clocks stopped long ago. Solid hulks of dark furniture blocked the way to the shop door. We'd come down the stairs from the flat and entered the shop from a door at the back, down a corridor and past a storeroom. I looked around, weaving my way cautiously between cases of stuffed birds and animals: dead feathers, dead fur, glass eyes staring at me. There were no dollies or fans here, no bright, pretty pieces of china, no bygone fripperies to lift the gloom, just cardboard boxes balanced everywhere, full of unidentifiable objects wrapped in newspaper. A stuffed owl glared.

'See? Shop is all junk,' Nick said happily. 'I get rid. Come to storeroom out back. I show you.' He led me back down the corridor and into a storeroom piled high with furniture: desks, stools, chairs and tables stacked crazily on top of one another. 'I need your help.'

I gazed around me and then turned to look at him. 'To do what, exactly?'

He chuckled and tapped the lid of a dark box like a small coffin on legs.

'You know what is?'

'A casket?' I ventured.

'Cellaret.' He flipped the lid open. Inside the box was lined with blue watered silk and fitted with brass holders and cut-glass decanters. 'See? All need polish.'

He pointed down to the cellaret's brass, lion-shaped feet. 'I have bad knees. I cannot get down there to polish any more.'

'You want me to polish it?'

'Yes, but no squirting.'

'Squirting?' I repeated blankly.

'No squirt polish. Wax polish only, very careful. I will

show you.' He closed the lid of the box gently and ran a loving hand across its surface.

'What kind of wood is it?' I asked.

'Walnut.' He pointed a thick forefinger. 'This cross-banding here is ebony.'

'And you're selling it?'

He nodded at the piles of stuff around us. 'All of this, I get rid.' He chuckled and pointed to himself. 'Too old now, my heart not good, I not remember what's in here any more. You help me. Find good stuff. Sell at auction, or on Internet.'

'But Nick, I don't know the first thing about all this stuff . . .'

'You learn. I teach.'

'It's just not the sort of work I usually do.'

'Why not?'

I hesitated. There was a part of me that really wanted to snoop about amongst all this stuff and have a good look, lift all the lids and open all the cupboards, find out what lay inside. And, despite his reputation, I liked Old Nick, with his twinkly eyes and rich chuckle.

'Why me?' I asked and he looked doubtful. 'Why are you asking me?' I explained.

'Ah!' he said, understanding. 'I see your van. Also, Mr Singh, he has your card in window. *No job too small*, it say.'

I laughed and gestured round the storeroom. 'Nick, this is not a small job! How often do you want me to come?'

'Every day.' He spoke as if it was obvious. 'I pay.'

'It's not that simple. I can't abandon my other clients. I

have people who depend on me – and dogs – look, I'll come whenever I can. How's that?'

'When?' he demanded with a scowl.

At that moment there was a knocking at the side door. Nick frowned and went to open it. 'Paul!' he cried, waving someone inside. 'Come in. Come in.'

'I've come to collect those chairs we spoke about.' A man appeared in the hallway and did a double take when he saw me.

'This is Juno,' Nick told him. 'My new assistant,' he added proudly.

'Really?' He raised a dark eyebrow. He was about my age, or a little older.

I was tall enough to look him in the eyes, but I'm used to that. Beautiful eyes they were too, very dark, set under long, level brows and fringed with black lashes.

'Paul,' he said, holding out his hand. We shook. Firm handshake, great smile – I felt a flicker, a definite vibe, and I knew from the way he held eye contact with me, that he felt it too. 'You're working for Nick?' he asked. His voice was pleasant, educated. In fact, there was something slightly public school about his whole persona: just confidence, perhaps. A cheerful strength emanated from him.

'That's the plan,' I said.

'Whatever you do,' he warned me in a murmur, 'don't drink his tea.'

'Too late.'

'Well, good luck!' He turned his attention to Nick. 'Now, where are these chairs?' They disappeared behind a pile of furniture at the far end of the storeroom and emerged, after a minute or two of shuffling things about, Paul carrying two heavy wooden chairs, thickly painted in white gloss, their seats covered with loud floral fabric. I know nothing about antique furniture but even I could see that a travesty had taken place.

'Nice to meet you, Juno,' he called back over his shoulder as Nick opened the door to let him out.

'Customer?' I asked when he'd gone.

'Paul?' Nick shook his head. 'He restore furniture. Those chairs, he take off paint, polish, re-cover. Bring back, good as new. You see.'

Well, I thought, with any luck I might. 'How about Saturday?' I suggested, although I don't usually like tying myself up at weekends. 'I could come on Saturday, just for the day, see how it goes?'

'How it goes,' Nick repeated, smiling and we shook on it.

'And no squirting,' I told him solemnly. 'I promise.'

CHAPTER FOUR

At three years of age I was found in a London underpass, a graffiti-scrawled subterranean passageway that stank of piss. I'd been there hours apparently, strapped in my buggy, screaming my head off, whilst on the floor beside me my young mother lay dying of a drugs overdose. I don't remember it. I have very little memory at all before my fifth birthday; no memory of my mother. I've blocked it all out, so they tell me.

When I was rescued from my buggy I was placed in the care of social services whilst a search was made for my family. My mother, it transpired, had been its little black lamb. Granted all the advantages: wealthy parents, an expensive education and a place at university, she'd thrown it all away, getting into recreational drugs, moving on to the hard stuff, dropping out, falling pregnant, and finally getting in trouble with the police. By the time she died, my grandfather hadn't seen her for four years, during which time my grandmother had passed away. No one had any idea who my father was.

My grandfather, once he was made aware of my existence, wanted nothing to do with me. He blamed his daughter, both for his wife's broken heart and her early death, and he was probably right. He was not prepared to assume responsibility for the spawn of a criminal or drug dealer. I remained in care.

But a cousin of my mother's, Brian, a high-flyer in the diplomatic service, home briefly on a posting from South Korea, learnt of my fate and came to see me. He told me later what a little savage I was, a screeching scarecrow of a child, all windmill arms and flying fists. I don't imagine I was an appealing prospect for adoption, and in any case, in his job, he wasn't in a position to consider it. But he paid for me to go to a very good boarding school. I think he felt that, if he'd been around at the time, instead of away in the Far East, he might have saved my mother from her fate.

School was a strict, no-nonsense place and I loved it. I boarded during term time but the long summer holidays were a problem. Brian only came home on alternate Christmases. I had nowhere to go.

It was another cousin, Cordelia, who saved me. Brian had contacted her, and although she had never met my mother, she'd offered to take me in. I was welcome to spend my holidays with her, in Devon.

He drove me down to Totnes and made the introductions. I was seven years old and amazed: Cordelia had hair just like mine. Not red – brown streaked with grey – but wild and curly, and she wore it in a great mass down her back, with no attempt to tame it, part it, or make it behave. I think I loved her on sight. She wore colourful skirts and dangling earrings and was unlike anyone I'd ever seen before. She looked deep into my eyes as she extended a long, bony hand to shake mine.

'You're an old soul,' she told me gently. Overawed, I'd gone quiet, and she smiled. 'You are a solemn little thing. When is your birthday?' I managed to tell her and she nodded wisely. 'That accounts for it, then. You're a Capricorn. Did you know that Capricorns are born old and get younger?'

'Still into the mumbo-jumbo, I see,' Brian muttered.

Cordelia smiled. 'If you mean astrology, Brian,' she responded, entirely without rancour, 'the answer's yes.'

Cordelia ran a little shop in Totnes, that thriving centre of what used to be called the New Age, right at the top of Fore Street. The shop was a place of wonder for me, draped with silk scarves and coloured shawls, crystals dangling on strings in the windows, sculptures of dragons and unicorns. The wooden counter was divided into compartments filled with beads. Cordelia would thread them on to silver pins to make earrings, or string them into necklaces and hang them on black velvet on the wall. She would let me do it too, playing with glass beads from India that glowed rich colours when I held them to the light; some as large as conkers, others as small as seeds, some silver and gold or painted and carved. I would play with this treasure for hours, watching the shop whilst Cordelia gave consultations in a little room behind a curtain at the back, for people who wanted their astrological charts interpreted, or their tarot cards read.

The opening hours of the shop were hit and miss. If she had no consultations booked and the weather was good, Cordelia would hang the CLOSED sign on the door and we'd hop on a bus that would take us over the South Hams or to the Otter Valley, or up on to Dartmoor, where we'd get out and walk miles, squelching our way in our sturdy walking boots across boggy ground, clambering rocky tors or splashing through frolicking streams, striding over the hills with a packed lunch in a backpack. It was Cordelia who gave me my love of the moor, of wild places.

In the evenings, if we'd been shut in the shop all day, she'd build a fire in a small brazier in her tiny back garden and we'd sit there in the dark and eat our supper and she would point out stars and tell me stories of all the places she'd visited, and of all the places she intended to go. She took me along with her to yoga classes, circle dancing, t'ai chi, vibrational healing and anything else that she happened to be going to. I was too young to understand what the hell was going on, but I had fun and I met some fascinating people.

I stayed with Cordelia every holiday until I left school for university. And the sad thing was, looking back on it, that by the time I was old enough to really understand all the things that she had to teach, I was no longer interested. My education had made me too sensible, too rational, to be taken in by her New Age philosophies. I felt I'd outgrown her, that I was more sophisticated. She was just an old hippy. I had begun, tragically, to mock her.

It was ironic that someone who'd back-packed solo around some of the most dangerous places in the world should lose her life through a moment's inattention crossing a Totnes street. Brian was not able to make it back from the Far East for her funeral, but sent flowers. Later on, I discovered that he'd tried to induce my grandfather to attend, as on many occasions in the past he'd tried to persuade him to meet me. After all, Cordelia was his family too. He'd refused. But all her friends were there and the church was packed.

She owned almost nothing. The shop and flat were rented and she was behind with the rent. I believe Brian paid her debts. Her amber earrings and a few books were almost all she had, and these she left to me. She was the nearest thing I had to a mother. I miss her every day of my life.

CHAPTER FIVE

'Receiving stolen goods, you said,' I reminded Ricky, spearing a garlic mushroom.

He and Morris had invited me out to lunch, ostensibly to thank me for helping them out with *The Wizard of Oz* costumes, but really because they wanted to find out how I'd got on with Old Nick the day before. I didn't object. Three-course Sunday lunch in the traditional country comfort of The Church House Inn at Holne is not something I can afford myself, and was worth trading for a little tittle-tattle.

'It was a long time ago,' Ricky responded thoughtfully, 'must be thirty years.'

Morris nodded as he chewed carefully on a bread roll. 'Whilst he was inside, his missus ran off.'

Ricky was nodding frantically, his mouth too full of crab cake to speak.

'She went to live with a sister, I think.' With a napkin, Morris carefully dabbed a droplet of scarlet soup from his tie. 'The girl would have been about fifteen by then.'

Ricky was able to speak at last. 'And there was a boy, a bit younger.'

I mulled this over. During my day working for Nick I'd asked him if he had any family, just making conversation, and he'd said no, he had none. None he wanted to talk about, obviously.

At that moment the waiter arrived to take away our first course and enquire if everything had been satisfactory. It had. When he'd carried away the plates, Ricky could contain himself no longer. 'So, how d'you get on yesterday?'

I hesitated. Something odd had happened and I wasn't sure how much I should tell.

Things had gone well to begin with; Nick had shown me some items he wanted to sell at auction: the cellaret and an exquisite little writing desk on slender legs, its doors inlaid with marquetry roses. Nick told me it was eighteenth century.

'See, it is beautiful, even on back? It not meant to stand against wall,' he told me, 'but in middle of room, pride of place – in lady's room. Is called *bonheur du jour*,' he added, speaking very carefully.

'*Bonheur du jour*,' I tried to translate, using my schoolgirl French, which is hazy to say the least. 'A good hour of the day?'

Nick chuckled. 'A daily delight,' he corrected me. Behind

46

the doors were rows of tiny drawers, and behind one of these, he showed me, a secret one. 'Here she keep her love letters, eh?'

I wanted to search for secret drawers in all the furniture then, but it was time to get to work. I began the job of polishing the cellaret, first washing it down with a solution of a special soap and buffing it dry with a soft cotton cloth, which quickly became filthy as I removed a century of grime. Then I got to work with the beeswax, Nick watching me like a hawk to make sure I always worked with the grain of the wood, never against. He had taken off its brass handles and was sitting in an old armchair with half the stuffing hanging out, polishing them, not with metal polish, but with salt and vinegar, scrubbing at the intricate design with a child's toothbrush.

'Is this *bonheur du jour* valuable?' I asked.

He made a hand gesture: so-so. I got the feeling he didn't want to tell me its real value and I made a mental note to look on the Internet when I got home and see if I could find a valuation website for antique furniture.

'You do good job, Juno,' Nick said approvingly. 'See how the wood begin to glow now?'

Suddenly, the doorbell sounded its death rattle, followed by an aggressive banging on the side door. Nick looked taken aback, as if he wasn't expecting anyone, and then gave me an uncertain glance. 'I see who is. You stay here, Juno,' he said and shuffled out to answer the door.

I'd been kneeling on the floor for some time and decided to use the interruption to stand up, stretch and relieve the pins and needles in my legs. Wondering if the visitor might be the rather interesting Paul, I tiptoed painfully to the storeroom door and took a sly squint into the corridor.

It wasn't him. The man standing in the doorway was shorter, powerful-looking, with blonde hair cropped very short, emphasising sharp cheekbones and small ears set so flat against his skull they gave him an alien, almost android, appearance. He was speaking to Nick with an urgent, hushed intensity, not in English, but something that sounded Slavic or Balkan. Nick was responding in soothing, conciliatory tones. The stranger wasn't happy.

It was no good my trying to eavesdrop and it was none of my business anyway. I was just moving away from the door to go back to my work when I unleashed a mighty sneeze. It must have been the dust I'd raised with all that polishing. The conversation by the door cut short and swift steps thumped down the corridor. I retreated to the cellaret as if I'd never left it, just as the door was flung open.

The stranger blocked the doorway, staring at me from eyes that were iceberg blue, and just as cold.

'Hello,' I said weakly and gave a little wave with my polishing cloth. He didn't move but continued his icy glare, silent and hostile. I felt frost crackling down my spine and suppressed a shiver. Nick was hastily shuffling down the corridor, making soothing noises. He appeared in the doorway and began talking. The stranger never took his eyes from mine, except once to demand something of Nick and jerk his thumb forcefully in my direction. He was wearing gloves, I noticed, black leather gloves. I couldn't understand the conversation that ensued but I got the general gist. He wanted to know who I was and what the hell I was doing there. Once he spoke to me directly, aggressively demanding something. I shook my head and shrugged. I think he was trying to trick me into a response, to assure himself that I didn't speak his language, that I could not have understood the conversation I'd overheard. It might have been in Transylvanian, for all I knew.

He spoke again, taking a step towards me, jabbing the air with his gloved fist. I can't say I didn't feel threatened, because I did: he was compact, strong and muscular, and together with his belligerent attitude and ice-zombie stare, seemed like a man who could do me damage and wouldn't think twice about it. I named him Vlad. I was considering the broken leg of a nearby chair as a weapon to smash over his skull if he invaded my space any further, but Nick managed to calm him down, talking to him in hushed, conciliatory tones, and coaxed him upstairs.

I went back to my polishing, trying to ignore the loud voices I could hear from the room above, and concentrate on the job. About twenty minutes later Nick's visitor came thundering down the stairs.

'Nice knowing you,' I muttered, thinking he was on his way out.

But then the door into the storeroom crashed open again and he stood in the doorway, scowling. I rose to my feet and held his stare, determined not to be intimidated, not to look away first. After a few moments he muttered something that sounded like a curse and swung out, slamming the door into the street behind him.

I noticed he had been carrying a small cardboard box under one arm. I'd have loved to have known what was in it.

Nick was hurrying down the stairs by then. 'Is everything OK?' I asked.

'Yes . . . of course!' he answered breathlessly, but he looked flustered, and seemed anxious to reassure me, taking my hand and patting it. 'My friend, he get excited. Is nothing.'

'He didn't seem to like my being here.'

'Is nothing. No worry.'

I could tell he was uneasy. I felt a little shaken myself.

'We finish today, Juno – more another time, yes?' He pulled a fat roll of banknotes from his cardigan pocket and began to peel them off.

'That's far too much . . .' I began but he hushed me, pushing them into my hand.

'You work hard, Juno.' He hesitated and then glanced at me slyly. 'My friend . . . you forget you saw him, yes?'

'If you want,' I told him. 'But he's none of my business, you don't have to bribe me.'

'No. No. You keep!' he insisted. 'I see you another day.'

'I need to look in my diary.'

'Yes, yes. You ring me,' he nodded, and couldn't hustle me towards the door fast enough.

'So, you never found out who he was?' Ricky asked, tucking into his Eton Mess.

We'd got through the sea bass, baby spinach and crushed potatoes by then. Morris and I were on to the crème brûlée.

'Nick's visitor?' I shook my head.

'Are you going to work for Nick again?'

'I think so. He's got tons more stuff that he wants me to clean for him, things he wants to send to auction.'

'Why doesn't he open his shop? I'd love a poke around in there.' Morris was an enthusiastic collector of teapots. The dresser in the breakfast room contained an army of them, all pointing in the same direction, spouts to attention.

'I think he's tired. Just doesn't want the bother of it. I'm giving him Chloe Berkeley-Smythe's slot on a Wednesday afternoon until she comes back from her cruise. After that we'll have to see.'

'Don't get too involved with him, Juno.' Morris wagged a finger at me. 'You don't want to get mixed up in anything dodgy.'

I should have taken his advice. But back then I didn't know then how dodgy things were going to get.

CHAPTER SIX

Verbena Clarke is not my favourite client. She lives in an expensive barn conversion on the Widecombe road, at a place where the countryside around begins to change. The trees thin out, the land opens up on either side as the hedgerows give way, replaced by grass verges and low, drystone walls. In the distance the green firs of a Forestry Commission plantation turn the horizon into a dark and spiky line. This is not yet the moor proper, but the land has lost the lush softness of the valley below. It has grown harder. Still beautiful, it has sharper edges, as if the moor's underlying granite is trying to push up from beneath.

I parked the van by the side of the road. Mrs Clarke does not allow me to drive in through her gates and park in her courtyard next to her Porsche and her Range

Rover. She says my vehicle is an eyesore. So I park it a hundred yards down the road, on the grass verge, where I'm certain she cannot avoid seeing it from the windows of her studio; although this small satisfaction is no compensation for having to stump back down the road in wet and windy weather.

Only a tantalising glimpse of the barn is visible, hidden, as it is, behind a high wall. Only as I come around the granite gatepost into the courtyard, is it possible to appreciate the beauty of the building, old walls and oak beams wedded seamlessly to modern screens of glass. Mrs Clarke is a design consultant, and what she has created from a cluster of derelict farm buildings is remarkable. Rumour has it – and by rumour, you understand, I mean Ricky and Morris – that there is an ex-husband lurking in the background, an ageing rock star, who stumped up the money for the barn development as a pay-off for dumping Verbena and her teenage girls and running off with a younger version.

To my surprise there was another vehicle parked beside the Porsche, an old lorry, surely not smart enough, I thought peevishly, to be permitted entrance to the courtyard. The tailgate was down and I peered nosily into the inside. It was empty. The front door of the barn was flung open, but I didn't know whether something was coming out, or something had just gone in. I got the answer when I stepped into the glass atrium and found a large, old-fashioned dresser, unattended, and blocking most of the hall. I called out a yoo-hoo as I squeezed my way past.

The lovely Mrs Clarke was sitting in the living room with a visitor. At least, with her halo of soft blonde hair and big blue eyes, she would be lovely, if she didn't have an irritating Home Counties schoolgirl accent and was so resolutely unsmiling. I couldn't help noticing that the visitor, presumably, judging from the overalls he wore, the man who had just delivered the dresser, was clutching a mug of coffee. Over the last two years I have worked two hours every week for Mrs Clarke, trudging in from the road where she makes me park in all weathers, and I have never been offered a cup of coffee, tea or any other form of refreshment.

'Hello!' The visitor hailed me in a loud and cheery voice. He was a pleasant-looking, elderly man, and judging from his loud voice, possibly deaf.

Mrs Clarke cast a look over her shoulder. 'Oh. Juno,' she greeted me in a desultory tone. 'Bedrooms.' Having given me my instructions, she wasted no more words on me, and turned back to her visitor.

'Aren't you joining us for coffee?' the visitor asked.

A questioning glance at Verbena's stiffened countenance told me that I wasn't paid to waste my time on pleasantries and I'd better get my ass up the stairs. ''Fraid not!' I told him and beat it up the staircase.

'Shame!' he said. As I reached the landing, I heard him enquire loudly, 'Who's the Titian-haired beauty?' Despite my ears being on stalks I only caught the end of her reply: 'cleaning woman'. She might as well have said 'serf'. Perhaps she'd like it branded on my forehead so future visitors would appreciate my lowly status and not attempt to engage me in conversation.

In the master suite I found the most pleasant member of the Clarke family, Perdita the pedigree Persian, stretched out on the bed. She rolled around luxuriously, showing off her gorgeous fluffy tummy and allowing me to adore her. I suspect that Perdita was only purchased because she looks so fabulous reclining on the furniture, although if she keeps bringing in dead voles and chewed-up baby rabbits from outside, she may well find she's on borrowed time.

When I'd finished in the master suite, with its white-marble bathroom, there were two more for me to clean. Frankly, I think Verbena's teenage offspring should be made to clean their own bedrooms' en suite. Picking up dirty knickers and grubbing long hair out of the shower plughole with a bent paper clip is character-building stuff.

By the time I'd finished, and came downstairs, the dresser was *in situ* in the breakfast room and Verbena's cheery visitor had obviously been gone for some time. Verbena was standing before her new purchase, considering the exact placement of a piece of chunky pottery. When she saw me, she reached reluctantly for her leather wallet. Every time she pays me, she goes through the same ritual, a sigh and a little shake of the head, as if I'm bankrupting her.

One day I pointed out to her that I cost a lot less than the plumber she'd just cheerfully handed over a wad of cash to for ten minutes' work. She had replied, somewhat reproachfully, that a plumber is a qualified professional with specialist skills. I didn't argue, just suggested that the next time she blocked up her waste disposal, she sent for me.

* * *

Afterwards I called on Maisie. They say that dogs and their owners look alike but this is not the case with Jacko and Maisie. Jacko is a bristly barrel of coarse fur on four short legs, an incompatible mixture of nasty terriers. I can't walk him with other dogs because he's a psychopath. Maisie, with her apricot curls and button black eyes, resembles a poodle more than anything else. She's ninety-four, and my job for her is to shop, walk her dog, fetch prescriptions and occasionally, clean. It's a flexible arrangement.

Her cottage is in Brook Lane, so called because of the Ashburn, a little tributary of the River Dart that slides sneakily under much of the town, emerges here and there to show itself as a tiny rill running along a ditch beside the road. It was possible to reach Maisie's gate only by stepping on a tiny bridge made from an old flagstone. Hers is one of just four cottages in the lane, and like many roads in country towns, once past the last house the tarmac degrades into a rough track, leading between fields.

Maisie was sitting on the cottage floor when I walked inside, her back propped up against the sofa, her little legs stretched out before her. I could see the soles of her pink sheepskin slippers, shiny with wear.

'Hello, lovey!' she sang out cheerily.

'What are you doing down there?' I kicked Jacko away as he ran forward, barking shrilly, and tried to hump my leg. 'Have you had a fall?'

'I skidded on a teabag.' She pointed towards the culprit, squashed damply on her kitchen lino. It was one of several littering the area around her overflowing pedal bin. I knelt down beside her. 'When was this?'

'Oh, an hour ago or so.'

'Have you hurt yourself?'

'No!' She began laughing like a pixie. 'I just couldn't get up, so I shuffled me old bum over here against the sofa to see if I could pull meself up on the seat, but I can't quite manage it. Hopeless, I am!'

'Heave-ho, then!' I grabbed her little hands, blue-veined and skeletal as claws, and pulled her up on to her sofa. She weighed next to nothing. 'Why are you still in your dressing gown? Hasn't the girl from the agency been?' It was close on twelve o'clock and an agency carer was supposed to come in between eight and nine each morning to help Maisie bathe and dress. She had difficulty getting her old bones going in the morning and if someone didn't give her breakfast, she'd forget to eat. She'd happily go through the day on a diet of tea and biscuits if I let her get away with it.

'Not yet,' she answered, unconcerned, 'but she comes a different time every morning. And it's not always her. Sometimes it's another one.'

'I'll make you a cup of tea.' It wouldn't be the carer's fault she was late. I'd worked briefly for a care agency and I knew the timetable was impossible.

'What do you want for breakfast?' I picked up soggy and dried-out teabags from around the kitchen floor. 'You're not very good at lobbing these in the bin, are you?'

'No,' she admitted happily. 'I'll have a piece of toast.'

I popped a slice in the toaster, bagged up the rubbish and took it outside. By the time I'd returned and put a fresh liner in the bin, the toast had popped up and Maisie had used her remote to switch on the television news. 'Who's that?' she pointed at the screen. 'He's always on, I don't like him.'

I glanced over my shoulder at the television as I spread the butter. 'That's the foreign secretary, Maisie.'

'Wanker!' she pronounced darkly.

I paused in mid-spread. 'What do you want on this toast?'

'Oh, I don't mind.'

'We'll make it marmalade, then.'

I don't know what the foreign secretary was talking about, but he caused Maisie to nod wisely and declare, 'Bad blood will out.'

God, I hope not, I thought to myself. When you're not sure what's running in your own veins, it's not a comforting thought.

At that moment a pretty girl in a blue overall hurtled in through the front door. Jacko launched an immediate assault on her ankles but I distracted him by rattling a packet of dog biscuits and hauling him off by his collar.

'Hello, Maria!' Maisie called out, waving her toast. 'You all right, darling?'

'Hello, Maisie! Sorry I'm late. I had to call an ambulance for Mr Wilson and I couldn't leave him, and that's put me behind. I'm sorry. I'll run your bath.' And with that, she rushed off into the bathroom.

I gave the kitchen floor a wash, checked the contents of Maisie's fridge, examining the sell-by dates for anything life-threatening, and then sat down with her to sort out her shopping list. 'How about a new pair of slippers?' I suggested. 'Something with a bit more grip?'

Leaving Maisie soaking in the bath under the watchful

eye of Maria, I set off for town with Jacko on the lead. Once outside of his own territory, Jacko is not too bad with people. But he seriously objects to sharing his pavement with other dogs or anything on wheels. Before we'd reached our destination he'd launched a yapping assault on a girl pushing twins in a buggy, frightened a kiddie on a tricycle, and given a nasty shock to an elderly spaniel and its equally elderly owner. By the time I'd dragged him around the shops in search of Maisie's ham and lettuce, I was fed up with apologising for him and tied his lead to a hook in the wall opposite Mr Singh's so I could go in and buy her jar of Ovaltine and bag of lemon drops in peace.

'I won't get you your pig's ear if you don't behave,' I threatened him darkly.

Suddenly he began to growl, deep in his throat, not his usual jaunty posturing, but a primeval rumble of fear and loathing. I saw Micky rounding the corner, dressed in his woolly hat, ancient mac belted round with string, and I understood. For where there was Micky, inevitably, a few moments later, there would be Duke.

Micky was a gentleman of the road – by choice, rather than the vagaries of fate – and roamed the moor at will, dossing down in a variety of hideaways of his own construction and shying away from people in general. He came down into town only when necessity compelled him. If he was heading to Mr Singh's, he was probably in need of some Rizlas for his roll-ups.

He raised a hand to me in silent greeting. A while ago he'd been involved in a misunderstanding with the police about the ownership of some recreational drugs, and had spent a month inside. I'd gone up on to the moor every day to find Duke and feed him.

No sooner had Micky disappeared through Mr Singh's swing doors, than Duke came limping around the corner. Duke was a cross between a Great Dane and a mastiff on one side and . . . well . . . *something else* . . . on the other, something huge, something a darker shade of black than any ordinary dog. His powerful body was battle-scarred and his massive head hung low. He'd have been perfect casting for *The Hound of the Baskervilles*.

By now Jacko was frantic, lead stretched taut, choking himself on his collar in a frenzied attempt to lunge across the road at Duke, who, oblivious of his presence, barged his way through Mr Singh's swing doors like a gunslinger heading into a saloon. Inside the shop was a stand of pick'n'mix, the bowls of sweets set temptingly at toddler height, the lids easy for a doggy snout to nudge aside. I began to count.

I'd only reached six when Duke emerged from the shop pursued by Mrs Singh in her sari and green cardigan, yelling 'Bad dog! Bad dog!' whilst hitting him across the back with a broom. She might as well have stroked him with a powder puff for all the notice he took. He flopped down on the pavement and concentrated on spitting out a shower of shiny sweet wrappers.

'He always goes for the Quality Street!' she informed me indignantly and scurried back inside.

I crossed the road to Duke and squatted, taking his great head in my hands. He let me have it, surrendering it to me as if it was too heavy and he was glad to be relieved of its weight. I stared into the dull fire of his amber eyes and we had a quiet word together while I massaged his torn ears. This was too much for Jacko, who was yelping and snarling, apoplectic with rage.

'Will you shut up, you suicidal little dog?' I hissed in his direction. If Duke turned on him he'd have no more chance than a rat. Fortunately, Duke wasn't interested in terminating Jacko's existence. His only object in life was to follow his master, who came out of the shop at that moment. Micky didn't speak, he rarely did, but he nodded at me and gave what passed for a smile: a creasing of the wrinkles around his eyes, a movement in the grizzled fungus of his beard. Duke got to his feet and limped after him. Once he'd disappeared from view, Jacko deflated slowly like a bristling balloon and I went into the shop to buy Maisie's lemon drops and mollify Mrs Singh.

CHAPTER SEVEN

'We go to view for auction tomorrow, me and Paul. Juno, you come with us, yes?' It was Nick's voice on the phone. I'd just come in from walking the Tribe and had to think a moment. 'It's Wednesday tomorrow. Am I not coming to work for you?'

'No work, is viewing for auction. You like to come, yes?'

'Well . . . yes,' I said, warming to the idea, 'why not?' I'd never been to an auction, or a viewing. And I had to admit the prospect of Paul going too was an inducement. 'Thanks. I'd love to come.'

'Good. You come, one o'clock. We go. And Juno,' he added devastatingly, before he put the receiver down, 'wear dress.'

So next day, after I'd walked the Tribe and delivered

them all, I came home, changed out of my doggie-walking clothes, showered, washed my hair, conditioned it within an inch of its life, and put on the only dress I currently owned, a cream silk button-through I'd bought in a vintage charity shop in Totnes. Quite suitable for an antiques auction, I thought. There was a small rust mark on one sleeve but it didn't show much. I left my hair loose and wore Cordelia's amber earrings. I stared at myself in the one full-length mirror in the house. I didn't look bad.

Old Nick didn't look his usual self either. When he opened the door to me, I took a step back in amazement. Instead of his cardigan and carpet slippers he wore a dark overcoat and highly polished, black shoes. 'I bet you didn't clean those with a toothbrush,' I said.

He laughed, donned an ancient trilby and proffered his arm for me to take.

'Our carriage awaits,' he told me, eyes twinkling. Up until that moment I hadn't given a thought to how we were getting to where we were going, just assumed that we'd be travelling in Paul's furniture van. But no, Nick informed me, we would be travelling in his own car. 'Well, you're full of surprises. I didn't know you had a car.'

'I keep in garage, round corner,' he said, pointing the way.

Of course, I should have expected an antique: a Riley, gleaming black on the outside, cream leather and a walnut dashboard within.

'It's beautiful,' I told him. 'How old is it?'

'1953,' he responded proudly. 'Much older than you ... ah, our driver!' he added, as Paul appeared. Apparently, he hadn't been asked to wear a dress. He was in jeans and an old blue sweater. He grinned at me as he took the keys from Nick and swung open the door with a mocking bow. As I slid on to the back seat I caught him running an appreciative eye over my cream silk.

I'd assumed we'd be heading for one of the auction houses in Newton Abbot or Exeter, but in fact we drove up through Holne and Buckland, and on to the moor. When we suddenly swept in between stone pillars topped with griffons, and up the long drive towards a grand country house, I realised this was not going to be the sort of shabby local auction I'd seen on television antiques programmes, usually held in some kind of old warehouse with pegboard on the walls. This auction was going to be posh. Judging by the cars we parked alongside on the gravel carriage sweep, it was going to be very posh.

We stepped into a marble hallway beneath a glittering chandelier the size of a greenhouse, where Paul collected a couple of thick catalogues from a pile on a table, and handed one to me. It contained lists of sale items, together with the auctioneer's estimate of what each one was expected to fetch.

'We leave you to wander, Juno,' Nick told me. 'There are things Paul and I must look at.'

I was still gaping like an idiot at my surroundings. 'Fine,' I told him. I wanted nothing more than a peaceful root around amongst the Aladdin's cave of treasures I could see displayed in rooms opening off the hallway. I wandered into a ballroom where the chandeliers hanging from an ornate plaster ceiling were only half the size of the one in the hall, but there were six of them. Ricky and Morris were going to love it when I told them all about this.

The ballroom was devoted to items of furniture, the room heaving with prospective buyers, the air fizzing with the kind of suppressed energy I'd only encountered in a casino or at a racetrack: big money was obviously involved. I looked in my catalogue. *Lot 294: George I, small walnut bureau cabinet with moulded swan-neck cornice, circa 1720. £37,000–£45,000.* I gave a silent whistle. A little later I found myself staring at a lot I recognised and hastily looked it up. *Lot 298: An Edwardian, lady's bonheur du jour in mahogany, with inlaid stringing and rosewood banding; marquetry roses inlaid. Circa 1850. £2,500–£3,500.*

My jaw dropped. The little writing desk might be small pickings compared to the grander lots on display, but I'd no idea it was worth anything like as much when I'd been on my knees, polishing it in Old Nick's storeroom. I looked around to see if I could spot Nick or Paul, but they were not in the room.

'Good God! What are you doing here?' a voice demanded.

I turned to see Verbena Clarke hovering by my elbow. Her eyes swept up and down my cream silk, although not in the same way that Paul's had done. She was plainly not pleased to see me.

'Hello,' I responded, as pleasantly as I could. 'I'm just here with friends.'

'Oh!' she muttered, an awkward blush colouring her cheeks, 'I didn't expect to see you.' Possibly caught out by her own rudeness, and unable to think of anything else to say, she turned and stalked away.

After a little more wandering among the treasures, I began to wonder what had happened to Paul and Nick. I hoped they hadn't forgotten me and gone home. Through the long windows of one room I could see across a courtyard to some stables, which were also stuffed with auction lots, and I strolled across. Inside, I found humbler fare: scrubbed pine, old tools and farm implements. I also found Paul and Nick, talking in a knot of people, including, I saw with some amusement, Verbena Clarke. Resolutely I made my way towards them.

'Good heavens,' one of them exclaimed loudly. 'It's the Titian-haired beauty!'

It took me a moment to recognise the man in an overcoat and trilby hat as the deliverer of Mrs Clarke's dresser. He tipped his hat to me. 'We met at Vee's the other day,' he prompted me as I joined the group, and introduced himself pleasantly as Tom Smithson.

I shook his hand. 'I'm Juno.' I turned to Verbena Clarke, and added, as if I'd only just noticed her, 'Oh, hello, Vee!'

She responded with a stiff nod.

'Juno is my assistant,' Nick told them all. There was a touching note of pride in his voice.

I found my hand being wrung by a tall, skinny man in a cravat and sports coat, who laughed loudly, showing yellow teeth like old piano keys. 'She's not Titian, old boy!' he cried, highly amused with himself. 'She's Pre-Raphaelite, definitely Pre-Raphaelite.'

I don't like having my personal space invaded: Piano Teeth was leaning in much too close, lingering over his unpleasantly limp handshake, whilst his pale-blue eyes undid the buttons of my dress. It was like being clung to by a piece of damp seaweed and ogled by a cod.

Paul was quick to pick up on my unease. 'Fancy a cup of tea, Juno?' he asked. 'There's a tea room in the old dairy.'

'Yes, you go, you two,' Nick urged us, an obvious signal he wanted us out of the way, and we left him to his cronies.

'So, you know Verbena?' I couldn't resist asking, as we strolled across to the tea room.

'Not really,' he answered, with what I took to be a pleasing lack of interest. 'She turns up at sales and auctions now and again. She's always on the lookout for bits and pieces.'

'Being a designer, I suppose,' I added.

He nodded. 'I've restored the odd bit of furniture for her.'

The tea room, which seemed to have been set up especially for the day, was a deep disappointment. After the grandeur of the house, I was expecting white tablecloths and fine china, hoping for dainty sandwiches, scones and serious slabs of cake. But the tea came out of an urn, set up on a trestle table and was served in plastic cups. We sat at a table sticky with spilt grains of sugar from torn paper packets, and grabbed the last two biscuits from a solitary plate. They were slightly soft.

'Not exactly National Trust standard, is it?' Paul asked, grinning. 'I suppose they don't feel they need to make an effort.' He nodded across to the house. 'The sale's what it's all about. That's what the people are here for.'

'I'd no idea that it was going to be such a grand affair,' I admitted. 'I didn't realise Nick dealt in such expensive stuff.'

Paul shrugged. 'Mostly, he doesn't. We don't come to this kind of sale very often. I just help him out from time to time with repairs and restoring things. We're not really in business together.'

I wondered if he knew anything about Nick's back-door dealings, specifically about Vlad, but I didn't ask. 'But you deal in antiques as well?'

'I suppose you'd call it that. I restore furniture. I don't seem to sell much.' He shrugged. 'I rent a space in Ashburton Art and Antiques Bazaar.'

I knew the place. This rather pretentiously named emporium was an old market hall that had been renovated, then divided up into units, which were rented out to individual traders, creating an odd mixture of antiques, arts and crafts, and local foodstuffs. I had an artist friend, Sophie, who starved there on a regular basis. I realised I must have seen Paul's things there, though not necessarily Paul himself. The traders took it in turns to look after one another's units, so they didn't all need to be there every day.

He sighed. 'I'm thinking of pulling out soon.'

I was about to ask why when Nick appeared in the doorway of the tea room and began shuffling in our direction. He was looking tired and a little grey and refused the offer of tea. 'We go home now,' he announced and I sensed the outing had been too much for him.

I threaded my arm through his as we walked back to the car. 'I spotted the *bonheur du jour*. It looks so different in this setting, really lovely.'

Nick chuckled. 'Hope it make lovely price. We see.'

'I didn't know you knew Mrs Clarke,' I added casually.

'Mrs Snooty Bitch,' he grunted, and I laughed.

'Will you come back for the auction?'

He shook his head. 'I watch online.'

'Will you be bidding for anything?'

Nick waggled his hand in a way that suggested *perhaps*. 'I see a few nice things.'

Then he turned to me, wicked eyes twinkling. 'See, Juno, selling, it is easy. Knowing what to buy' – he tapped the side of his nose knowingly – 'that is the difficult part.'

CHAPTER EIGHT

'I have good idea.' It was Nick on the phone, again, next morning. 'You come round and see me, yes?'

'I come round and see you, no,' I responded. I'd just got back from my morning's travails and was trying to grab a sandwich before I had to go out again. I was only listening with one ear, the phone tucked into the crook of my neck whilst I sorted through that morning's post – all highly uninteresting – a pile of bills and a mystery package, a free gift from an overseas charity. 'I'm busy,' I told Nick firmly, extricating the contents of the package, which turned out to be a cheap pen with my name embossed on it in gilt lettering. If the charity thought I was going to use it to write them a cheque, they were out of luck. 'I'll see you tomorrow.'

'No tomorrow,' he insisted. 'Come today.'

'What's it about?' I asked crossly.

He chuckled down the phone. 'You see.'

I gave in with a sigh, abandoning all hope of a sandwich. 'Oh, all right. See you in ten minutes.'

'Is good,' Nick responded, and put the receiver down.

I was still muttering grumpily to myself as I approached Nick's door, but it was opened by Paul and my bad mood vanished as he smiled and stepped back to let me in.

Nick was standing in the corridor leading to the storeroom, next to a pair of beautiful, Edwardian balloon-back chairs made of a dark, glossy wood, with deeply buttoned seat cushions of rich green velvet, edged with a fringe.

'Those aren't the same chairs!' I cried, gaping.

Nick chuckled and nodded. 'Paul do good job.'

'He certainly has.' I turned to look at him. 'What will you do with them?'

'They're Nick's chairs,' he said, 'but I'm taking them to—'

'Yes, yes!' Nick interrupted him excitedly, 'that is why I want you, Juno . . . come upstairs . . . we talk!'

'Don't worry,' Paul murmured in my ear as we followed him up, 'I'll make the tea.'

'Do you know what this is about?' I whispered.

'I do.' He looked a bit sheepish. 'I'm afraid it's my fault.'

Nick started as soon as I sat at the kitchen table. 'Juno, I have great idea. Paul, he go to—'

'Have you heard of Somerset's Summer Antiques Fair?' Paul interrupted, setting the kettle on the stove and then turning back to look at me.

'Vaguely.' I knew a fair was held on some disused airfield in the middle of the Somerset Levels each year, but I'd never been.

'Is big market!' Nick interrupted. 'Famous! People come from all over country . . .'

'It's a great place to sell,' Paul went on, opening cupboard doors in search of mugs. 'In fact, it's difficult to get a pitch – you have to apply months in advance and go on a waiting list. This year I've managed to get one, only an outdoor one, but . . .'

'And that's where you're taking the chairs?' I still didn't see where I fitted in.

'Is good pitch,' Nick told me. 'Double size . . . So when Paul tell me, I say I pay half rent, he put things on for me . . .'

'That's a good idea!' I said innocently. Looking back, I can't believe how blindly I fell into his trap.

'Is good!' he agreed, chuckling. 'So, you go? Yes?'

'Sorry?'

'You go fair, with Paul. Sell stuff.'

I gaped at him. 'Just a minute . . .'

'I'm sorry, Juno.' Paul had finished fiddling with the tea things and he sat at the table. 'I can't do it on my own. It takes two to run the stall all day. The friend who was going to come with me can't make it. I've asked around but I can't find anyone who's free on Friday—'

'We're talking *this* Friday. Do you mean tomorrow . . . ?' I interrupted.

'No, no,' he reassured me, 'next week. Nick's obviously not up to it, but when I mentioned it to him, he thought that you might be available.'

'Well, that's because Nick likes to forget that I work for anyone other than him!' I responded, narrowing my eyes at him.

Nick just chuckled. 'But you like it, Juno. Is fun.' He patted my hand. I could cheerfully have slapped him. 'You take only few things for me. Rest, you choose.'

'What?' I asked suspiciously.

'You choose, from junk. Take things you like. Sell. We split money. Fifty-fifty.'

'I can't.'

'But you will like, Juno. I know.'

'That's not the point, Nick. I can't let my Friday people down.' I frowned. 'Why can't they hold this fair on a Saturday?'

He shrugged. 'It's traditional.'

Paul was pouring tea by then. He waggled the can of evaporated milk at me, dark eyebrows raised questioningly. I shook my head. 'Why don't you give Juno a chance to think about this?' He slid a mug of tea towards me. 'Let us know if you can work things out. If you want to, that is,' he added, grinning at me warmly. Strangely, I did want to, and it had nothing to do with selling Nick's junk.

'Nick's right, it can be a lot of fun,' he went on. 'But it's a long day, out in the open and if the weather's bad, and you're not selling, it can be bloody grim. The other thing that he hasn't mentioned is that we'll need to set out about four in the morning.'

'Why?' I demanded crossly.

'We need to get there early. We have to park the van immediately behind our pitch to unload. Later I'll have to move it to the car park, but it takes quite a while to set the tables up and be ready in time.'

'So, you go, Juno? Yes?' Nick asked.

I glowered at him. He had a bloody cheek, expecting me to sacrifice a day's work, and inconvenience my Friday clients, just to earn him a few rotten quid on his junk. On the other hand, it could be an adventure and the thought of spending the day with Paul had its attractions. 'I'll think about it,' I muttered. 'I've got to go now,' I added as Nick opened his mouth, and made my escape before he could press me any further.

By evening I'd worked out that if, the following week, I did Maisie's shopping on Thursday afternoon, instead of Friday morning, I really only had one problem left. I trotted down the stairs and knocked politely on my landlord's door. Adam answered.

'Good evening,' I said sweetly.

'Can I help you?' he asked, eyebrow raised in suspicion.

'Depends. How would you feel about taking a few dogs for a walk?'

The most difficult part was deciding what to take. Nick had let me choose what I liked from the boxes of junk in the shop. I knew that room in Paul's van would be limited and it had taken me days to decide. In the end I'd packed up a half a dozen boxes of assorted china and glass, most of it imperfect, and a few bits of brass.

I brought it all back to the flat to clean it. The brass needed polishing, newspaper wrappings had left black smudges on the porcelain and the glass was dusty. I made a list of all the items in my chosen stock, and copied it out as a record for Nick.

The problem was that I had no idea what to charge for anything. I'd read history at university, and at one time I could have written you a mean essay on life in the pottery towns in the nineteenth century, but when it came to identifying their products, I admit I was dismally ignorant. I couldn't tell pottery from porcelain, salt glaze from slipware, bisque or cream ware from a hole in the ground. I couldn't interpret the cryptic marks on the base of many of the pieces, and unless it was written in plain English, couldn't tell Clarice Cliff from Bristol or Bow.

Nick was no help at all. When I told him I didn't know what to charge for anything he just shrugged and told me I would learn. The only person who was of any use was Morris, who'd come around one evening, eyes on stalks, in the hope of adding to his teapot collection. He went through everything with me, reassured me that I didn't have any priceless treasures in my stock and gave a few rough suggestions about price.

'Take a good look around the market when you're there,' he suggested, 'see what other people are charging. You know, Juno, I'm sure Nick wouldn't trust you with this stuff if he was worried about you making a loss, my love. It's just bric-a-brac, really.'

Among Nick's stock I had also found a biscuit tin full of old glass brooches, the sort of thing that Maisie wears pinned to her coat on her rare trips out. Many of them had their catches broken or stones missing, and I'd spent hours cleaning them with soapy water, scrubbing them with a soft toothbrush and sticking in loose stones with epoxy glue. When I'd finished, I laid them all out on the kitchen table, on a piece of black velvet, the same piece that Cordelia used to display jewellery in her shop, and was busy pinning them on when I was interrupted by a knock on the living-room door.

It was Adam. 'Police downstairs for you,' he told me, his face deadpan.

I thought he was joking. But sure enough, when I followed him down, there were two lady coppers standing on the doorstep.

'Juno Browne?' one of them asked me pleasantly. 'Could we have a word?'

Mystified, I showed them up into the living room, where they sat side by side on the sofa, one skinny and dark, one plump and fair. 'Would you like tea?' I asked. 'I've just boiled the kettle.'

Fair said she wouldn't, and Dark said she would, so I went off into the kitchen to fetch a mug, all the time wondering what on earth had led two police constables to be sitting in my living room, side by side on my sofa. I delivered the tea and sat in the armchair facing them. 'What's this about?' I asked.

'Are you acquainted with Mrs Verbena Clarke?' Fair did the talking, whilst Dark clutched her tea.

I felt a stirring of disquiet immediately. 'Yes, I've known her for about two years. I clean for her once week.'

'It's just that there appears to have been a robbery. Certain valuable items have gone missing from Mrs Clarke's home, and an amount of cash and she—'

'Hold on, just a moment!' I held up a hand. 'She's not accusing me . . . ?'

'Not at all! Let's be absolutely clear about that,' Fair said hastily, so hastily in fact, that I didn't believe her for a moment. 'It's just that Mrs Clarke can't be certain exactly when these items went missing, and as you were there on . . . Tuesday, was it . . . ?' – she glanced down at her notebook – 'She wondered if you might be able to help.'

I wondered why, if she wanted my help, Mrs Clarke couldn't have phoned and asked me herself, but I didn't say so. 'You said there appeared to have been a robbery?'

'There was no sign of a break-in but a quantity of cash was taken from her wallet.'

'She does leave it lying around.' Whenever we went through the ritual of my payment, Verbena had to search for the blasted thing and it was usually to be found lying on the coffee table, or the breakfast table, or one of the kitchen worktops. 'She never locks her back door, either.'

'She did admit to that fact,' the blonde officer went on. 'She thinks that the thief might have stolen it whilst she was working in her studio. I understand it's separate from the main building, across the courtyard, in what was the old stable block.'

'And those windows don't face the courtyard,' I added. 'It would be easy enough for someone to sneak in without her seeing them. But it doesn't make sense, does it? Why take the cash, not the whole wallet?'

The constable shrugged. 'Credit cards aren't much use to a homeless person. Drug addicts are only interested in cash. But also,' she went on, 'certain items were taken from upstairs.'

'Can you tell us, Juno,' Dark Hair spoke up, leaning forward and fixing me with grey eyes, her mug still clutched in her hand, 'whether you noticed anything unusual on Tuesday?'

'Well, a new dresser had just been delivered,' I told her.

'The man who delivered it didn't go upstairs,' she responded, staring at me. 'You did.'

I was silent a moment. If that wasn't an accusation, it sounded very close to one.

'Did you go into Mrs Clarke's bedroom?' she asked.

'That's what I was there for,' I answered steadily. 'I cleaned her room, as I always do, and her en suite bathroom. And her dressing room,' I added. 'I hung up some of her clothes.'

'Did you clean the dressing table?'

'Yes.' Verbena's dressing table was concealed behind a pair of soft-close doors, which opened up to reveal a fitted vanity unit surrounded by soft lighting and mirrors. It was like a shrine.

'Do you remember seeing any jewellery on the dressing table?' Fair asked.

I knew that most of Verbena's jewellery, the valuable stuff, was kept in a small safe with a combination lock on it, in the bottom of one of her wardrobes. On the dressing table she kept a Chinese porcelain dish, into which she dropped her jewellery when she took it off at night, items that presumably she didn't feel compelled to lock up straight away. I knew what was in it each week because I had to move the dish to polish the table underneath. On Tuesday, there had been a gold-coloured leaf brooch she often wore to secure scarves. Nothing else.

'You didn't see any earrings?'

'Have earrings been taken?'

'Some diamond drops, apparently.' The constable handed me a photograph, obviously taken at some time for insurance purposes. The drops must have been three inches long, strings of diamonds set in a series of zig-zags. I'd certainly never seen them before.

'Unusual,' I commented.

'Unique, apparently,' the constable told me. 'A present from her ex-husband, especially designed for her.'

I handed her back the photograph. 'Shouldn't they have been kept in the safe?'

'Mrs Clarke left them on the dressing table overnight, intending to put them in next morning,' the constable informed me. 'When she found they weren't there, she assumed she must have done it the previous evening, after all. She'd been out late at a party, it seems, and she wasn't remembering the details too well. Anyway, she didn't check until much later in the day.'

'Well, I didn't see them.'

The constable closed her notebook and thanked me, smiling. 'That's all we need to know,' she said. 'Sorry to have bothered you.'

'I'm sorry I couldn't be more help.' As she and her colleague got to her feet, I made to take the mug that Dark Hair was clutching.

'No, no,' she said. 'I'll take it to the kitchen.' A few

moments later her voice floated through to the living room. 'Ah! You are interested in jewellery, then?'

I went into the kitchen, followed by her colleague. The constable was standing by the table, looking down at the black velvet on which the pinned brooches glittered accusingly. 'Are all these yours?' she asked.

'None of them are,' I said, feeling irrationally uncomfortable, 'I'm selling them for a friend.'

She raised her eyebrows at me. 'You buy and sell jewellery?'

'They're only made of glass,' I told her, wishing they didn't look quite so much like a haul from De Beers.

'And you're selling them?' Fair asked.

'I'm taking them to an antiques market,' I stated emphatically, 'for a friend.'

'And what friend would that be?'

They were both staring at me. I hesitated. Why was I feeling so guilty when I hadn't done anything wrong? 'Mr Nickolai.' I tried not to sound defensive and failed miserably. 'You can ask him if you like. He has a shop in Shadow Lane.'

The dark-haired constable was smiling. 'Oh yes,' she said, glancing sideways at her colleague. 'We know all about Mr Nickolai.'

I was too bloody furious to even think about going to bed. After I'd seen the police officers out, I knocked on Adam and Kate's door. I needed to vent my feelings, and anyway, I reckoned they had a right to know why the police had been in their house. In their student days they'd been passionate animal rights campaigners and their involvement in protests had led to them being arrested more than once. In any case, Adam thought all rich people were bastards, so on hearing my story, he and Kate were ready to sympathise with me as an innocent victim of police oppression, if not actual brutality. Over a glass of organic red wine, we happily tore Verbena Clarke's character to shreds.

I went upstairs feeling a lot better but I still couldn't sleep. Several times in the night I had nearly got up to phone Mrs Clarke. I felt like telling her to stuff her job. But my quitting suddenly might not be a good move. The police might tell me the theft was the work of a random, opportunist thief, but I suspected they really thought it was an inside job, committed by someone who knew where Verbena kept her valuables. And she had pointed her finger straight at me.

CHAPTER NINE

Next morning, I took a shortcut through Ashburton Art and Antiques Bazaar.

I found Paul's unit in one corner: all furniture items, beautifully restored – except for a single wooden chair, split down the middle, one half-restored, the other covered with chipped paint and old varnish; a clever 'before and after' advertisement.

'Did you want Paul?' A voice behind me made me turn. 'Only, he's not here at the moment.'

The voice belonged to Sophie Child.

'Hello, Sophie. I'm only being nosy. How's things?'

Sophie was an artist who produced exquisitely detailed watercolours, typically of hedgerows full of wild flowers. She could make a muddy ditch filled with dead leaves look enchanting. Despite her talent, she was not doing well. 'Quiet today,' she sighed. She was an elfin little waif with serious dark eyes behind enormous specs, her face framed by an urchin cut of dark hair. Today she was fluffed up against the cold in a fuzzy sweater several sizes too big for her. She looked like a baby owl. It might be summer outside, but it's always freezing in the stone-flagged market building.

A gaggle of day trippers had gathered around her unit, their chattering voices echoing loudly as they examined her work. 'There might be some customers amongst that lot,' I said.

'They look like p-p-p's to me,' she muttered glumly. She grinned when she saw my puzzled face. 'Pick-up, put-down and piss-off,' she explained. 'I suppose they might buy a few greetings cards.'

I nodded towards the cafe in the corner, the only business in the market that made any steady money. 'Can I get you a coffee?' She looked like she needed warming up.

'No thanks, I've had two cups already this morning. Actually, could you do me a favour and watch my stall while I go to the loo?'

'Lovely, aren't they?' I said of the paintings as I squeezed myself behind Sophie's display table so I could face the assembled horde of trippers. We chatted about how beautiful they were, but unfortunately how expensive, and my pointing out that each one was unique and hand painted didn't make them any more affordable. There was a lot of shaking of heads. 'Some of them are reproduced as greetings cards,' I indicated the spinning card rack. 'They're very reasonable.'

Sadly, all of the ladies turned out to be p-p-p's except one, who bought a card for her sister's upcoming birthday. Sophie reappeared as her customer drifted away and I told her that her takings had increased by two pounds fifty. ·

'Which card did she buy?'

'The one with the hare,' I told her.

She nodded. 'It's popular, that one. I need to get some more printed but . . .' she tailed off lamely. She didn't need to finish. She needed to get more printed but she couldn't afford the printing costs.

I invited her around to supper, just to cheer her up. But Sophie declined. 'That would have been lovely, Juno, but they've offered me a shift waitressing at The Dartmoor Lodge tonight and I can't afford to turn it down.'

'Well, perhaps next week.' I was just about to go when a thought occurred to me.

'Isn't Verbena Clarke a customer of yours?'

'Don't!' Sophie shuddered. 'The thought of her makes me want to reach for my inhaler.'

'I thought she bought some paintings from you.'

Sophie rolled her big dark eyes. 'Not quite. She got me all excited and cost me loads of money.'

Intrigued by now, I perched my bum on the edge of her table. I wanted to hear this.

'She was working on refurbishing a big hotel up on Dartmoor,' Sophie explained. 'She'd seen my stuff in here and thought my hedgerow paintings might fit in with the new decor. So she took a couple up there. Well, the owners really liked the paintings, they wanted me to paint two more, but they didn't like the frames. So I offered to change the frames on the existing two, and frame the new ones to match. It cost me a fortune because they wanted heavy gilt mouldings, really expensive.'

'But they bought them in the end?' I asked.

Sophie shook her head. 'No, they didn't. Verbena brought them back. She said the hotel had decided they weren't right after all. I was really pissed off after what the frames had cost me, so I rang the hotel to have it out with the owners. And it turned out that they'd turned the paintings down because they were too expensive. Verbena had put a whacking great commission on top of my asking price,' she said indignantly. 'In fact, she would have made more money on the paintings than I would.'

'Didn't you tackle her about it?'

'Course! She just shrugged and told me that it was the same commission that any gallery would have added if they'd been selling the paintings for me. Unfortunately, she's right about that.' Sophie sighed. 'The world is full of bastards,' she added glumly.

I didn't disagree. I stopped on my way out of the bazaar, at the stall run by Honeysuckle Farm, a local animal sanctuary for injured wildlife, abandoned farm animals and pets. The wall behind the stall was decorated, if that's the right word, with sheets of printed photographs and information about guinea pigs, ponies, ducks and other waifs and strays who needed a loving home. I nodded a hello at Pat, who ran the sanctuary with her sister and brother-in-law.

Pat looked like a waif and stray herself, thin and spare and angular, an old crocheted cardigan buttoned across her bony chest. A homely woman, not blessed by any physical bounteousness, she wore a permanently woeful expression that disguised great fortitude and a heart of gold. She was sitting behind the table, nose red with cold, knitting.

I frowned. 'Didn't your stall used to be over there – on the opposite wall?'

Pat nodded, her knitting needles not missing a click. 'I've been moved,' she answered, aggrieved. 'They complained about me.' She nodded again, this time her nod aimed at two dealers across the aisle, whose displays of bric-a-brac and collectables occupied a large area of the bazaar. 'They say I'm not art or antiques and I shouldn't be in here,' Pat went on, her voice trembling with emotion. 'They say I look like a jumble sale, that I lower the tone.'

I made sympathetic noises but I could see their point. The ladies who dealt in antiques had been to some trouble and expense, their pretty porcelain and silver displayed in glass cabinets, their tables artfully and tastefully arranged. Pat had just thrown an old blanket over her tabletop. Beyond a few paperbacks, second-hand children's toys and old *Blue Peter* annuals, she had almost nothing to sell. There was a small basket of costume jewellery, most of it plastic, and that was that. Her table looked like something from a car boot sale. It was never going to raise any money for the animal sanctuary, and probably barely made the rent. The best items were a few beautifully made babies' clothes that Pat had knitted herself, for sale at ridiculously cheap prices because nobody buys layettes for their babies any more.

'Trouble, is, Pat, you haven't got enough decent stuff to sell.'

'Well, I know that, don't I?' she agreed. 'But I have to rely on donations. And we're not allowed to sell our farm eggs here any more,' she went on crossly. 'Now they're talking about putting the rent up. And with the cost of animal feed going up all the time . . .' She shook her head hopelessly.

'Well, don't worry, Pat, they can't just throw you out.'

'I'm not so sure,' she muttered. 'That one there' – she jerked her head at one of the antiques traders in question – 'she's on the Chamber of Commerce.'

'Well, tell her to get stuffed,' I recommended.

Cordelia must have given me a nudge at that moment. I noticed something coiled up in the basket of plastic jewellery. I pulled out an old three-string necklace, mostly composed of glass beads and held it up. 'I haven't seen these for years.' I fingered the beads. 'See this pale-green glass? It comes from Czechoslovakia . . . or it did. You can't get it any more. You can only find it in old jewellery. There's nothing else that's quite this shade of green. Cordelia used to love it.'

Pat knitted on, unimpressed.

'How much?' I asked her.

She sniffed dolefully. 'Pound?'

'Done.' I gave her the money, picked up my necklace and left.

At the door of the bazaar I stood back to let a young mum go through, pushing a buggy. A little girl dressed up like a fairy was riding in it, complete with tiara and wings, and brandishing her plastic magic wand. I pointed at the spot where Sophie and Pat were chatting. They had come together to commiserate, joined in mutual despair. 'Wave it over that pair,' I said, tapping the wand, 'there's a love.'

Half an hour later I was standing in North Street, across the road from the pharmacy, gazing intently at Maisie's shopping list, when I became aware of a genteel thumping noise close by. Ricky and Morris, sitting at a table near the window of Taylors, a genteel and elegant tea room and one of their favourites, were knocking on the window and gesturing for me to join them.

By the time I got inside, Ricky had already signalled to the waitress to bring me a coffee. 'You'd better bring another cheese scone as well,' he called to her, 'a big one.' Sometimes I love that man.

Morris moved his bags of shopping from the seat of a vacant chair so that I could sit down. I hadn't seen either of them since the auction, so I brought them up to date on that, and told them all about Verbena Clarke and my visit from the police the previous evening. 'I've worked for that damn woman for two years,' I told them, busily slathering butter on my cheese scone. 'But she's always treated me like filth. You should have seen her face when she spotted me at the auction.'

Ricky and Morris began chuckling.

'What?' I asked suspiciously.

'She just didn't like the competition, love,' Ricky told me.

'Aw, come on!' I gaped at him. 'Are you trying to tell me she's jealous?'

'I remember her when she was a kid,' he told me. 'She could get anything she wanted by flashing those baby blues. Now she's a woman with teenage children and a husband who's dumped her and time's marching on. The baby blues don't work so well any more and it's a bit late for her to cultivate charm. She's left wondering why people don't like her.'

'But I'm her cleaner,' I objected. 'We're not engaged in a popularity contest.'

Ricky gave a derisive chuckle. 'You might not be. She is.'

Together with my scone, I chewed this over. 'So, do you think she used the robbery as an excuse to get rid of me? Because if she genuinely wasn't sure when her earrings had been taken, she could have rung me before she set the police on me.'

Ricky and Morris exchanged a look.

'There might be another reason, love,' Morris suggested sadly.

'What do you mean?'

'What he means is,' Ricky answered, 'that she might have done just that, rung you for a chat, if she hadn't seen you a few days before, at that auction, in the company of Old Nick.'

'Receiver of stolen goods,' Morris added softly.

'You mean, she put two and two together and made five?' I asked, aghast. 'But it was ages ago, wasn't it, that Nick went to prison?'

'Before your two young coppers were born,' Ricky agreed. 'But they still knew all about him, didn't they?'

'So he might have been in trouble since?'

'Who knows? The police are always suspicious of antiques dealers. After all, they're a dodgy lot. But the point is, Princess,' he said emphatically, 'he's got a reputation. And mud sticks.'

'You need to think about that, love.' Morris blinked mournfully over his spectacles. 'You've got to think of your own reputation.'

I was silent a moment. I was known to be honest, trustworthy. I got good references from all my employers. I had spare keys to many of their properties. But if Verbena Clarke went around Ashburton shooting her mouth off, if it once got about that I was suspected of being light-fingered, all that could change, and the business I had worked so hard to build up would be in danger. Then another thought occurred to me. 'So, that means, then, when those two coppers came round to see me, they already knew I worked for Nick because Verbena had told them?'

'Maybe that's why they decided to call,' Ricky nodded meaningfully.

'Perhaps, when you've done this antiques market, you ought to think about giving up working for Nick,' Morris suggested gently.

I shook my head. I enjoyed working for him. Why should I give up working for him just because Verbena Clarke was an evil, suspicious cow? On the other hand, I did not enjoy the police asking me strange questions and giving me stranger looks. I sipped my coffee thoughtfully.

'It looks as if this might be a two-scone problem,' Morris ventured after watching me a moment.

Ricky nodded and held up a hand to catch the eye of the waitress. 'I think it might.'

* * *

Back in the flat I stared gloomily into the interior of my fridge. It was lucky Sophie wasn't coming for supper. The lighted void contained nothing but two eggs and a small piece of cheese. It was a good thing I'd eaten those scones earlier. In fact, if Ricky and Morris didn't feed me every time they saw me, and Kate didn't give me regular leftovers from her kitchen, I'd probably starve. Cheese omelette for supper, I thought, making the best of it. Perfect.

The phone rang as I was grating the cheese into a bowl. I abandoned the grater and went into the living room to pick up. A voice like a refined foghorn hooted down the line. 'Hello, Juno dear! Chloe here!'

'Mrs Berkeley-Smythe, as I live and breathe!' I declared. Her voice sent me into a slight panic and I began reaching for my diary. 'You're not back already, are you?' The day before she returned from her cruise I was supposed to let myself into her house, dust, put her central heating on, switch on the fridge and buy her some basic groceries. Had I missed the date?

'No, no! I'm ringing you from Malta,' she assured me, laughing.

'Well, you're loud and clear. Are you having a good time?'

'Marvellous! And that's why I'm ringing. The dear old cruise line has offered me fifty per cent off if I stay on for the next trip. And they'll upgrade my cabin. I think they call it a no-brainer . . .'

'They do,' I told her. 'So where will you be going?'

'Oh, it's only another whizz round the Med, but I thought I might as well . . . so, that means you don't need to worry about me for another month.'

At that moment Bill strolled in from the kitchen, a shred of grated cheese hanging in a yellow ringlet from his eyebrow. I hissed at him.

'What?' bellowed Chloe.

'Nothing. So what date are you coming back?'

'It's either the twenty-third or the twenty-fifth, but, don't worry, I'll let you know for sure.'

I wished her another bon voyage, which she seemed to find hilarious. I like old Chloe. She was blithely and unrepentantly cruising her way through her children's inheritance and I didn't blame her. They weren't very nice to her and had more than enough money of their own. She was determined to live at sea as long as she could, and die on board if she could manage it. She said that cruising cost less than living in a care home, and that the service was better. Her delayed arrival suited me. Once she returned, I'd have to rearrange my schedule all over again, if I was still going to fit in working for Old Nick, something I was still considering the wisdom of. I put the phone down and glared at Bill, smugly licking his paws. Plain omelette, then.

CHAPTER TEN

We bumped our way into the old airfield in Paul's van and trundled down the cracked concrete of what must once have been the runway. I get up pretty early to walk dogs but I'm not usually awake before the sun, which was just venturing over the horizon, blushing the grey sky with pink. I yawned.

Parallel rows of stalls, as yet just skeletal frameworks, edged the runway on either side. A few already had vehicles parked beside them, traders, wrapped up against the early chill, busily unloading their stock. Each empty stall displayed its number and we drew to a stop by number forty-seven. I was quite excited. I'd never done anything like this before.

Paul nodded in the direction of a large aircraft hangar,

its interior already lit up and shining brightly through open doors. 'That's where the posh folk live,' he told me, 'rich bastards who can afford stalls inside. It's also where you can find the loos if you need them.'

'I'm OK,' I assured him.

'Right.' He grinned as he opened the van door. 'Let's get to it.'

The first thing we needed to haul out of the van was the tarpaulin to cover the overhead framework of the stall in case it rained. It was a heavy thing to lug skyward. Paul stood on the wooden tabletop, securing it with giant crocodile clips to the steel frames, stretching the tarpaulin across the two tables that made up our stall, whilst I fed the bulky waterproof fabric up to him from beneath.

Vehicle doors slammed all around us as more traders began to arrive. The sky began to lighten, the air filled with the smell of hot fat and the sound of sizzling as nearby catering vans revved up for business. The wind blasted across the open airfield and I was glad I'd taken Paul's advice and worn plenty of layers.

I didn't own a tablecloth, so I'd brought a white sheet to put down on my table and unpacked my boxes on to it. I laid out the rectangle of black velvet, pinned with all the brooches and grouped my pieces of china and bric-a-brac as attractively as I could. Overall, I was pretty pleased with the effect.

Paul had placed some small items on his table, and things that needed protection from the weather, like the chairs with their green velvet seats; larger items of furniture he simply stood on the concrete at the side.

'Will you be OK for a minute? I'd better go and park the van. On the way back I'll bring some coffee.'

'Oh, please!' I rubbed my hands together, wishing I'd brought my gloves and wondering if it was possible to get frostbite in June.

'Did you bring any change?' he asked.

I'd come prepared. I rattled my plastic sandwich box, in which I'd put my carefully counted float. I was keeping it out of sight, under the table. 'But they're not letting the public in yet, are they?' I checked my watch. The fair didn't open officially for another hour yet.

'Traders will be round, looking for an early worm.' He climbed into the van. 'If a man called Dennis comes looking for me, tell him I've got the stuff and I'll be back in a minute.'

I gave him the thumbs up as he drove off, although I hadn't got a clue what stuff he was talking about.

The market had sprung to life whilst I'd been engrossed in putting out my stock. There were four separate lines of stalls down the runway, most of them being dressed and in various stages of completion. I was gagging for a look around. I waited for Paul to return, stamping my frozen feet, hoping that it wouldn't rain and that I'd have some customers, I didn't want to go home at the end of the day without having sold anything.

I got my first customer within a few minutes. A woman in a padded jacket and fur hat, another trader I assumed, came to run an eye over my stall. She picked up a blue jug, studied it for a minute and asked, 'What's your best on this?'

'Fiver?' I suggested.

She nodded wordlessly, handed the money over without ado and wandered off. Well, I thought, that was easy. With childish glee, I wrote my first sale of the day in my notebook. Paul returned, carrying coffee. I clasped my frozen hands gratefully around the plastic cup and told him proudly about my sale.

'She didn't argue about the price?' he asked, eyes narrowing doubtfully.

'No, not at all,' I told him happily.

He grimaced. 'Traders always haggle. You probably had it priced too cheap.'

I must have looked crestfallen and he told me to cheer up. 'Why don't you wander around? Go inside the hangar and warm up. Get some breakfast. We may be busy later.'

I needed no further bidding. All agog, I wandered the avenues between stalls selling any amount of old tat. At least that's how it seemed to me. But I'm not inspired by Dinky cars, train sets, medals, coronation mugs, toys, tin or plastic, or figurines of little animals. Some people, it seems, will collect anything. Eventually, I found more interesting stalls, some selling costume jewellery, and took careful note of prices. One displayed nothing but kitchenware: wooden breadboards and rolling pins, chipped enamel jugs and breadbins, scales with brass weights, in fact, a lot of stuff that Nick still had in his kitchen: all highly collectable, apparently.

I also found the little blue jug, or one identical to it, that I had just sold for five pounds. On this stall it was marked at forty-five. I looked around to see if I could spot the lady with the fur hat but she wasn't anywhere in evidence. Perhaps she'd seen me coming and was hiding. Anyway, it was my own fault. I'd stepped into a minefield for the unwary, with very little knowledge to protect me.

Chastened, I wandered away into the hangar, which, although it was really a draughty building open to the elements at both ends, felt like a cocoon of warmth compared with the chill outside. I headed for the loo. I'd brought my washbag with me so that I could freshen up. I don't bother with much make-up at any time, but at four in the morning the best I could manage was to splash water on my face and clean my teeth. So I stood in front of the mirror, flicked my lashes with a mascara brush and rubbed on some lip gloss. After a brief struggle, I gave up my hair as a bad job and went to the cafe, where I bought two breakfast rolls stuffed with egg and bacon, carrying them away on a precariously flimsy cardboard tray.

Inside the hangar, the stalls were in a different class. None of your shabby-chic, tin advertising signs in here, none of your *Star Wars* memorabilia. Here were the rare collectables: gold watches, silver and precious jewellery, fragile furniture, fine porcelain and crystal that couldn't be risked out in the windy weather, rare books and maps, samplers, bisque dolls, fans and old lace. Everything was gleaming, sparkling, delicate and fine. Feeling like a poor relation, I hurried on outside. I didn't want our breakfast to get cold.

But before I reached the door, I was forced to make a detour. I heard a loud laugh close by me and spotted a face I recognised. It was he of the Piano Teeth, who'd been all over me at the auction viewing. Reluctant to be the victim of another ogling or damp clinging handshake, I swerved, dodging behind a row of stalls. As it turned out, I needn't have worried about his spotting me. His attention was fully engaged by a voluptuous young woman, discussing a large brass plate, which, I noticed, she was holding up in front of her like a shield.

'Oh, you beauty!' Paul exclaimed as I returned. I would have liked to think he meant me, but his eyes were fixed firmly on his bacon and egg roll.

We munched in companionable silence. A well-stuffed bacon and egg roll is not an easy thing to eat with any delicacy and requires concentration, not conversation. When I'd finally chomped my last and licked my fingers, I told him about seeing the jug, and Piano Teeth.

'Oh, Albert's here, is he?' he asked, grinning.

Before I could reply a voice called out, 'Paul, me old mate!' A man in a flat cap and padded jacket was strolling towards us. Paul introduced me to Dennis.

Dennis doffed his cap. He was distressingly bald. I'm not talking sexy, stubbly bald, I'm talking shiny, slightly pointed bald. I felt an overwhelming urge to tap him on the head with a spoon.

'You got those paintings I phoned you about?' he asked, putting his hat back in place.

Paul produced from under the table some oil paintings, which I realised I'd not seen since we loaded my stuff on the van. He'd been keeping them back for Dennis and now he laid them out on the table – six traditional farmyard scenes: old breeds of spotty pig and horned sheep, a cockerel and hens, a donkey looking over a stable door, and so on.

'Lovely!' Dennis chuckled. 'Well done, my son.'

'Watch that one,' Paul pointed. 'It's still a bit wet.'

I thought he was joking. The paintings were obviously nineteenth century, or even earlier, their colours darkened, muted with age and grime. I laughed.

'What signature did you put on?' Dennis asked, donning a pair of specs, and bending low for a closer look.

'Henry Wain.'

'Ah, good old Henry! He's got quite a following, you know, in town.' He pulled a bulky wallet from his pocket. 'The usual?' he asked, thumbing notes off a wad.

'A pleasure to take your money, sir,' Paul grinned, folding the notes away in his pocket.

'And can you do me another half-dozen Arnold Bishops?' Dennis asked, picking up his purchases and tucking them under his arm.

'Seascapes?' Paul asked.

'Yes, lovely! You give us a call when you've done 'em and we'll sort out when we pick them up. Nice to meet you, Juno,' he added, and then looked me up and down and grinned. ''Ere Paul, what d'you think to a few classical goddesses? Juno here could model, couldn't you, love?' And he went away, chuckling, highly pleased with himself.

I turned to gape at Paul. He stared back, trying to look serious, his dark eyes shining with mirth.

'*You* painted those?' I managed at last.

'Yup,' he responded, grinning.

'But they were *old*!'

'About a week.'

'But how . . . they were *old* – they were faded and dark . . .'

He beckoned me close. 'Darkolene,' he whispered softly in my ear. I shook my head at him dumbly. 'It probably went out of production before we were born,' he explained. 'Before the days of polyurethane varnish, it's what folks used to darken their wooden floorboards. A coat of Darkolene adds a hundred years to a painting – at a stroke, as it were.'

'And you paint these . . . *antique* paintings . . . to order, for Dennis, who sells them as genuine, in his shop . . . to customers who think they're buying an antique?'

'Not always,' he answered unrepentantly. 'He sells some to other traders as well.'

'And they know where they've come from?'

'No. They don't know *where* they've come from,' he told me firmly, 'but they know they're not genuine antiques.'

His cheerful dishonesty shocked me. I must have looked flabbergasted.

Paul laughed. 'Look, Juno, I'm not a forger. I don't put real signatures on those paintings, I just make them up.' He shrugged. 'And if it makes you feel any better, my criminal career can't go on much longer, anyway.'

'Why not?'

'Darkolene is getting very difficult to come by. I buy up old tins of it wherever I can find them but one day the supply will run out. And modern polyurethane varnishes are no good at all. They don't have the same effect.'

'I see.' I didn't know what to say, really. I suppose I've led a sheltered life.

'I'm not the only one who makes their own antiques,' he told me. 'Did you notice a stall selling *Victorian* panoramas?'

'Oh, yes I did!' I remembered a display of glass-fronted boxes, each a little larger than a shoebox and painted inside like the room in a doll's house, with peg dolls and tiny teddy bears sitting on miniature furniture; charming – if you like that kind of thing.

'That's Carol. I bet you she'll be round later, asking if we've got any taxidermy.'

'Taxidermy?'

'Stuffed animals come in glass cases.'

I suddenly thought of Nick's shop, of the glaring owl. The light began to dawn.

'*Old* glass cases,' Paul nodded, seeing I was catching on. 'Carol's very careful. She paints the backgrounds in watercolour, uses vintage fabrics to dress her dolls, and she never puts too many of her *panoramas*' – he made quote marks in the air with his fingers – 'on display at once.'

'I must go back and have a closer look,' I said.

'If anyone asks, she'll be perfectly honest about the fact she makes the things. But very few people do ask . . .'

'And they're happy to pay a high price because they think they're buying something old,' I completed for him. 'And stuffed animals are unfashionable, so I suppose she can pick up the cases cheaply?'

'That's right.'

Clever Carol, I had to admire her ingenuity.

Our conversation had to stop then, because a couple came up to look at Nick's balloon-back chairs. Whilst they were examining them in minute detail and Paul was filling them in on their history, I had my second customer of the day.

'How much for the celery glass?' a pleasant lady asked me, holding up a wide-necked vessel with a pedestal base.

For a moment I stared like an idiot. I hadn't realised it was a celery glass.

I'd thought it was just a vase. I recovered my wits and named my price. She made a slightly lower offer, which I accepted, and the money changed hands. I wrote down my second sale in my notebook. *Celery glass*. I had a lot to learn.

The fair filled up – a record attendance, apparently. I sold several brooches and a ribbon plate. I was hardly going to make my fortune, but I found selling was fun. I also sold a pink glass dressing-table set, glad I'd revised the price upwards after I'd seen another for sale. Paul, meanwhile, offloaded a small Edwardian dressing table and a wooden campaign chest.

But it was a long day. In between customers we filled our time with chatting and taking it in turns to fetch refreshments. After chips from one van, and custard doughnuts and hot chocolate from another, we decided that the eating had to stop and Paul went off to look around the fair, leaving me in charge, with a list of rock-bottom prices on his stock, below which I was not allowed to stray, if anyone asked.

I learnt quite a lot about Paul in the gaps between customers. As the crow flies, he lived only a short distance from my front door. In fact, I could reach his place in two minutes if I scrambled through a hedge and across a field; although a more civilised route would have been to carry on past Maisie's cottage and down Brook Lane. This would bring me directly to his gate.

He lived in a field, or rather, in a caravan in a field. He'd bought an acre of land with the idea of building his own house. He wanted to create an off-grid, eco-dwelling, constructed of straw bales and cob. He was really enthusiastic about the whole project. I'd never heard anyone talk about ground-source heat pumps and wind turbines with such energy and passion. The question I really wanted to ask, of course, was whether anyone else lived there with him, but I couldn't think of a way of phrasing the question that didn't sound embarrassingly obvious and inept. He hadn't mentioned a partner, but it would be strange if such an attractive man didn't already have someone in his life. If I didn't want to make a clot of myself, I had better proceed with caution.

Three years after buying the land, he told me, he was still wrestling with the council over planning permission. 'If I wanted to put up a conventional modern house it would be fine.' He shook his head in frustration. 'I'm trying to build something that will make a far less destructive impact on the environment and the bloody fools won't let me do it.'

'But they allowed you permission for the caravan?' I asked.

'That was already there when I bought the land and there was already a barn on-site. I use it as a workshop. I put a tank in there for dipping and stripping.'

'Dipping and stripping?'

'I've got a friend who owns an architectural salvage business. Most of my bread and butter comes from stripping doors and stuff for him. The good stuff I do by hand, but large items, like the doors, have to go in the tank.' His dark eyes smiled. 'You must come over one day and have a look.'

He returned from his wander around the fair, looking pleased, even though I had no further sales to report. He was gripping something in his fist. 'The problem with places like this is that if you're not very disciplined, you can end up buying as much as you sell.' He opened his fingers to reveal a small, pale object squatting on his palm. It was a little toad, an ugly creature with bulging eyes, its tongue sticking out. It had a hole in its head running through to its tail.

I picked it up. 'Is it Chinese?'

'Japanese. It's a netsuke, probably nineteenth century. The Japanese used to wear them tied on their sashes. That's what this hole is for, for threading it on.'

'Is it valuable?'

'Not this one. They can be expensive, depending on what they're carved from – ivory or jade – and who carved them; this one's just wooden.' He shrugged. 'But it's a nice addition to my collection.'

'You collect them?'

'My private passion.' He winked as he slipped the thing into his coat pocket.

'How many have you got?' I asked.

He frowned thoughtfully, 'About twenty.'

'Have you got them on display?' I asked mockingly.

He gave a crack of wry laughter. 'In the caravan? No. They're stuffed in a cardboard box.'

Netsuke. I tasted the word on my tongue: another thing I was going to look up on the Internet when I got home.

CHAPTER ELEVEN

I decided I would stay away from Paul in future. I fancied him too much. And after what happened at the end of the fair there was obviously no future in that.

We were busy packing away. It was almost time for the fair to close, the customers were drifting off home and all the stallholders were packing up around us.

A woman approached. I'd seen her on one of the stalls inside the hangar. I remembered her startling green eyes. She'd been engaged in a lively discussion with a customer over a *cloisonné* vase and her accent was French. She didn't look like a market trader, certainly didn't look like a woman who had spent the day out in the weather, as I looked, windswept and bedraggled. She looked glossy, well groomed and elegant. 'Ah, Paul!' she cried, as she hugged him and kissed him on both cheeks.

Paul introduced her as Sandrine. Her gaze swept me up and down and returned to my face. She gave me what I can only describe as the look of filth.

'So, Paul,' she asked, still maintaining eye contact with me, 'where is your lovely wife?'

I turned away and carried on stowing away my unsold stock, wrapping things in newspaper and putting them in boxes, keeping my head down, apparently not listening in to their conversation, my ears on stalks. There was a moment of silence before Paul replied. Did he glance in my direction?

'Carrie's staying up in Nottingham,' he told her, 'with her mother.'

'And Josh too?' she purred sweetly. 'How old is he now? Two?'

'Nearly three.'

'Ah,' Sandrine babbled on, 'the time, how it flies!'

Ah, the heart, how it sinks! Now I had the answer to my question. My face felt hot, I was blushing like an idiotic schoolgirl. And why, I asked myself? Paul and I weren't on a date. During the day he had asked me if I'd be interested in working some other fairs and markets with him, which I'd taken as a sign that things might be moving in an interesting direction, but I'd no reason to feel embarrassed. It just seemed very strange that he'd told me all his plans for his new home and the kind of life he wanted to live there, and said nothing about a wife and child. Surely they would be mentioned, hinted at somehow? I felt irrationally irritated with him, and even crosser with myself.

Glossy Sandrine made her departure with, 'Do give my love to Carrie when you see her!' and drifted away. I carried on packing and tried to smother the desire to strangle her with my bare hands. After all, she'd done me a favour.

Paul's attention was taken by a woman interested in a little table of his, and so we were saved the awkwardness of conversation for a while. I didn't know what to say anyway. Better to shut up and leave it to him to raise the subject.

Which he did, but not until we'd packed everything, loaded it in the van, folded away the tarpaulin, and were sitting in a queue, trying to exit the airfield with all the other traders, after the fair had closed.

'You OK, Juno?' he asked, glancing at me because I was silent.

'Fine,' I assured him. Less said the better, I felt.

'You enjoyed today?'

'It was great, thanks.'

There was a brief pause before he spoke again. 'I didn't mention Carrie before because . . . well, it's a bit painful at the moment. Truth is, she's left me . . .'

'She doesn't understand you?' I suggested sarcastically. I regretted it immediately, could have bitten off my tongue.

He grunted. 'I suppose I deserve that.' He was silent a moment. 'It was our dream, you see, building our own place and raising our kids in a natural environment. At first, Carrie was just as passionate about it as I was. But then she got pregnant with Josh – well, it's not easy, coping with a small baby in a tiny caravan. Last winter was really hard, we were broke . . . and the weather . . .' He shook his head at the memory. 'It was freezing cold, never seemed to stop raining. The caravan was damp. The mud was awful. Well, when we found Carrie was expecting again . . .'

Ah! I thought, something the glossy Sandrine didn't seem to know . . .

'She said she couldn't go through it again, not unless we were living in a proper house. She decided to go back to her mum for the duration of the pregnancy.'

'But she'll come back, won't she?'

'I don't know,' he admitted hopelessly. 'I suggested we modify our plans to build a more conventional house. The council might let us get on with it. But even that could take a year to build, longer if we get delays. She wants us to abandon the whole idea, sell up and buy a new property.'

'And you're not prepared to do that?' I was feeling sorry for him by now, just trying not to show it.

'Of course I will, if I have to. But I'm just hoping, once the baby's born, if I can persuade Carrie to come back down here again, she might change her mind.'

'I'm sure she will,' I said, although I didn't know if I would if I were in her position: having children changes things, changes people. Not that I know anything about it. In fact, I don't seem to know much about love and relationships in general. It must be the Capricorn in me, perhaps I'll get better at it when I'm younger.

'So, we're still friends?' Paul asked. We'd deposited all my boxes outside my front door and I'd assured him I could manage them from there.

'Of course we are.'

'Give us a hug, then.' He opened his arms wide and I let him envelop me in a big friendly embrace. And that was stupid, because, as he planted a brotherly kiss on my cheek, I felt the warmth and strength of his body, like an electrical charge. I had to resist the desire to melt my body against his, to brush my lips against that warm, tanned neck.

I decided then I would maintain a distance as much as possible. He was a married man. I'd been down that road before and I wasn't about to make the same mistake again. So, I wouldn't do any more markets with him and I wouldn't go round to see his place as he suggested. I would maintain a polite distance, stay away.

I watched him drive off. And I wouldn't have gone near him ever again, if it hadn't been for what happened the day after.

CHAPTER TWELVE

I called around to see Nick the morning after the fair, keen to tell him about my day. Considering the amount of money he'd made with the *bonheur du jour* at auction, I thought he might be disappointed with our paltry pickings, but not at all. He seemed pleased. 'I've brought back the rest of the stock,' I told him. 'It's in my van.'

'No, no. You keep, Juno,' he told me. 'You keep it till next time.'

I wasn't so sure there was going to be a next time. And I didn't want to keep the boxes. I didn't have room in my flat to store them and I couldn't leave them in the van because I needed the space for the Tribe every morning. But I wanted to ask him a favour, so I mentally resigned myself to lugging the wretched things back home.

'You know that nasty, ratty-looking stuffed weasel you've got down in the shop? It's not likely to sell, is it?'

'You want?' Nick frowned at me, puzzled. 'You want weasel?'

'I don't want weasel, but I would like the case.'

'What for you want case?' he asked suspiciously.

'It's just an idea I have, something I want to mess around with. I'll pay you for it.'

He shrugged. 'It's yours. Take it.'

'Are you sure?'

'Yes. Go, fetch,' he said, as if I was a dog. 'Juno,' he called out as I started off down the stairs. 'You take weasel. You no take case and leave me with weasel.'

'OK!' I called back, wondering if the council refuse collectors would take away a stuffed rodent if I left it in a bin.

The weasel was up on the top shelf in the shop, which meant climbing up a dangerously rickety wooden stepladder. Whilst I was wobbling about on the top step amongst the dust and cobwebs, I examined some other taxidermy items. The glaring owl and its case were much too big for my purposes, but there was a badly stuffed, furious little creature, which might once have been a red squirrel, baring its teeth at me. Its case was about the right size.

So engrossed was I in the consideration of objects that I don't normally get a chance to see up close, that I didn't hear the sick rattle of the doorbell, or Nick going down to answer it, until it was too late. Voices sounded in the hallway, speaking in a foreign language: one was Nick's, but the other I was certain belonged to Vlad. There was also a new voice, much deeper. I reckoned Nick wouldn't want Vlad to know I was there, and I wasn't keen on encountering him again myself, so I kept very still whilst I heard heavy footsteps climbing the stairs. I listened until they reached Nick's living room, their footsteps directly over my head.

Then I sneaked quietly down the ladder. I could slip out of the front door without being noticed but I'd left my bag in Nick's kitchen. My keys were inside so I couldn't get into the van, and if I walked home, I couldn't get into the house. I slid my hand into my jacket pocket. My fingers found my mobile phone, but nothing else.

I stayed put for a minute, listening to the voices upstairs. A lively discussion was rapidly escalating into a heated argument. I crept to the door and peered out into the corridor. A voice suddenly raised in anger – Vlad's voice, aggressively loud, bullying, accompanied by a series of thumps: his gloved fist pounding on a table, or something worse? Then came a tremendous crash, like a piece of furniture being thrown over, and the unmistakeable sound of a slap. I heard Nick cry out.

I raced up the stairs, slipping my phone from my pocket, and held it against my ear. 'Police!' I yelled, rushing into the room. I held the phone out at arm's length. 'I've called the police!' I hadn't of course. No signal. I just hoped Vlad and his companion didn't realise that.

I had the advantage of surprise. They had no idea I was in the building and for a moment they stared, speechless with shock. Then Vlad let out an oath. His companion, solid as a church door, black hair crinkling over a low brow – let's call him Igor – stood still and gaped at me. He was gripping a bunch of Nick's shirt front in one massive fist, the other raised in preparation for a blow.

'Get out!' I screamed at him, pointing the way down the stairs. I tried to control my voice but it was shaking and way off the scale. 'Go!' I waved the phone at them, screeching like a harpy. 'Police! I've called the police!'

They might not know much English, but they understood 'police' all right. Igor slowly released his hold on Nick.

For one heart-stopping moment I thought that Vlad was going to call my bluff. A derisive smile slowly spread across his face and he took a step towards me. If his icy stare was bad, his smile was worse, like the grin on the face of a wolf that has spotted a limping lamb. But at that moment, somewhere out on East Street, a siren wailed. I could tell it was only an ambulance, but it was enough to spook the Brothers Grim. They exchanged glances, decided that discretion was the better part of valour and beat a retreat down the stairs, Vlad making vile and hateful mutterings on the way.

At the foot of the stairs, he turned, glared up at me, jabbed at me with one finger, then drew it emphatically across his throat. The message couldn't have been clearer.

I held up my phone, pointing in his direction. I might not have a signal to make a call, but I could still take a photograph. The camera flashed. Vlad's face turned white with rage as he realised what I'd done. For a moment I thought he would rush the stairs and wrench the phone from my hand. But then the siren sounded closer. He muttered, and banged his way out of the door after his companion.

I flew down the stairs behind him, slammed the front door shut and thrust the bolts home. My heart was hammering and I felt sick. I took a deep breath and ran back up to the living room, where Nick had slumped into a chair. He looked ashen.

I knew he kept bottles of booze in a cupboard. I hunted around, found brandy and a glass, poured, and placed it on the table next to him. He was breathless and I gave him a moment to recover himself, picking up the table that had been thrown over and collecting the pieces of a shattered ornament.

'Oh, Juno . . . Juno . . .' he gasped at last, shaking his head. 'You should not have done that.'

'I don't know what would have happened if I hadn't.' I knelt beside his chair. He reached out and gripped my hand weakly. His touch was clammy, his breathing ragged.

'I'm going to call a doctor,' I told him.

'No, no,' he protested feebly. 'I have pills . . .' He pointed to the mantelpiece. Searching amongst the clutter of ornaments and old envelopes on the shelf, I found a small brown bottle and shook two tiny tablets out into his trembling palm. He put them under his tongue and after a minute he seemed to be breathing easier.

'Who are those men?' I asked him. 'What do they want?'

He slid a shifty glance at me. 'They are just . . . business associates.'

'Business associates?' I repeated scornfully. 'I'm going to call the police.'

'No! No police,' he gripped my hand again. 'You promise . . . Juno . . . call police . . . things get very bad.'

115

'Either you tell me what's going on, Nick, or I call them right now.'

'And tell them what?' he demanded, rallying. 'You hear argument . . . you don't . . . know . . . what is about. Old man get punched . . .' He shrugged. 'You think they care?' He gave the ghost of a chuckle. 'Is just misunderstanding, Juno . . . is all right.'

I went to the window, threw up the sash, and looked up and down the street. I couldn't see Vlad or Igor anywhere but that didn't mean they weren't lurking somewhere. They'd be back, I was sure of that. But Nick was deaf to all arguments. The mention of police only made him agitated and I didn't want to make his condition worse than it already was. In the end, I promised I wouldn't call them. Yet.

'Is all right, Juno, they gone.' Nick chuckled. 'Angry goddess scare them away. You go now, huh?'

'I'll go when you're fit enough to follow me down the stairs,' I agreed reluctantly. 'You lock and bolt the door after me. And don't you let them in again, you promise me?'

Nick nodded. 'I promise,' he agreed meekly.

It was half an hour before I cracked open the front door. I peeped out cautiously, in case the two bogeymen were in the alley. When I was sure the coast was clear, I shut the door behind me and waited until I heard Nick push the bolts into place before I hurried across Shadow Lane and climbed into my van, locking the door after me. I sat for a moment, tapping my fingers on the steering wheel as the full idiocy of what I'd done came over me. I'd have been no match for either of those two if they'd decided to turn on me. And there'd been no mistaking the meaning of Vlad's departing gesture. I could have ended up battered and bruised, and very possibly floating down the River Dart.

I considered breaking my promise and going straight to the police but there didn't seem much point. I knew if they followed it up with Nick, he'd only downplay the incident, or even deny it took place at all. I sighed. I wasn't happy, but there didn't seem to be anything I could do. Reluctantly, I pulled away from the kerb.

I was booked for that afternoon, gardening for the vicar. I usually love working in the vicarage garden, surrounded by warm stone walls hanging with old-fashioned roses, clusters of scented Rambling Rector and Himalayan Musk nodding in the breeze. In fact, a couple of hours working in any garden can make me feel better about most things. But dead-heading the roses and staking the delphiniums didn't work for me that afternoon. Birdsong and bees bumbling amongst the lavender failed to lift my spirits. All I could think about was Nick. When I got home, I parked the van, but didn't bother going back into the house. I passed the garden gate, walked down the lane and scrambled through the hedge and across the field.

Paul was in his workshop. I called at the caravan first, but it was locked up, so I made my way down to the big corrugated iron shed. The door was standing open. I went inside and stood for a moment surrounded by a jumble of old furniture. I could hear water splashing somewhere, what sounded like a powerful jet or hose. I called Paul's name and wandered through the shed into an old, attached stone barn. I called again. The sound of the water stopped abruptly and he appeared, coming through a small door, wearing wet gumboots, the trousers of his overalls splashed with wetness, a pair of protective goggles pushed up on his forehead. 'Juno!' he cried, smiling. He stripped off a pair of heavy rubber gauntlets and tossed them on a workbench. 'I wasn't expecting to see you so soon.' His smile faded as he looked at my face. 'What's wrong?'

I began to relate what had happened that morning, but he stopped me and made me sit down. He pulled up a stool beside me and listened whilst I poured out what had happened.

'And you've no idea who these men were?' he asked at last.

'That's why I came to you. I thought you might know them. Nick might have mentioned them, or said something . . .' I showed him the photograph of Vlad I'd taken on my phone. It was a charming study, his face twisted with malice, caught just at the moment he was drawing his finger across his throat.

'Never seen him before.' Paul frowned and rubbed his chin thoughtfully. 'I know some of the dealers he knows, local people, like Tom Smithson and Verbena. But I've never come across this pair.'

'Nick won't tell me what they want. I'm frightened he's going to get hurt.'

Paul thought for a moment. 'Tell you what, Nick and I need to settle up for the things I sold for him at the fair yesterday. I'll go around tonight, see if I can find out anything. He might open up to me.'

'Thanks.' I smiled and he smiled back.

'So,' I said, deliberately breaking eye contact and looking around me, 'this is your empire.'

'Allow me to show you around, madam.'

The barn was workmanlike and tidy, the space taken up by an enormous saw bench and stacks of furniture in various stages of restoration. Chisels and files hung in specially fitted racks on the walls and there were plastic bins for wood shavings and sawdust. Rows of tightly fitted tins stood on the shelves and there was a strong smell of resin, beeswax and spirit varnish. There was also an oil painting on an easel, of a barge with red sails on a swelling grey sea, its colours bright and fresh.

'Is this a genuine Arnold Bishop?' I asked.

Paul grinned. 'The very same.'

'Where's the Darkolene?'

He pointed to a battered, ancient-looking tin with dribbles of dried, dark-brown varnish down the side. 'That's my last one. I'm starting to panic.'

Chaos was allowed to reign in one corner only. Dirty coffee mugs jostled for space on a wooden draining board next to a cracked china sink, with an old kettle, an exploded bag of sugar and half-opened packets of biscuits.

'I don't think much of the catering arrangements,' I told him frankly.

'What's up here?' I climbed a wooden ladder to an old hayloft but there was nothing to see but more furniture.

Back down on ground level, I went through the little wooden door Paul had come through earlier. It took me into a lean-to with a glass skylight in a corrugated metal roof. The concrete floor was shiny with wetness, the powerful hose Paul had been using lying like a huge serpent on the concrete. Beneath the skylight stood a large metal tank, about the size of a builder's skip. 'Is this the stripping tank?' I had to stand on tiptoe to peer in. It was half full of cold, clear liquid.

'Careful!' Paul warned me, following me through the door. 'Don't get too close.'

'What's in it?'

'Sodium hydroxide,' he said, stooping to coil up the hose. 'Caustic soda.'

'Nasty stuff! Isn't it bad for old furniture?' I asked. 'Doesn't it ruin the wood?'

He laughed, coiling the hose over a reel mounted on the wall. Its brass nozzle drizzled slightly and he gave a final turn to a large tap on the wall beside it, making sure the water was turned off. Then he came over to join me by the tank. 'Leave anything in too long and it'll fall to pieces. It dissolves all the glue in the joints. I heat the tank first, then things don't have to stay in so long, and it doesn't damage the wood so much. I never use it for the good stuff.' He pointed to a pine cupboard lying on its side on the wet concrete. 'I've just taken that out. I was rinsing it off when you called.'

'How do you get the stuff in there?' I looked up. Above the tank a big metal grid, like an old-fashioned laundry airer, hung on chains.

'If you stand aside a minute, I'll show you.' He grabbed one of three levers on the side of the tank. 'This one raises and lowers the grid,' he demonstrated. The chains squeaked and rattled as the grid went up and down. 'This one opens and closes the lid.' He pulled the second lever and the two metal halves of the lid closed in a neat seam over the top of the tank.

'And what does that one do?' I asked, pointing at the third.

'Ah, this is the one you have to watch,' he told me. 'Mind your head, it swings out a bit suddenly. This lever swings the whole rig out sideways. Then you can lower it to the ground to put whatever you want to go in the tank on the grid . . .'

'And then raise it with the other lever and swing it back again,' I completed for him.

'That's it,' he said. 'Want a go?'

I took over the levers and played happily for a couple of minutes, raising and lowering the rack and swinging it into place until the novelty wore off.

'It's a bit risky isn't it, using this stuff?' I asked. 'It burns horribly, caustic soda.'

'When I put the tank in, I had to lay a special drain,' he explained. 'If you don't dispose of the waste properly you can get a big fine.'

'What would happen if you fell in?'

'You'd never get out again, that's for sure. Left there long enough, you'd dissolve.'

I suspected him of pulling my leg. 'Seriously?'

'It used to be used for disposing of animal carcasses – human ones too, I expect, on the quiet. I heard a story once about a bloke who fell in a tank and couldn't get out. They found him next morning – nothing but jelly.'

I took a step back, shuddering. In the safety of the workshop once more, my thoughts returned to Nick.

'Will you phone me when you've seen him tonight?'

'Don't worry.' He gave a sudden grin. 'Perhaps these guys won't come back. It sounds like you made a good job of scaring them off.'

CHAPTER THIRTEEN

When I got back to the house I still had to unload Nick's boxes. As I was making my fifth trip from the van to the front door with my arms full, Adam came out to give me a hand and told me I could store them in a space under the stairs. I began to feel a lot happier. Then Kate came out from the kitchen and asked me if I'd like a spicy vegetable pasty for my supper and my happiness bordered on ecstasy.

I ate it warm from the microwave, standing in the kitchen, Bill weaving figures of eight around my ankles. I put the plate in the sink and dusted crumbs of flaky pastry from my boobs. I had things to do.

I hunted under my bed until I found what I was looking for – a carved wooden box that belonged to Cordelia. I put it on the kitchen table and opened the lid.

'Aha!' I declared, picking out a tiny pair of pliers. The rest of the box was stuffed with self-seal plastic bags containing long metal pins, hooks and various types of bead: Cordelia's earring-making kit.

I fetched the green glass necklace I had bought from Pat. I'd cleaned it prior to taking it to the antiques fair so I was able to start work at once, snipping each of the three strings that made up the necklace and letting the beads fall out on to a tray. I picked up three, ascending in size, and threaded them on to a long silver pin, putting a tiny silver bead from Cordelia's kit in between each one. Bill, who had leapt up on the table, watched with interest as I used the pliers to bend the top of the pin over into a loop and hang it on to the hook that went through the ear. I pinched the loop into place. '*Voilà!*' I dangled the result in front of him. 'One earring!'

Over the next two hours I made twenty-four pairs of green glass earrings, using either gold or silver beads to separate the glass ones, varying the design with additional beads from Cordelia's box. Bill lost interest after whisking a marble-sized bead on to the floor with his paw, chasing it around the kitchen floor and losing it under the fridge, obliging me to fish about among the dust with the handle of a broom. Then he curled up, inconveniently, on my lap.

I was pleased with my night's work, if a bit boggle-eyed. No two pairs of earrings were the same. And I still had beads from the necklace left over. I also had a stiff neck. I stretched and let down my hair just as the phone rang. It was Paul.

'Is Nick OK?' I asked.

'Yup. He was being careful, wouldn't open the door to me until I called to him through the letter box.'

'Did he tell you anything?'

'I asked him straight out. He was cross with you for talking to me and he clammed up at first. But eventually he opened up a bit, said that he'd dealt with these guys in the past . . . "moved things on for them", is how he put it. He said they come down now and again from London to do business with him and he's never had any trouble with them before.'

'Well, he was having trouble with them this morning.'

'This time, there was a problem over the price of some stuff he'd sold for them. He'd put it in an auction for them and whatever it was – he wouldn't tell me – didn't reach the expected price. They're after Nick for the difference.'

'That's not fair,' I objected. 'It's not his fault.'

'I don't think *fair* comes into their vocabulary.'

'Probably not,' I agreed. 'What's he going to do?'

'Pay up and get them off his back, he says. He's going to set up a meeting. I offered to be there as security. They're not likely to turn violent if he's got a witness.'

'I want to be there too.'

I heard Paul laugh down the phone. 'You might scare them off! I wish I'd been there this morning, I hear you were a sight to see.'

'I don't know about that,' I muttered, embarrassed.

'By the way, you didn't notice their car this morning, did you?'

'No. Why?'

'It's probably just coincidence. There was a black BMW parked down the street this evening, I noticed it when I came out of Nick's. There were two men sitting in it. When I walked down the street in their direction they drove away, pretty sharp.'

'Did you get a look at them?'

'Not really. It was too dark. When I got in my van, I drove around the block a few times in case they'd come back, but they didn't. Like I say, it was probably just coincidence.'

'Let's hope so.'

Paul yawned. 'Well, I'm off to bed. Try not to antagonise any more dangerous thugs if you can help it.'

I remembered Vlad standing at the foot of Nick's stairs, glaring at me and drawing his finger across his throat. 'I'll try,' I promised.

Next morning, I popped into the bazaar and gave a mournful Pat a quick lesson in how to make earrings. The ones I'd made the night before hung in rows on an old photo frame I'd padded with black velvet and turned into a display stand.

'Juno, they're lovely!' she cried.

'Shove over, then, cos I'm going to show you how to make them.'

It was, as I told her, dead easy, once she'd mastered the knack of bending the top of the earring pin over into a loop with the pliers. The real skill came in choosing the beads, putting colours and shapes together. Judging from the pretty baby clothes she'd knitted, I reckoned Pat would be good at that, and she was. Her big, bony hands worked with surprising dexterity.

'I must pay you for all these beads and things,' she said, looking anxious.

'Nope, treat it as a donation to the animals.' I left her with all the spare beads, plus lists of jewellery-making suppliers. I loaned her Cordelia's little pliers, with a warning that I'd want them back. They had sentimental value.

'Oh, Juno, thank you ever so much!'

'My pleasure, Pat. Just get cracking! I've got something else to bring you next week.'

CHAPTER FOURTEEN

Paul was wrong about the BMW. It wasn't black, it was blue. I was coming back from Tavistock on the B3357, the road which bisects the moor. Summer had finally started in earnest and I'd given myself a day off for a snoop around Tavistock. It's a lovely town with an old, stone-built market hall, which yielded some interesting goodies. But I spent more than I intended, so instead of treating myself to lunch in a cafe, I settled for some shop-bought sandwiches and decided to take the scenic route home across the moor and stop for a picnic.

Despite the glorious weather, I seemed to have the moor to myself save for a few black-faced sheep grazing amongst clumps of gorse. I pulled in off the side of the road and parked on the car park, little more than a level area of gravel beyond the grassy verge. There were no other cars there.

Little grew up there above the height of bracken and gorse, and the treeless moorland gave me sweeping views. I stared across the landscape, a stiff breeze flirting with strands of my hair, and breathed in deep. To the north of the road, the rocky outline of Great Mis Tor dominated the skyline. To the south, the land fell away gently, and I gazed across hills that were tinged with bronze, russet and purple, fading to blue in the far distance. I locked the van, walked away from the road over short grass scattered with tiny black piles of sheep droppings and found a sun-warmed rock, where I could park my bum and eat my sandwich. I shed my jacket, folding it under me for a cushion and watched a pair of buzzards circling in the immaculate blue above my head.

Perhaps I have the soul of a cleaning lady after all. A hundred yards or so ahead of me a stunted hawthorn tree, grown hunchback against the prevailing wind, clung with gnarled roots to a low cairn of rock. It would have made a wonderful photograph, a symbol of the struggle of poor living things against the pitiless elements – except that tangled in its branches was a shredded plastic bag.

I couldn't bear the sight of the thing flapping away like a flag, the thought that it might be there for years, a horrible intrusion in an otherwise unspoilt wilderness. I had to remove it. I left my bag and jacket where they lay and threaded my way through the gorse to the cairn of rocks. I could see where the sheep had made a path before me, leaving tiny clouds of wool hanging on the tips of the thorns.

Reaching the foot of the tree involved some awkward clambering, treading carefully, searching for footholds among the knotted, witch-like fingers of its roots. It was a few minutes before I managed to scramble to the top. Moss grew thick on the northern side of the trunk, a sign of clean air. I breathed in deeply and then turned around to get another look at the view: then dropped down behind the tree, crouching as low as I could behind the rocks, my heart thumping with shock.

Vlad and Igor were walking across the grass towards me. They must have spotted the van parked by the side of the road. They could scarcely miss it. I always park across the lane from Nick's shop and they'd probably seen it there. It wouldn't take a brain surgeon to work out who it belonged to.

I risked a look over the rocks in front of me. Right now they were going through the pockets of my jacket, and laughing. I saw my bunch of keys tossed in a glittering arc into the bracken. Igor began rooting through my bag. He found my phone and passed it to Vlad, who stood scrolling through, looking for something: the photograph I had taken of him. He gave a bark of laughter and showed something to Igor. He must have found it. I didn't need to see his thumb working to know he was pressing delete, before he flung the phone into the bracken along with my keys.

Meanwhile, Igor was happily chucking things out of my bag. He found my silent dog whistle and blew it several times, shrugged when it made no noise, and tossed it over his shoulder. A tampon went flying, then my diary; then he found my purse, opened it and emptied out the change.

I dodged back behind the rock, out of sight. Perhaps now Vlad had got what he wanted and erased the photograph, they might both drive off and leave me alone.

'Juuunoooo.' It was Vlad calling, his voice mocking. 'Where are you hiding, girlfriend?'

He and Igor weren't going to go away. They were coming to find me.

What the hell was I going to do? There was no one else for miles around, no cover to hide me beyond the rocks I was cowering behind. I couldn't stay where I was and there was nowhere I could run to without them seeing me. Even if I could make it back to the safety of the van, my keys were gone. I crouched silently, willing myself to stay calm, to breathe evenly, not to give in to the panic that was fluttering in my throat. They must know where I was hiding; before long, they'd be coming to get me.

I dared a glance over the rocks. The two of them were striding towards the cairn.

I looked around: short grass, broken rocks and stunted thorn bushes; open country, nowhere to hide. I glanced up at the tree. I could climb it, but it was so small and stunted that its branches wouldn't put me beyond their reach. I could sneak in amongst the rusty bracken, crawl on hands and knees, but my movement through it would be slow, noisy and easy to detect. Better to run, try to reach the road and pray a car might come along, pray the driver would stop for a wild-eyed woman with wilder hair, out on the moor, crazily flagging him down.

'Juuunoooo.'

They were closer now. I bolted, veered away from them

in a wide arc, racing across the grass towards the road. They spotted me as soon as I emerged from the shadow of the rocks and shouted. I kept running. I'd been a good runner once. If only I'd kept up the training. They split up, Igor breaking into a shambling jog after me, Vlad sprinting on ahead to cut me off before I could reach the road. I stopped, breathing hard, blood roaring in my ears, then jinked back the way I had come, back towards the cairn, forcing them both to change tack.

But we all knew they had me. I couldn't keep this up for long. Sunlight flashed on something silver in Vlad's gloved hand: a blade. I scrambled back up the rocks to the tree, stood up and screamed for help at the top of my lungs. A cruel wind whipped my voice away, carrying it off like a lost soul, rendering my screams useless. Igor and Vlad were closing in on me from either side.

I bent down, picked up a rock the size of a tennis ball and hefted it, assessing its weight. Igor laughed. But I wasn't going down without a fight and he didn't realise he was dealing with the captain of the school cricket team. Let's see how funny he found it when he was wearing a chunk of granite in his teeth. I bowled it overarm, aiming at his head. But throwing a rock is not the same as throwing a cricket ball. It fell short. I was out of practice.

Out of practice and out of luck. I scrabbled among the stones at my feet, searching desperately for another likely missile. Too small would do no damage, too big would be impossible to lift. My hand closed on one, sharp and pointed, barely more than a chip. I stood up and aimed it like a skimming stone, straight at Igor's head. It spun through the air and struck him on the cheekbone. He bellowed, stopping to clutch at his face. When he took his hand away I could see a trickle of blood. He snarled and broke into a stumbling run towards me. Frantically I hunted for another stone, my breath coming in short, panicky gasps.

As I struggled to dislodge a rock lodged between two roots, a long mournful howl echoed across the moor. For a moment I froze, then looked up. Igor and Vlad hesitated, glanced uncertainly at one another. Then there was silence, the only sound was the faint mewing cries of the buzzards, circling in the sky above. They shrugged and started towards me again, Vlad grinning as his hand closed more tightly around his knife. I clawed at the rock by my feet, scrabbling with my fingers, tearing my nails as I fought to prise it loose from the earth.

But something had heard those blasts Igor had made on the silent whistle. Something was answering the call. Another baleful moan sounded, only this time it was closer. A thing unseen was crashing through a stand of nearby bracken, making the ferns rustle and wave wildly, a thing that growled and snarled and sent the sheep scattering in all directions. The bracken parted and a great black shape came thundering out.

It stopped in front of them, blocking their way: a mass of quivering muscle, fur bristling around mighty shoulders and ridging along its spine, its torn ears flattened against a broad skull, lips drawn back from fearsome fangs. It growled, rumbling rage deep in its throat, fury blazing hot in its eyes.

'Duke!' I whispered in awe.

Vlad and Igor took a step back and Duke let off a volley of raw, threatening barks. They stood motionless, Vlad's grip tightening on the blade. Duke sank low, his belly almost brushing the ground. He crept forward, shoulders pumping like a lion stalking its prey, gathering himself for a spring, all the time a terrible, low moaning tearing itself from deep within his throat. I could see Vlad weighing up the odds. He might manage a lucky stab, but he risked getting his tonsils ripped out.

Slowly, almost imperceptibly, he and Igor began to inch backward, Igor making stupid 'nice doggy' noises, neither of them taking their eyes from Duke, who inched ever closer as they crept back.

Without warning, he charged. Both men turned and fled. Duke leapt at Igor, felled him like a tree, then shook him, crushing his forearm in the vice of his jaws. I could hear the bones crunching from where I stood. He screamed out, but Vlad had kept on running, and was already climbing into the BMW.

Duke released his grip, chasing off towards the car. Vlad slammed himself inside as the dog launched himself at the driver's door, claws slipping, scrabbling against the window as he slathered and snarled through the glass. I heard the engine start up. Sobbing and gibbering in pain, Igor floundered to his feet and lurched across the grass. Vlad reversed sharply, shaking Duke off and swinging the car around so that Igor could clamber in the passenger side. I yelled at Duke to come to me, terrified that Vlad would run him over.

Igor wrenched the door open with his good arm and flung himself aboard. Before the door was closed, the car lunged forward in a crash of gears. There was a crunch of tyres spinning on gravel, a spraying up of tiny stones, and then the car sped off up the road. Duke gave chase for a few long, loping strides, but slowed and lost interest. I stumbled down over the rocky cairn and my legs gave way beneath me. I sat on the ground and sobbed. Duke baulked of his prey, ambled over beside me and lay down in a disgruntled fashion. I threw my arms about his neck and hugged him.

'Awesome!' I whispered in his ear. 'You were awesome!'

It wasn't me who called the police. I don't know how long I sat, clinging around Duke's neck, blubbing into his fur, but after a while he'd endured enough, got heavily to his feet, and snuffled among the gorse where he found and devoured the half-eaten sandwich I had put down on the rock what seemed like a lifetime before.

That brought me to my senses. I needed to find my keys, and my phone. I picked up my bag and began hunting around in the scrubby bushes. I located my empty purse, my diary and the tampon, and was still scrabbling among wicked thorns, trying to find my keys and phone, when I heard a piercing three-note whistle in the distance. Duke's head came up, he gave a single slow wave of his tail and barked in greeting. I recognised the whistle too. It was Micky. I scanned the horizon but couldn't see him. He was probably still far away, his whistle carrying long-distance.

Duke began to lope off. He stopped at the top of the cairn and looked back at me uncertainly. The whistle came again. And with no further thought, my hero disappeared over the cairn and was lost to sight.

I continued searching painfully among the thorns, my fingers bleeding from repeated stabbings. I had to find my keys. I wanted to get off the moor, I wanted to go home. But more urgent than any of that was the need to ring Nick, to warn him that Vlad and Igor could be on their way. I had to find my phone. Happily, I located the dog whistle. I couldn't be sure whether it was that, or all my screaming and hollering that had drawn Duke's attention, but I didn't intend to leave it behind.

'Have you lost something?'

I looked up. A couple of walkers with woolly hats and backpacks were striding in my direction.

I put on a smile as they came towards me. 'I dropped my bag and lost my phone . . . it's here . . . somewhere,' I added, looking around helplessly. 'You don't have a mobile on you, do you? Would you mind phoning my number?'

The woman had already produced her phone. I gave her my number and within a few seconds mine began to vibrate noisily among the yellow flowers of the gorse. We located it about three feet from where I'd been looking. Thank God, Vlad hadn't torn out the sim. It would still work. We also found my keys. I thanked the couple profusely.

'Are you sure you're all right?' the man asked, eyeing me doubtfully. I probably looked a wreck.

'I'm fine,' I responded, sucking blood from my finger. 'I'm going home now. I think I've had enough of the moor for one day.' Concerned, they wanted to stay and chat. I just wanted them to get going so that I could phone Nick.

'Well, if you're sure you're OK . . .'

'Yes. Thanks again.' I waved at them and hurried away towards the van.

It had a flat tyre. Vlad must have stuck his knife into it when he and Igor arrived. I couldn't help thinking about the old quarries and mine workings there were roundabout, all the places my body might have been dumped, never to be found again. I phoned Nick's number, unlocking the van door and tossing my bag inside whilst I paced fretfully, willing him to answer.

'Nick, are you all right?' I blurted as soon as he picked up.

'Is Juno?' he asked. 'Yes, yes, I'm fine.'

'Vlad and Igor—' I began.

'Who?'

'Your friends . . .'

'No need to shout! I see them this morning. We talk. We come to arrangement. Everything is all right now. They go home.'

'I . . . I don't understand . . .' I said stupidly. 'You've *seen* them?'

'We friends again,' he told me happily.

I couldn't believe what I was hearing. 'Friends?' I shouted down the phone at him. 'They just tried to kill me!'

'No, no, Juno . . .' Nick began soothingly, before the phone was obviously snatched out of his hand.

'Juno, where are you?' It was Paul's voice.

'I'm up on the moor,' I told him.

'Are you all right?'

'I am now.' I gabbled an account of what had just happened to me, ending with the flat tyre.

'I'll come and get you. Tell me exactly where you are.'

I told him where I was. 'But it's all right, I can manage, I've got a spare.'

'I'll be there in about half an hour. You sit tight.' And he rang off before I could argue any further.

Suddenly drained of energy, I sat in the van, and rested my head against the steering wheel. After a few minutes, a car pulled up beside me, blue light flashing, and I started nervously. It was a police car with two officers inside. The driver wound down his window and gazed at me from pale-blue eyes. 'You all right, miss?'

'Yes, I'm fine, Officer,' I lied, trying to sound bright, as he climbed out of his vehicle. 'I've just got a flat tyre.'

The other officer also got out and together they walked around, making a great business, it seemed to me, of surveying the van. 'So you have,' he remarked pleasantly. 'Have you been sitting here long?'

'I'm waiting for the AA.'

'Ah!' The driver glanced at his colleague. 'It's just we had a rather strange report about twenty minutes ago. A call came in from a gentleman birdwatching up there.' He pointed towards a distant tor. 'He was using powerful binoculars. He said he'd seen something strange going on, a woman being chased by two men, a woman with long red hair,' he added, scrutinising me with eyes narrowed, 'like yourself.'

'Really?' I gazed at him, all innocence, raking a hand through the tangled mass of my curls and pulling out a frond of bracken.

'I think he must be quite an elderly gentleman,' he

went on. 'He felt he was too far away to render you any assistance and so he called us on his mobile phone. He also mentioned something about a huge black dog.'

I gave what I hoped was a convincing laugh. 'It wasn't that big! I think it was a Labrador. It belonged to the two men. I was just over there having a sandwich and the dog came bounding up to me . . . very friendly. They'd stopped their car you see, to let it out for a walk. They were just running about, playing with it.'

'And were you running about too?'

'Oh yes!' I was aware of just how idiotic I was making myself sound. 'I love dogs,' I ended lamely.

'And you didn't scream for help?'

'Well . . . yes! But it was only a joke . . .'

'So, it was all a game, then?' The officer was eyeing me dubiously. 'Are you sure?'

'Well, I can understand that perhaps to someone watching from a distance it might have looked a bit strange . . .'

'And this dog didn't bite anyone?'

'No, no!' I assured him, laughing. 'It was all just a game.'

The police officer favoured me with a long, thoughtful stare and I knew that he didn't believe a single word that I had said. But there were no mangled corpses lying anywhere, so I don't suppose he cared. 'Well, as long as you're all right, miss,' he said eventually.

I saw Paul's van approaching and let out a grateful sigh. 'Ah, here's my friend coming to my rescue, come to change my tyre.'

'Oh really, miss?' The driver smiled as he slid into the front seat and closed the car door. 'I thought you said it was the AA you were waiting for.'

'So, why didn't you tell them the truth?' Paul asked.

It was later, much later. We were lying in bed in his caravan, my head on his shoulder, his fingers playing idly with a strand of my hair.

'I don't know really,' I admitted, sighing. 'I didn't want it all to rebound on Nick. If I'd told the police, he would have had to answer a lot of questions. I didn't want to get him into trouble.' More than that, if I'd told the truth, I knew they would have gone looking for Micky and Duke. The police don't like dogs that attack people, even people intent on murder.

Paul laughed softly. 'You didn't want to get Nick into trouble? Earlier on you said you were going to kill him.'

'I still might,' I muttered.

It was his refusal to take me seriously that had enraged me. Once we'd changed my tyre, Paul and I had driven our respective vans back to Nick's place and I had told him everything. First of all, he pretended he didn't believe me, as if I'd imagined the whole thing.

'What they do on Dartmoor?' he asked. 'They go back to London.'

'Perhaps they were stopping off to visit some of their nice friends in prison,' I suggested sarcastically. 'I don't know! All I know is, they stopped when they saw my van.'

'They would not hurt you, Juno,' he kept saying.

'Vlad had a knife!' I told him furiously. 'He'd slashed my tyre so I couldn't get away.'

'They just want to frighten you . . . You make them look small . . . They want teach you lesson . . .'

'Oh, that's all right, then! They might have stopped short of stabbing me. They might have been content with beating me up and raping me, or perhaps just carving their initials on my face.'

'No, no . . . Juno,' he said soothingly. 'They not do that.' He tried to take my hand and pat it, patronising old bastard, but I snatched it away.

'You told me . . .' I spoke softly but my voice trembled with rage, '. . . when I wanted to ring the police, that day when those two were here threatening you . . . you said that if I rang the police, things could get very bad.'

He didn't have an answer to that and I just nodded. 'I'm out of here! Bye, Nick.'

'But Juno, wait!' he called out as I thumped angrily down the stairs.

Paul caught up with me as I stood out in the alley, taking deep breaths. 'Look, he really is shocked and frightened about what happened to you today. He just doesn't want to admit it, that's all.'

'He's talking as if I'm making it all up!' I said furiously.

Paul risked a smile. 'Why don't we go and get a drink?'

'That's the best idea I've heard today,' I told him, and we walked down to The Silent Whistle.

'So, what happened this morning?' I demanded crossly. 'Why didn't you tell me you were setting this meeting up?'

Paul looked a little sheepish. 'We didn't think it was a good idea to involve you,' he confessed.

'Oh, really?' I tossed back a drink. I don't usually drink double brandies but I reckoned I deserved one. 'Quite ironic in the circumstances, don't you think?' I croaked, my throat scorched with burning alcohol. I plonked the glass back on the bar and signalled the barmaid to pour me another.

'It was a strange experience,' Paul admitted. 'I'm standing there in stony silence, trying to look like a hard man, whilst Nick and . . . Vlad . . . is that what you call him . . . ?'

I nodded. I'd broken into a bag of crisps and my mouth was too full for me to speak.

'Well, they argued for quite a while,' he went on. 'Of course, I couldn't understand a word, and behind them, the other guy . . .'

'Igor,' I muttered, trying not to spray him with shrapnel.

'*Igor* stood in silence, like me, doing his hard-man act. And I have to admit,' he added ruefully, 'his was a lot better than mine.'

'But they settled their differences, in the end?'

'I suppose. Nick handed over a thick envelope of cash. I watched Vlad count it and I reckon there was at least three thousand in there. They seemed happy, even shook hands. Which makes me wonder . . .' he tailed off thoughtfully.

'What?'

'Why did they come after you?'

I'd been wondering about that myself. 'I can't believe they followed me all the way to Tavistock and back. I think I was just unlucky. I don't know what they were doing on that road, but they must have spotted the van. It's difficult to miss it. Vlad didn't like having his photograph taken. I suppose he seized an opportunity to get rid of it.'

'And to scare you enough to stop you going to the police,' Paul added.

'Or get rid of a witness altogether.' I was still convinced he and Igor would have killed me if Duke hadn't come to my rescue.

'They don't like having witnesses to what they're up to, that's for sure. I don't think they'll come back,' he added, putting his empty beer glass down on the bar and helping himself to a crisp, 'I doubt if they'll want to deal with Nick again.' He grinned suddenly, his dark eyes lighting up. 'They didn't reckon on Boudica and the Hound of the Baskervilles.'

'And do we know what they're up to?' I asked, pointedly ignoring this unflattering reference. 'Do we know what Nick was trying to sell for them?'

Paul shook his head. 'He's very tight-lipped about that.' For a few moments, he gazed thoughtfully at our reflections in the mirror behind the bar. I gazed too, and in the reflection, our eyes met. For a moment, we just stared. Then Paul spoke and broke the spell.

'Just as they were leaving, Vlad spoke to me. I'm stupid, I suppose, but I didn't realise he could speak English.'

'It came as a bit of a shock to me,' I admitted. 'What did he say?'

'He came right up close to me, looked me in the eye and asked, "Are you bodyguard?" He smiled in a way that made me want to kill him – derisively, I suppose, and said, "You tough guy, eh?" Then he laughed, the other guy joined in, and they both left.'

'Did you say anything?'

'I opted for dignified silence.'

'But Nick was all right?' I asked. 'When they left, he was happy?'

'He seemed very relieved.' Paul smiled suddenly. 'He was right about you, though.'

'What do you mean?' I asked, wishing his smile was not so warm.

'When you're angry, you're a sight to see – a real flame-haired goddess.'

Our lovemaking that night was more of a celebration for my being alive and unharmed, rather than outright lust, that and being more than slightly drunk. Not that the night was without passion. We made the little caravan rock on its springs. But in the morning, we both knew that it hadn't been a good idea.

When I awoke, Paul was sitting on the edge of the bed, staring at a picture on his phone. He wasn't aware that I had woken and I was able to study the muscular contours of his back and shoulders, smooth skin made golden by the early sun, and the sad, lost look on his face. I sat up and rested my chin on his shoulder so that I could see the picture too. A pretty, brown-haired woman pointed towards the camera, crouching next to a dark-haired toddler who looked just like his daddy. 'How long is it since you've seen them?'

'A few weeks.' His voice was laden with longing.

'Then go and see them now. Today. Take some time off.'

He turned to me, dark eyes full of guilt. 'Juno, I don't want you to feel used.'

I silenced him, placing a finger against his lips. 'Look, we had a great time last night, but I'm not stupid.' I smiled, taking his chin between my hands. 'Go and see your wife and child.'

He frowned. 'Will you be all right? I don't think you need to worry about those two Russians. I don't think they'll be back.'

'I'll be fine.'

He smiled and stroked my cheek. 'You're great, Juno.'

'Yeah, yeah, I'm a real goddess!' I shivered and pulled the duvet around my bare shoulders. 'Now make me a cup of tea, you swine. I've got to go and walk dogs in a minute.'

CHAPTER FIFTEEN

To be truthful, it took a while for me to stop looking over my shoulder for Russian thugs. I stayed away from Nick. He kept phoning, trying to persuade me to go and see him but I didn't answer his messages. I tried to forget all about him.

But I had twelve boxes of his stock piled up in the hallway to remind me of his existence every time I went in the front door and I needed to do something about them. In the end, I sorted out some pretty things and took them around to Pat for her Honeysuckle Farm stall. She was doing quite well with her earrings. I told her I wanted fifty per cent on any of Nick's stock that she sold. This fifty per cent I would eventually give back to him. It meant that I didn't get anything out of the arrangement, but I was past caring by then.

I had a second reason for keeping Nick at a distance. When I'd got back from Paul's caravan that morning, I found a message from Verbena Clarke, telling me that she no longer required my services. I needn't call again.

I was livid. I'd resisted the temptation to contact her about the visit from the police, looking forward to a free and frank discussion when I saw her next, which should have been the following morning when I went to work for her. Her abrupt termination of my employment was as good as an accusation.

I tried to ring her back but she didn't pick up and she'd turned off her answering machine. I considered storming around to her house, but after five minutes of fuming consideration, I decided that I was well shot of her. And if I was, as Ricky and Morris suggested, guilty by association, then I was well shot of Nick too.

I got back into my pre-Nick groove, concentrating on my clients. Chloe Berkeley-Smythe had come back from her cruise and I returned to cleaning for her in her old weekly slot. To be truthful, I never got much work done for Chloe. She would have been quite happy to pay me to chat, pore over cruise brochures, and help her plan her next romp around the Caribbean. I had to be disciplined, doggedly working on while her foghorn voice bellowed over the noise of the vacuum-cleaner, telling me that it must be time to stop for a little drinkie by now.

I put in more time for Ricky and Morris, who were kind enough never to say 'I told you so' about Nick. Only once in the following weeks did I find myself driving down Shadow Lane. I had to stop and pull over on to the pavement, to let a car travelling in the opposite direction go by, our wing mirrors almost touching as the driver squeezed his vehicle past in the narrow roadway. For a few moments I was forced to halt opposite Nick's shop and my attention was snagged by a tall, skinny man emerging from the end of the alleyway that led to Nick's front door. He looked furtive, his watery gaze shifting from right to left before he stepped out from the alley, as if checking the coast was clear. For a moment, our eyes met and he smiled. Not a friendly smile, but more a nervous rictus at realising he was being observed. I recognised him then. I remembered his loud laugh, his big yellow teeth like old piano keys, his gelatinous handshake. I'd spotted him again at the antiques fair. Albert, I think Paul had called him. Now it seemed he was one of Nick's back-door customers. He was carrying something awkwardly, trying to conceal a package under his coat. More dodgy dealings, I thought contemptuously, and drove on.

A few days later I was in Ashburton on foot, shopping for Chloe Berkeley-Smythe. She'd forgotten she had a friend coming to lunch and asked me to fetch emergency rations from the delicatessen on North Street. I came out with a variety of local cheeses, thinly sliced beef, olives, home-made pâté, pastries, handmade chocolates and other mouth-watering spoils that I could never afford to buy for myself.

It was starting to rain, sudden large drops that made everyone hurry into doorways and the shelter of awnings. The van was parked several streets away, so I thought I'd take a shortcut down the alley that joined Sun Street and Shadow Lane, past Nick's front door.

I threaded my way along the narrow space between the wheelie bins, taking care not to knock the bags of shopping, not really looking where I was going, shoulders hunched against the increasingly heavy rainfall. It was the *tap-tap* of high heels that made me look up. Someone else was using the alley as a shortcut, coming straight towards me from the other end.

Verbena Clarke stopped dead in her tracks; her face turned white, then scarlet. She stared, hesitating a moment, pushing back her cloud of fluffy blonde hair with a gloved hand.

'Hello,' I said. 'I want to talk to you.'

She didn't give me the chance, turned on her heel and fled, back the way she had come. I hurried on after her, past Nick's door.

At the end of the alley I was forced to halt abruptly, teetering, as a mother pushing a baby in a buggy along the pavement, almost wheeled over my toes. This gave Verbena the time she needed to yank open the door of her parked Porsche and slide into the front seat, muttering as she slammed the door after her. By the time I had crossed the street and reached the car she had already locked herself safely inside. I knocked on the side window, but she ignored me, revving in a way that warned me to keep my distance, and pulled away. Thwarted, I fumed at the pavement's edge. I watched her drive off down the street, far too fast. As the car disappeared round the corner, I heard a sudden screech of brakes. No satisfying crump of metal on metal, though, just a near miss.

It was just as well she'd evaded me. A kerbside brawl was probably not wise. But she needn't think she'd escaped me completely. One day, when I could no longer think of the incident without smouldering, I would pay Mrs Clarke a visit. Revenge, they say, is a dish best eaten cold. And I intended to enjoy every mouthful of mine.

CHAPTER SIXTEEN

Pat was not impressed with my attempt to make a Victorian panorama from two wooden clothes pegs and the case of the stuffed weasel, although I dressed the peg dolls carefully and painted little faces on them.

'That one's cross-eyed,' she told me, peering at it through the glass, 'and the other one looks simple.'

I accepted this withering criticism of my creative efforts without affront. 'I'm sure you could do a better job.'

'This case is a bit tatty.'

'It was all I had. Look, it's just the *idea* I'm showing you, Pat,' I explained. 'I thought you might be able to do something with it.'

'Our Ken could make a better case than that.'

'Great!' I was beginning to feel impatient with Pat's lack

of enthusiasm. I'd started off the day feeling reasonably mellow, but my mood had been soured by a driver in a flashy car who'd nearly wiped me out, and the van full of dogs, by careering around a sharp bend on the back road into town. Technically, he might have been below the national limit but he was still driving at a speed only a reckless fool would attempt on such a blind corner. We missed crashing head-on because I swerved the van into the hedgerow, my halt accompanied by a lot of yelping from the back and the sound of dogs being flung about.

I jumped out to check. They were shaken and whimpering. There didn't seem to be any bones broken, but without the wire safety grille I was convinced Schnitzel the dachshund would have joined me on the front seat. What really infuriated me was that the other driver didn't even bother to get out of his car, just rolled down his window and laughed.

'No damage done?' he'd called out cheerfully.

Other than vandalising a bit of ancient hedgerow and upsetting me and the canines, no there wasn't. 'No thanks to you,' I'd replied through gritted teeth. 'You might like to consider slowing down.' I jerked my head back in the direction I'd come from. 'There are horse riders back there. Crash into one of them and they might make a nasty mess of your motor.'

'Thanks for the advice,' he responded smoothly and drove off, leaving me seething by the roadside, clearing broken brambles and squashed blackberries from my windscreen.

'I'll leave it with you then, Pat,' I said, gathering up my things.

She was gazing at the panorama, deep in thought. 'Yes thanks, Juno,' she said, without looking up.

'You're welcome,' I told her, standing up to leave. 'How are the earrings going?'

Pat looked up at last. 'Oh, they've sold really well! I've ordered some more beads and Ken's making me a bigger display stand.'

'Excellent!' I muttered and stalked away, leaving Pat still staring pensively into the panorama's painted interior.

My next call was on Maisie in Brook Lane. As I creaked open the garden gate I could see her standing in the porch of her cottage, busy fussing with a feather duster amongst the shelves, flicking it around the prickly army of potted cacti that defended her front door, whilst Jacko dozed in his favourite spot on her windowsill. She scowled when she saw me and tottered inside. She was sulking because the day before I'd insisted on putting her stinky old dressing gown in the washing machine.

'Your friend's in hospital,' she told me as soon as I went inside. There was a waspish sting to her voice. 'Did you know?'

'What friend?' I asked.

'You know.' She sat down. 'Thingy.'

I viewed Maisie's pink cheeks and bright eyes with suspicion and crossed the room to lay a hand on her cheek and then her forehead. 'You're not feeling feverish, are you? You are drinking plenty? We don't want you getting dehydrated again. Remember what happened last time.' I went to the fridge for a bottle of squash and poured her out a full glass. 'Drink this.' I held it out to her. 'All of it.'

Anyone who thinks little old ladies are feeble wants to try wrestling with one suffering from a urinary tract infection. This is brought on by dehydration and produces symptoms that can easily be mistaken for dementia. I called the paramedics the first time it happened. Maisie was already in fighting mood when they whisked her off to hospital. I followed in the van after packing her an overnight bag. By the time I got to the ward she'd turned violent and was going three rounds with one of the orderlies.

'Who are you bossing about?' she demanded belligerently, not taking the proffered squash. 'Bossy cow,' she muttered under her breath.

'Fine.' I set the glass down on a table. 'I'll ring Janet then, shall I?' Janet is Maisie's daughter who lives up north in some town that sounds like heck-as-like, and is always the ultimate sanction when Maisie misbehaves.

She picked up the squash hastily. 'No, no. I'm only having you on.' She sipped as if she suspected it was poison.

'So, what friend were you talking about?' I asked her. 'Who's in hospital?'

'You know, him with the rag-and-bone shop.'

'You mean Nick?'

'That's him. Stroke, three weeks back.'

I stared. 'How did you find this out?'

Maisie had got the story from a friend at her church coffee morning, who'd got the story from Mr Singh. Apparently, Nick had rung him to ask him to bring round some groceries but when he'd arrived at Nick's flat, he couldn't get an answer. He'd called the police, who'd had to break in, and they found Nick on the kitchen floor.

'And he's been in hospital three weeks?' I asked, aghast. 'Where is he? Exeter?'

'Paignton. He's in the rehab unit,' Maisie went on, pleased to be able to air her knowledge. 'Mr Singh's been visiting. He says they won't let him come home cos he lives alone and there's no one to look after him.'

This is not my problem, I told myself firmly, as I watched Maisie drink. But I decided that I'd pop round to Mr Singh's shop, anyway, and get the full story.

CHAPTER SEVENTEEN

I lied to the staff at the hospital. I told them I was Nick's niece.

Maisie's information was only partly correct. It turned out that he hadn't suffered a major stroke, just a TIA – what they used to call a mini-stroke – and was, according to Mr Singh, as right as rain after a day or two. And he'd only been in the rehab unit for ten days, not three weeks. But social services weren't prepared to allow him home unless there was someone there to look after him. I lied again. I would take him home, I said, I would look after him.

As soon as I laid eyes on him, I felt like turning around and leaving him to their mercy. It wasn't so much the *Juno-I-knew-you-would-come*, with which he greeted me, but the twinkly-eyed, knowing grin that accompanied it that infuriated me beyond reason.

Nevertheless, I heard myself apologising for not coming before, for not knowing what had happened to him.

'Do not leave me here, Juno,' he begged me in a whisper. 'I go mad.'

I glanced around me at the day ward, empty except for two old ladies dozing in their chairs, undisturbed by a television blaring in the corner, and an old fella nodding and chatting away to himself whilst he tried to fill in a jigsaw puzzle.

'Is awful here,' Nick confided. 'All stinky old ladies. No one even play chess.'

I heard real desperation in his voice and I relented. 'Don't worry. If we can't get past the guards on the gate, we'll tunnel our way out.' I looked around for a nurse. 'Leave this to me.'

Three-quarters of an hour later, accompanied by a bag containing pyjamas and slippers (thoughtfully brought in by Mr Singh), a walking frame that Nick had refused to use, but which I wedged in the back of the van to save any arguments with the staff nurse, and his new medication, I assisted him into the front seat of my van.

He began to perk up as soon as the van passed through the hospital gates. I could sense him growing restless. He was excited. There was something he wanted to tell me.

'Juno, I have great idea,' he said at last.

'Oh yes?' I kept my eyes on the road.

'We open shop.'

'Sorry?'

'My shop. We sort out junk – throw away old rubbish – smarten up, open it . . .'

I interrupted him. 'Just a moment . . . you told me that you shut the shop because it was too much for you . . . you're too old, you're not well, you can't cope with it any more. And now, when in addition to all that you've just had a stroke, you want to open it again?' This wasn't my objection at all. It was his use of the word *we* that had me worried.

He was nodding vigorously. 'Yes, yes! Life too short, Juno . . . I not ready to be with stinky old crazies . . . eat baby food . . . walking frame. We clean shop. Make nice.'

And then he added. 'I am not ready to be ghost.'

I ignored this last remark. 'It'll need more than cleaning. It'll need redecorating inside and out . . . Mind you,' I conceded, 'if you cleaned the windows and washed down the paintwork . . .' Nick was nodding enthusiastically and I realised I'd better shut up. If I wasn't careful I was going to talk myself into agreeing to what he wanted. 'And if you did open it, who's going to run it?'

'You and me!' he said, as if it was obvious.

I sighed. 'I have my own work, my own business. Why can't you get this through your thick head?'

He gave a snort of contempt. 'Looking after old ladies . . . walking dogs . . . is not business! Is nothing!' He slid a wicked glance at me. 'Is no job for goddess.'

'If you don't shut up,' I warned him, 'I am going to throw you out of this van.'

He chuckled, but surrendered into silence whilst I drove us back to Ashburton.

All this was my own fault. Months ago I'd tried to persuade him to open the shop. You've got all that stock just sitting there, I'd said to him. If you gave this place a lick of paint, some clever lighting, you could make it look really inviting. And when he pointed out that it was in a poor trading position, I'd suggested something stupid like putting a cafe board on the corner of North Street, pointing visitors in the direction of Shadow Lane. I only had myself to blame.

Fortunately, when we got back to Nick's, we had more immediate things to think about: for example, whether he was actually fit enough to climb the stairs. It took a little longer than usual but he made it, breathlessly. Once I had got him into his armchair, I took his key from him so that I could let myself back in, and went round to Mr Singh to pick up some essential groceries and give him a full report on the patient. By the time I got back, Nick had already risen from his chair and poured himself a whisky.

I frowned. 'Are you allowed that on your medication?' He just flapped his hand at me as if I was an irritating fly, so I decided to let him get on with it.

'Mr Singh will be round first thing in the morning,' I continued, 'to see you're all right.'

'Why you no come?' he demanded.

'Because I am not your slave and because I have dogs to walk and jobs to do for other people. I'll pop round later. I owe you some money, anyway.'

He frowned. 'What for you owe me money?'

I told him about the stock I was trying to shift for him through Pat in the bazaar and his face wreathed in smiles. 'You see, Juno, you like antiques business.'

I ignored this and ploughed on resolutely. 'Now, do you think you can get down the stairs in the morning, to let Mr

Singh in, or do you want me to take this key back to him, so he can get in by himself?'

'What you think? I am not cripple. I have key.' He held out his hand for it. 'I be OK.'

I placed it in his waiting palm. 'Do you want me to make you a sandwich before I go?'

'No.'

A thank you would have been nice. 'I'll be off, then. Ring me if you want anything.' And I left the ungrateful old bastard to his own devices.

I could hear the phone ringing as I climbed the stairs, so I dropped everything to fumble for my keys and then flung myself across the living room to reach the receiver before it stopped ringing.

'You said ring you if I want anything.'

I sighed. 'What is it, Nick?'

'I want to open shop.'

'Goodnight,' I said firmly, and I heard him chuckle as I put the receiver down.

At 2.47 a.m., according to the glowing green numerals of my bedside clock, I abandoned all attempts to get to sleep and got up to make a cup of tea. Bill, who'd been curled up next to me like a warm, furry bolster, wandered into the kitchen to join me. I might have made it into the land of Nod if I could have stopped myself mentally reorganising Nick's shop. I would paint the interior a soft white and light it with shaded table lamps to give it a warm glow. I'd get rid of the stuffed animals and remove the heavy items of furniture to the stockroom. With all the wood and brass polished, and some pretty pieces of china dotted around, I was sure it could be made to look inviting. Once, that is, the sign above the door had been repainted properly and the hideous wire mesh removed from the windows.

There was a lot I hadn't told Nick. He didn't know that I'd started going around car boot sales, looking for things to buy, that I was doing my homework, watching antiques programmes on TV, studying *Miller's Antiques Guide*, that I'd bought a little book on silver hallmarks: that I'd been bitten by the bug.

I'd even started a collection of my own: hatpins. Daft, really, as apart from one brown woolly one, I don't possess any hats, but I'd become hooked on hat pins. My collection was small at the moment: one with a pearl head, a dainty silver one, the end shaped like a swallow, and a long spiteful job that ended in a great knob of red glass. I'd made a velvet pin cushion to stick them in and I wouldn't be satisfied until it was bristling like a hedgehog. I was quite taken with lace bobbins as well, but decided that one passion was enough for any woman.

I sat in my armchair, sipped tea and mulled things over. I had four vacant work slots at the moment. Chloe Berkeley-Smythe was on the high seas again and wouldn't return for several weeks. I'd lost a gardening job, due to a client moving away and I hadn't replaced Verbena Clarke. Maisie had her daughter Janet coming to stay, so she wouldn't be requiring my time just now. I could give those four half days to Nick.

I rang him next morning, not having achieved much

in the way of sleep. 'I will help you get the shop ready to open,' I told him.

I heard him chuckle down the line. 'I knew you would.'

This made me want to slam the phone down on him straight away but I persevered. 'There are conditions,' I warned him. 'First of all, you do no more *selling on* for Russians . . . or any other nationality for that matter.'

'I promise,' he said dutifully.

'No more dodgy, back-door customers,' I went on, remembering Piano Teeth.

'No, no, no,' he assured me.

'Secondly, you pay me for all my time.'

'Of course, Juno.' He tried to sound offended. 'What you think?'

'And once it's open, I am not giving up my work to sit in your shop all day, waiting for customers to come in. That job is yours.'

He began to speak but I told him to shut his mouth and wisely he complied.

'I'll redecorate inside,' I went on, 'but only if you get a professional painter to do the outside and repaint the sign properly.'

There was a pause. 'OK,' he agreed.

'And we will need to get someone to shift the really heavy stuff out before I can start painting the walls.'

'Paul,' Nick said instantly. 'He do it.'

It was my turn to pause. 'Paul may not be around. Since his baby's been born he's up and down to Nottingham a lot.'

'I ask him.'

'OK,' I said.

'OK,' he said.

And I put the phone down, knowing I'd made a horrible mistake.

I was right. It wasn't until Nick's shop was cleared of all the furniture and junk that I realised what a huge area it was. I fitted in painting when I could but there was so much paintwork. The doorway, and the big windows on either side of it promised to be days of work, what with rubbing down, undercoat and gloss. And then there were the walls.

The painting became a real chore, my progress was interminably slow. The end of summer slipped away under innumerable coats of paint. I got sick of the smell, felt stifled by the shop and the narrow, cobbled alleyway. I longed to escape for a day up on the moor, in my walking boots, tramping over open ground, breathing fresh air, watching clouds roll across a wide sky. But I knew I wasn't going to get it. Evenings were drawing in and the leaves were already on the turn. Nick was threatening to go back on his promise to employ a professional signwriter for the shopfront, arguing that I could do just as good a job for a lot less money. I knew he would, of course, and told him he was a cheapskate.

Walking the Tribe each day saved my sanity, got me out while it was still early and the morning air was cool and fresh. I spotted Paul's van one morning, parked in the lane outside his field. He hadn't been around for weeks. I kept the dogs on leads. I didn't want any of them racing ahead of me and running amok inside his workshop. As it turned out, the workshop door was safely shut but I could see the door of the caravan was open, so I strolled over, calling his name.

As I approached, a large green rectangle was suddenly propelled through the open door and landed with a soft thump on the ground outside. I recognised it as the mattress of the sofa bed, on which he and I had once enthusiastically bounced around.

'Hello?' I called. I didn't want to risk putting my head around the door, I didn't know what might come flying out next.

Paul's voice came from within. 'Juno? Hello!' He jumped down from the caravan, grinning, gave me a brotherly kiss on the cheek and patted the heads of canines of various sizes who were circling round his feet, tails wagging and demanding attention.

'I didn't know you'd come back.'

'I'm just down for a few days, picking up a bit of work. I hope you weren't planning on bringing this lot inside,' he said, nudging aside a nosing doggy snout. 'It's enough of a mess as it is.'

'Spring cleaning?' I decided to risk a glance into the interior. It was bedlam. It looked as if he'd been throwing everything around, pillows, bedding and clothes all over the floor, the fold-down table piled high with boxes, items of junk spilling out all over the place.

'Not exactly,' he explained. 'I've lost something.'

'Anything important?'

'Just one of my netsuke. I was packing them away and I must have dropped one.'

'Well it can't have gone far. Do you want me to help you look?'

'No thanks, it's not important. Like you say, it can't have gone far. It must be in there somewhere. Anyway,' he said, closing the door on all the chaos, 'how's things?'

The dogs, bored with standing still, were whining and straining at their leads. We released them to romp about the field, sniffing around unknown territory, whilst we followed on at a walking pace. I told him about Nick's stroke, and how I was working on the shop, and how Verbena Clarke had sacked me because she suspected I'd pinched her earrings.

He looked horrified. 'She can't believe that, surely?'

'Well, the damn things are missing,' I told him, 'and it looks like I was the last person to go in her bedroom.'

'But she hasn't accused you directly?'

'No, she just sent the cops around to question me. Although Ricky and Morris don't believe they'd have gone that far if I wasn't an associate of known criminals.'

Paul laughed. 'What? You mean Nick?'

'Well, I don't know any others – apart from you, of course. And he was in prison once, wasn't he, for receiving stolen goods?'

'More than once, but I don't suppose he was doing anything a lot of other people weren't doing, and it was all a long time ago.'

I frowned. 'You ever hear Nick mention his family?'

He shrugged. 'I didn't know he had any.'

'A son and daughter, apparently . . .' I stopped to yell at Schnitzel, who was eating something in the long grass, probably something nasty.

'I've never heard him mention them,' Paul responded. 'Why?'

'It's seems sad, that's all. He's old and alone and vulnerable. He could do with some family support.'

'He's not alone.' Paul grinned and patted me on the shoulder. 'He's got you.'

Later on, we met for a drink. Paul showed me pictures of the new baby, Molly. He was planning to stay up in Nottingham for a few months, coming down now and again to pick up work. He was still trying to persuade Carrie to accompany him home, still battling her parents, who were exerting all their pressure to make her stay where she was.

I made the right cooing noises about the baby. But I was relieved he was going back. Seeing him again was like being prodded with a sharp stick, reaffirming my desire and a sense of solitude that I was not often conscious of. He told me he was planning to head off to Nottingham that evening. Just as well, I thought.

CHAPTER EIGHTEEN

I arrived early at Nick's front door, enthusiasm summoned for another long, back-breaking day's painting, and reached out to press the bell. But the door was already open and swung wide at my touch. Nick never left his door unlocked, never left it open. I hesitated for a moment, calling out as I headed up the stairs.

'Hello, Nick! You there?' I stopped on the landing and tapped on the bathroom door. There was no movement behind the frosted glass panel, no sound of running water, no reply. 'Nick?' The silence, the stillness, was beginning to unnerve me.

I could see the light was on in the living room. I trotted up the last few stairs and stood in the doorway.

I will always remember everything about that moment:

the rumpled rug, the patch of rubber missing from the sole of Nick's slipper, the blue and white striped legs of his pyjamas, his brown dressing gown with its twisted cord: his skull smashed in like the shell of a meringue. Blood had seeped over the collar of his dressing gown, splashed over the fender and the green glazed tiles of the fireplace; there was blood on the rug, spreading out in a puddle from behind his head, dried rusty brown and soaked deep into the pile, a sharp, metallic smell.

My knees gave way and I clutched at the door frame, holding on while the room reeled sickly and a dizzying wave swept up from the soles of my feet. I clung on, staring, hearing the ticking of the clock in the corner. It was slowing down, a heartbeat of time between each swing of the pendulum. For Nick, time had stopped altogether. His white fingers had stiffened into cold claws digging into the carpet. His face was half turned towards me, one blue eye, for ever frozen, staring like the eye of a creature in a glass case.

I choked back bile with a shudder and fled, stumbling down the stairs, yanking open the door, desperate to get out. I couldn't breathe. I lurched into the alleyway where I staggered like a drunk, leaning against the wall to steady myself, bent over, hair falling over my face, whilst I struggled to heave air into my lungs. Then I plunged out into North Street, heading for the nearest shop.

A neat young man rose from his desk as I burst in. Behind him were boards displaying photographs of houses, and I realised, as I gaped around me foolishly, that I had blundered into an estate agents. As he took me in, his expectant smile faded. He wasn't very old, in his first job probably. In his grey suit and tie he looked like a school prefect. I couldn't force my words out. There was a choking lump in my throat and I couldn't stop shaking. 'Are you all right?' he asked anxiously.

'Nick . . .' I tried to point but my arm wouldn't hold steady. 'He's dead.'

The receptionist, a mature lady, got up and steered me efficiently towards a chair. 'Who's dead, my love?' she asked patiently. 'Mr Nickolai, d'you mean, around the corner? You'd better go and have a look, Darren,' she told her young colleague firmly. 'See what's the matter.'

Darren did not look enthusiastic, but he straightened his shoulders manfully and left the shop.

'Police . . .' I gabbled to the receptionist, 'We must call the police . . .'

'We will, dear,' she told me soothingly, as if I were a small child, 'just as soon as Darren's been to check.' She looked as if she might be the grandmother of small children, her natural motherliness painted over with make-up that didn't suit her, her plump body squeezed into a uniform of starched white blouse with buttons straining over her bosom, and black pencil skirt.

'He's dead,' I repeated, trying to get her to understand.

'Yes, dear, you've had a bit of a shock.' So had Darren. He came back into the shop, all colour drained from his face.

'I think,' he began huskily, lowering himself to sit on the edge of his desk and loosening his tie, 'we'd better call the police. There's been a murder.'

* * *

169

They made me go back into the flat, hours later. By then I'd repeated what I'd found over and over. First to a uniformed policeman, who'd sealed off the entrance to the alleyway with blue and white tape, and posted a colleague at Nick's front door; and then to Detective Inspector Ford, who'd listened sympathetically while I garbled it all out again between sips of hot, sweet tea.

He listened patiently, nodding now and again, as if he were mentally sifting grains of what might be useful information from the chaff of my outpourings. 'Would you describe yourself as a business partner of Mr Nickolai?' he asked at last.

'Not really.' Despite myself, I smiled. 'More of a dogsbody.'

'But you'd got to know him quite well? You might know who his friends are . . . other than these foreign gentlemen whom you've described.'

'Yes . . . I suppose . . .'

'You see, what I'm getting at, Juno, is that there doesn't appear to be any sign of forced entry, which would indicate that Mr Nickolai opened the door to his killer. It would be helpful if we knew who his regular visitors were so that we could eliminate them from our investigation.'

'Yes . . . I see,' I said lamely, although apart from Paul and dear old Mr Singh, I couldn't think of anyone who visited regularly.

'Later on, we'll ask you to look at some photographs of known offenders, to see if you can identify these Russians.'

I nodded miserably. If only Vlad hadn't deleted that photograph.

'You do realise,' the female detective constable sitting next to him cut in suddenly, 'that if you'd mentioned these Russians to our officers that day when you encountered them on the moor, they might have been arrested and this might never have happened?' She stared at me with her strange-colour eyes and her little mouth twisted. 'Mr Nickolai might still be alive.'

I gasped as if she'd punched the air out of my lungs.

'That will do, Constable!' The inspector turned on her furiously. 'Go and check on forensics, see how they're getting on.' Her little mouth shut like a trap, but as she got up from the table, the look she cast me was triumphant.

'I want you to disregard what my colleague just said,' the inspector said when she'd left the room.

'Even if it's true?' I asked brokenly.

'We don't know that, at this stage. We don't know anything.' He leant forward. 'But you could be very helpful to us, Juno. At the moment, it doesn't seem that robbery was a motive, but you've been in the flat many times, you might be able to tell us if anything had been disturbed, or if anything was missing.'

'You want me to go in there and look?'

'The forensic team will still be working but Mr Nickolai's body has been removed,' he assured me. He stood up and held out a hand.

'Now?' Panic squeezed my insides.

'Please.' Polite, but clearly a command.

He guided me across the road from the back door of the estate agents, his hand, supporting but firm, on my elbow. A little knot of people had gathered on the pavement, drawn like insects to the flashing of blue lights. Ordered back by the police, they'd retreated as far as the nearest corner. Amongst them, the tall, turbaned figure of Mr Singh stood, looking worried and confused. At the sight of me he raised a hand to catch my attention, but I could only throw him a helpless glance as the inspector walked me inexorably to the point where we ducked under the blue and white tape with DO NOT CROSS printed on it.

At the door, a man in white overalls was brushing powder around the doorbell with a soft paintbrush. We stopped and were made to put white elasticated bags on over our shoes so that we wouldn't contaminate the crime scene. I was warned not to touch anything. As we began to climb the stairs, I made to grip the handrail for support, but remembered just in time, and stopped myself.

Inspector Ford paused. 'All right?' he asked, and I nodded, taking a deep breath.

At the entrance of the living room he made me stop and asked me to wait whilst he held a whispered conversation with the detective constable and another of the white-suited forensic team. I could see into the room. Some of the rugs had been removed, leaving pale rectangles on the old carpet underneath. Most of the blood had gone with them, although splashes on the fireplace remained, each one ringed by a circle of white chalk.

The inspector drew me into the room, stood me on one of the pale rectangles, and again, asked me not to touch anything. 'I just want you to stand here and look. Take your time. Look all around you. If there's anything at all that strikes you as—excuse me.' He was beckoned into a further conversation with a white-suited one who had been photographing bloodstains, and went over to inspect the fireplace, whilst I stood looking around, wondering what I was searching for.

Nick had been cleaning the brass escutcheon plate from a wooden tea caddy. It lay among the jumble of cleaning materials on the table. His spectacles were there too, not folded neatly, but set down as if he had just taken them off, which he had done probably, when he got up to answer the door to his killer. Tears stung the back of my eyes and I looked away.

'His computer's gone,' I said aloud.

'Ah, that's been removed by forensics.' Inspector Ford returned to me with a slight smile. 'Perhaps you can help us here. On this mantelpiece there's a clear mark in the dust, as if something has been standing there, something that's not there now . . .'

'I don't remember,' I began feebly.

'Something with a square base,' he continued.

I realised what he was getting at. 'You mean, it could be the murder weapon?'

He didn't confirm it. 'Can you remember what was there?' he insisted, his eyes fixed intently on mine.

I remembered the mess that something had made of Nick's skull. Something heavy. I stared at the fireplace, trying to recall all the times I must have looked at whatever it was, the time when I had searched through the clutter on the mantelshelf, hunting for Nick's pills. Something had stood there then. I couldn't think. I felt numb, like a dumb animal. 'I'm sorry.'

'That's all right. It may come to you later.' The inspector gave me his card. I was to ring him if I thought of anything. I could go home. He'd arrange for a uniformed officer to drive me.

The news of Nick's murder had got there ahead of me. It was already late in the afternoon. I realised I'd lost all track of time. I must have been with the police for hours. Kate and Adam were waiting, opening the door as soon as I got out of the police car, sweeping me into their living room, where I sat and sobbed wetly whilst they plied me with alcohol and wrapped me in a blanket of sympathy and concern. Kate wanted to feed me but, for once in my life, I wasn't hungry. Morris and Ricky phoned, having been trying to get through to me at my flat without success, but I asked Adam to tell them I'd speak to them tomorrow.

When I finally managed to convince Adam and Kate that I really did want to be on my own, I went upstairs and soaked myself in a long, hot bath, staring numbly at the glistening bubbles until the water grew cold. I was just hauling myself off to bed when the phone rang. I meant to ignore it, but ran to answer it when I heard Paul's voice leaving a message.

'Juno, are you all right?' he asked when I picked up. 'I've been worried sick about you.' His voice sounded shaky.

'Oh . . . you've heard?'

'Yes. God, Juno! It's terrible! Poor Nick . . . I'd . . . I'd have phoned earlier but I've only just got back home. I've been with Nottinghamshire police all evening. They sent officers round to tell me what had happened and took a statement. Not that I could tell them much.'

174

'Did they ask you about the Russians?'

'Yes. I told them all I knew, not that it amounts to much.' He hesitated a moment. 'They took my fingerprints.'

'That's just for elimination,' I explained hastily. 'They took mine too. I had to tell them of anyone I knew who'd recently been in the flat.'

'They also asked me to account for my movements last night.'

I caught my breath. 'But . . . they can't suspect you! You were in Nottingham . . .'

'Well, I was on my way. Fortunately, I stopped for petrol at Gordano Services and I was able to show them the receipt with the time on it. And they can check the service station CCTV, if they want to. Actually, there was a crash on the motorway and I was held up, didn't get home until the early hours.'

'Jesus, Paul! I'm sorry!'

'They wouldn't have been doing their job properly if they hadn't asked, I suppose. But it's you I'm worried about . . . I'm sorry you had to go through that. It must have been horrible.'

'I'm all right.' I could hear my voice cracking. I wasn't all right. I was struggling not to start sobbing down the phone. 'Poor Nick,' I managed at last. 'D'you think—?'

'I think you should try and get some sleep,' Paul interrupted gently. 'We can talk about this some more tomorrow. I'll phone you.'

I wanted to ask when he'd be coming down again. I suddenly wanted to see him very much. But I held back. He was ringing from Carrie's family home. It wouldn't have been fair. We said our goodbyes and rang off.

To my surprise I slept. Waking early, I watched the sun slanting in through my curtains, falling on the little iron fireplace on the bedroom wall. The mantelshelf was barely wide enough for any ornament to stand on, but I'd found a slender china candlestick at a boot sale that just fitted on it and I watched the sun cast its shadow beside it on the wall. I got up and phoned the police station, left a message for Inspector Ford.

'A candlestick,' I told him, when he phoned back later. 'It's a candlestick that's missing from Nick's mantelpiece.'

He asked me if I could describe it.

'It's silver,' I told him. 'William IV.'

'Heavy?'

'Oh yes.' I thought of its solid square base, its corners, and winced as I remembered Nick's crushed skull. 'Heavy enough.'

CHAPTER NINETEEN

According to everyone I knew, I needed time to get over the shock, so I took a few days off. But all I could think about was finding Nick's murdered body, so I went back to work to take my mind off it. Unfortunately, his murder was all anyone wanted to talk about, especially Ricky and Morris. But after hours of hunting through rooms full of ballgowns for *The Merry Widow*, it was a relief to take a break and talk, to sit in their cheerful breakfast room with the long windows open to the fresh garden air, the sunlight streaming in from the outside. 'The police still think it was premeditated, then?' Morris asked, dispensing the refreshment.

'I don't know what they think.' The police weren't exactly confiding their thoughts to me. 'But there was no sign of forced entry. Whoever his killer was, Nick let him in.' I stared thoughtfully into my teacup. 'And we know he was killed late at night. He was in his pyjamas and dressing gown, presumably, ready for bed so . . .'

'It must have been someone he knew, wouldn't you think?' Ricky asked, squinting as he lit up a cigarette. 'Someone he trusted?'

'Well, you wouldn't let a complete stranger in late at night, would you?' Morris added.

I sighed. This was one of the questions that had been turning endlessly in my mind, throughout the small hours. 'The other thing is, there was no sign of a struggle. There was no robbery – and no attempt to make it look like one. The only thing taken was the murder weapon. It doesn't seem that Nick fought for his life . . .' I felt tears welling up suddenly and stared down hard at the flowers embroidered on the tablecloth. Morris reached out a comforting hand and laid it on my arm. I pulled myself together and went on, 'He was just . . . felled. Hit once, from behind . . .'

'You think he trusted these Russians after all that had happened?' Ricky asked.

I shrugged. 'Nick insisted they parted as friends. He refused to believe they intended to do me any harm that day on the moor.'

We were all silent for a minute, sipping tea, then Morris spoke again. 'What if, his killer simply crept up on him?' he asked, peering at us over his specs. 'What if he didn't know anyone was in the flat at all?'

Ricky's eyes narrowed behind a thin spiral of cigarette smoke. 'If his killer had got into the building earlier in the day, say if Nick had gone out, Nick could have locked the place up at night, not knowing his attacker was in there with him.'

I shook my head. 'Nick hardly ever went out, and he never the left the place, even for a few minutes, without double-locking the door. Do you know, the police found cash hidden all over his flat? Hundreds of little packages, rolled up in rubber bands, amounting to thousands, apparently . . . he was hoarding it under the carpets . . . no wonder he didn't want me poking about with a vacuum cleaner!' I took a sip of tea. 'But it was so . . . efficient – the killing, I mean.'

There had been no trail of bloody footprints, just a few drops of blood on the stairs, presumably left by the murder weapon as it was taken away. Inspector Ford seemed satisfied that this was the missing candlestick, that it could have inflicted the wound that killed Nick: death in a single blow. The killer hadn't gone into the kitchen or Nick's bedroom, or down into the shop. He'd come in, killed Nick, and gone, taking the candlestick with him. It was like an execution.

In my mind, Vlad was the executioner. He was cold-blooded, too careful to leave telltale traces behind him. He would have worn his black gloves. But the police had little to go on. Searches in Nick's flat, and through his bins outside, revealed no clue. Police enquiries amongst antiques dealers and pawnshops, appeals to the public on local media, had given them no useful information. Even Nick's computer did not contain anything of value. He used it to track online auctions, for almost nothing else. He didn't engage in social media and he didn't communicate by email.

I couldn't give the police much information either. Inspector Ford had rung me to ask if Nick had owned a dog. Forensics had dog hairs on the rugs that they'd removed from the flat, coming from several different breeds.

'That must be something to do with me,' I'd admitted awkwardly. I'd explained about the Tribe and we'd agreed that I could have carried dog hairs in on the hems of my trousers or the soles of my shoes. I wondered if I left a trail of dog hair everywhere I went, effectively making those places I was paid to clean, dirtier.

Morris peered at me, wearing a worried frown. 'You know, Juno, you're looking very tired.'

'I'm not sleeping so well,' I admitted. When I did sleep, I dreamt about poor Nick, lying there on the rug. And I didn't care what he might have done, I missed him.

'Perhaps you should see a doctor.'

I shook my head. 'He'll only want to give me sleeping pills.'

'I know it's difficult, but you must try and forget it, leave it all behind you.'

'I'm all right,' I assured him. 'I just need to keep busy.'

Ricky stubbed out his cigarette, exhaling as he got to his feet. 'C'mon then, back to work. These bloody frocks won't pack themselves.'

Later that night I stood in Shadow Lane. It was close on midnight, no one around. The rain was light, but steady, the cobbles wetly sheened, glistening silver in the glow of a single street lamp. I stood in the shadow of a doorway opposite Nick's shop, just watching. I didn't know why I had gone there really, knew I was being stupid. But somehow I felt drawn there. The empty building looked sad, the windows dark, no Nick sitting up in his cosy little flat, listening to his radio. Poor old Nick. The police tape with DO NOT CROSS on it that sealed the entrance to the alleyway had worked loose in one corner, a pale ribbon lifting and flapping in the breeze. I wondered how much longer it would be there. How long before the police gave up on an investigation? I felt I ought to be doing something to help, but I didn't know what.

More than once I'd thought about breaking in. There was a window in the storeroom, high up in the wall. But the thought of smashing the glass, wriggling my body through the narrow frame, dropping down into darkness on the other side, crashing into God-knows-what furniture stacked underneath, raising a racket and risking injury, put me off. Or, to be honest, the inevitable interview with the police if I got caught was putting me off. The thought of explaining myself to Inspector Ford, or worse, his horrible detective constable, made me shudder.

I was about to do the sensible thing, stop standing in the rain and go home, when the figure of a man emerged from the end of the alley, pushing the broken tape aside with one hand and looking furtively around him. Instinctively, I ducked further into the shadows and held my breath.

In the darkness I could only make out a tall, spindly figure, coat collar pulled up around his ears, a dark cap obscuring his face. Then, as he turned his head, the lamplight gave me a brief glimpse of his features. It was enough. Piano Teeth. He gave one more nervous look around him and then emerged from the alleyway, sticking the tape back and tapping it into place with his bony fingers. Then he thrust his hands in his pockets and, with an air of assumed innocence, sauntered jauntily towards North Street.

I hurried after him and peered around the corner. I wanted to see where he was going. But more than that, I wanted to see what he'd been up to. I watched him until he disappeared from view then nipped back to the dark mouth of the passage.

I pulled away the police tape and fumbled in my bag for my torch, aimed the beam of light down the alleyway, flooding the ground ahead, and trod cautiously, dodging the puddles. The rain was leaking from a gutter, pattering on to the plastic lids of wheelie bins and I weaved my way between them, down to Nick's front door and ran the torch beam over it. The police tape was still fixed in place, the door solidly shut. I gave it an experimental push. Nothing seemed to have been disturbed. I walked on a little further, until I stood beneath the stockroom window, high in the wall, and shone the torch at it.

I was so intent on looking upwards I didn't notice the bloody beer crate until I nearly fell over it. Someone had emptied it of its bottles, stood them carefully against a wall, turned the crate upside down so it could be stood on, and placed it immediately beneath the window, to give himself a leg-up. Now, who would do a thing like that? I asked myself, as I placed my own feet on its surface. I gave a tentative bounce. The crate was made of plastic, but seemed sturdy enough.

My nose just about level with the window frame. I shone the torch around. There were plenty of dirty cobwebs, but no broken glass, no splintered wood. If Piano Teeth had considered breaking in this way, he must have thought better of it. As I inspected the frame more closely, I discovered that the window was actually screwed shut from the inside. It would have been impossible to force it open without tools, and perhaps he hadn't brought his breaking-and-entering kit with him. Or he was a coward, too scared to break in, just like I was.

I heard voices and hastily flicked off the torch. Some late-night revellers were carousing down Sun Street, crossing that end of the alleyway. A drunken voice suggested that bugger the police tape, they should take a shortcut. Time I was gone. I jumped down off the crate, knocking over the beer bottles and sending them rolling, clinking noisily across the cobbles. 'Shit!' I cursed in a whisper.

'Somebody's down there,' the drunken voice announced loudly.

'Prob'ly a cat,' someone else suggested.

I didn't wait to hear the rest of the conversation. I dashed down the alley, back the way I'd come, not stopping to put the tape back in place. I ran down Shadow Lane, slowing my pace as I turned the corner, and began walking home, shoulders hunched against the falling raindrops.

Now, what could Piano Teeth have wanted so desperately that he was prepared to break into a crime scene to get it? To remove evidence of his having been there? It was a bit late for that. The police knew he'd been

183

in Nick's because I'd told them I'd seen him. I didn't know his real name, but Paul did: Albert something. Assuming they'd been able to track him down, they would already have interviewed him.

The sensible thing to do, of course, would be for me to ring the police as soon as I got home and tell them what I'd just seen. But would they be interested? After all, I hadn't really caught him trying to break in, and there was no real evidence he'd tried. An upturned beer crate didn't count for much. I could just imagine what the police would say. It was dark, could I be sure the man I'd seen was really him, what was I doing there anyway? No. If I wanted to know what Piano Teeth was up to, I was going to have to ask him myself.

CHAPTER TWENTY

'Of course I remember you, Juno!' Tom Smithson shook me warmly by the hand. 'You came to that auction viewing with Paul and poor old Nick.' He shook his head sadly. 'Awful business!'

'The police have been in touch, then?' I asked.

'Yes. Please sit down. Sit down.'

Dartmoor Antiques was set in an old warehouse on the outskirts of Exeter, a concern very like Ashburton Art and Antiques Bazaar but larger and more impressive. Tom Smithson was the proprietor. I'd tracked him down on the Internet. Most of the ground floor was filled with his stock.

'Dark-brown furniture,' he waved an arm at a collection of wardrobes, desks, assorted bookcases, tables, chairs and dressers, 'not fashionable at the moment, of course,' he added wryly as we sat down at a mahogany table. He turned to me and smiled. 'So, what can I do for you?'

I felt a bit awkward. 'I expect I'm only going to ask you what the police have already asked,' I told him. 'But time is going by and the case doesn't seem to be going anywhere. I wondered if you'd ever come across Nick's Russian customers.'

'You're right, they did ask but I'm afraid I couldn't help them. I didn't have that many dealings with Nick myself and I hadn't seen him since the auction.' He frowned at me. 'You're convinced, are you, that these Russians are responsible?'

I sighed. 'Pretty much.' I recounted my meetings with them, first at Nick's flat, and then on the moor.

Tom Smithson listened, his genial features displaying more and more alarm.

'They certainly sound like a pair of wrong 'uns. But I've never come across them, and I don't know what Nick's connection to them might have been.'

'There was another dealer with you and Nick, that day at the auction,' I began tentatively, getting to the real reason for my visit. 'Tall, thin, with . . . um . . . large teeth . . . I think his name is Albert. I saw him coming out of Nick's place one day, by the back door.'

'You mean Bert Evans.' He thought for a moment and his shoulders shook with laughter. 'Poor old Bert! He has been known to dabble in what you might call murky waters, but if you're fancying him for a murder suspect, Juno, I'd think again. He's got a brilliant alibi.'

'What?' I asked.

'He was having dinner with us the night that Nick was murdered. There was a whole group of us, we went on until the small hours. In fact,' he added, grinning, 'I remember that you came into our conversation that night.'

'Me?'

'You made quite an impression on Bert. He was asking if anyone knew anything about you. He's a sad soul, been widowed twice. He's always on the lookout for the next Mrs Evans.'

My face must have been a picture. It made Tom laugh, anyway. 'But seriously,' he added, 'I think you can forget him as a suspect. He's got a very weak heart, he's waiting for a bypass operation. He'd run a mile from any violence – has to avoid stress at any cost.'

Then what, I wondered, was he doing poking around a crime scene?

'He's got a unit here, as a matter of fact,' added an amused voice, 'although we very rarely see him.' A lady was strolling towards us, silver hair cut into a shiny bob, her long, purple skirt swinging as she walked. She carried a sad-looking teddy bear under one arm, and had small gold-rimmed specs perched on the end of her nose.

'Vicky love, come and meet Juno.' Tom Smithson held out a hand. 'Juno, this is my wife, Vicky.'

'I'm trying to thread this bloody needle,' she told us, holding it up at arm's length and squinting at it, 'so that I can repair poor Bruin here.'

'You need stronger glasses, old girl,' he advised her.

'No, I just need longer arms.'

I volunteered to thread the offending needle, whilst Vicky wandered off to make us all a cup of tea. Despite the autumn sunshine the air was fresh, and it was cold sitting in the warehouse, the door wide open to attract customers. A few possible buyers could be seen browsing amongst the old garden implements and stone ornaments displayed outside.

I sat drinking tea and chatting with Tom and Vicky for another half-hour. They were lovely people, and any idea that I might have cherished that Tom might have been involved in Nick's murder seemed ridiculous.

'Of course, if you want to talk to Bert, we can give you his number.' Tom chuckled. 'I'm sure he'd be pleased to see you, fancies himself as a bit of a ladies' man.'

'On what basis?' I asked, incredulous.

'Oh, you'd be surprised.'

Yes, I would. I thought I'd change the subject. 'Have you seen anything of Verbena Clarke lately?' I asked, as Tom scribbled Bert's number on a scrap of paper.

I explained that she and I had parted company, without explaining why. He nodded sagely. 'Not an easy character, our Verbena.'

'Do you know her well?' I asked.

'No, no, only through the trade.'

I would have liked to ask more, but customers began drifting in through the door, and I felt I'd taken up enough of Tom's time. But Vicky offered to show me around and I couldn't resist the chance for a good snoop. Apart from the piles of brown furniture, collectibles and stuff that could be dismissed as junk, there were units containing more expensive items, most of them locked safely inside glass cabinets, many of these cabinets internally lit, with mirrored shelves to show off the contents to best effect. I peered in, mulling lustfully over silver jewellery, snuffboxes, vinaigrettes, and a long hatpin ending in a translucent lump of glowing amber. I read the price label, and sighing sadly, looked to the shelf above. And there stood a candlestick: square base, heavy, silver, William IV.

'You OK, Juno?' Vicky asked. 'You've gone white.'

'I wonder if I could have a closer look at that.'

She raised an eyebrow. 'It's rather expensive.'

'I've got an uncle with a big birthday coming up,' I told her, lying glibly. 'It's the sort of thing he'd love.'

'Of course . . .' Vicky searched for the key to the cabinet among the heavy bunch that she carried, unlocking the glass door and sliding it open.

'This isn't Bert Evans unit by any chance?' I asked, still staring at the candlestick.

'No, no,' she assured me, as she reached in for it. 'This cabinet belongs to Olivia. She's not here today.' She glanced at the price tag. 'But I'm sure she'd be open to offers.'

She held the candlestick out for me and I realised I was holding my breath. I took it and turned it round in my hands. It looked identical to the murder weapon, but had been well polished, the overhead spotlights dancing off its gleaming surfaces. I turned it over and studied the base. The rectangle of green baize that covered it was pristine.

'I don't think that baize is original,' Vicky said, 'probably a replacement.' She smiled. 'You're holding that as if it's an unexploded bomb.'

I smiled too, but weakly.

'Would you like me to ring Olivia?' she asked. 'Ask what her best price is? I'm sure she'd be willing to do a deal, the thing's been sitting there for at least a year.'

I felt a surge of relief. The question I had been going to ask next, where Olivia had got the candlestick from, was now irrelevant. If it had been in the cabinet so long, it couldn't be the murder weapon. I looked at the price tag. 'I'm afraid it'll still be too rich for my blood.'

I handed it back to Vicky, she replaced it in the cabinet and we made our way back to the warehouse entrance. 'If you think it's the kind of thing your uncle might like, I could keep an eye out for another one,' she volunteered, 'something a bit cheaper. You never know when one might come in. I could always phone you. Would you like me to do that?'

I turned to her and smiled. 'Yes, thanks.'

'Hold on,' she called, just as I was walking out, 'didn't you want to talk to Bert?'

I waved my scrap of paper. 'Tom gave me his number.'

'We can do better than that.' She searched a drawer under the counter. 'Here,' she held out a business card. 'We keep them for all our traders.'

I took it from her. It read, in elegant, curling script: *Bert Evans, Antiques and Objet's d'Art*. Either he had no grasp of the apostrophe or he ought to sack his printer. But the card gave his telephone number, and his address.

CHAPTER TWENTY-ONE

My plan to call on Bert Evans next morning was thwarted by Maisie and her washing machine.

'It's done it again!' she wailed at me on the phone. 'It won't open. It won't let me have me washing!'

'Don't try and force the door, Maisie, not again. We don't want another flood. Just wait till I get there. OK?'

Maisie was muttering as she put the phone down. She believed her washing machine to be possessed of a malign spirit. It wasn't of course, she'd just pressed the wrong button, again, but why washing machine manufacturers can't understand that elderly people cannot see tiny white buttons on a white background, is a mystery to me. By the time I'd gone round to her cottage, drained the washing, sorted out the correct cycle, let the machine do its stuff and hung her clothes out on the line for her, it was lunchtime.

I was promised to Ricky and Morris for the afternoon, but I phoned them and cried off, promising to work tomorrow instead. This left me free to call in on Mr Evans, unannounced. His place was a little way away in Lustleigh, in a pretty village where many of the properties were detached, thatched and worth a small fortune.

I drove around a couple of times before I eventually found the private road leading to his house. There was a board on the corner with the name of three properties on it, *Teniriffe* being one. It seemed Bert couldn't spell either. But whatever Tom Smithson had meant by dabbling in murky waters, Bert was doing very well out of it. His gravelled drive led to an impressive house with mullioned windows, a pretty front garden surrounded by mature trees, and a double garage with two cars and a large motorhome parked outside.

I pulled the van up behind it, got out, rang the doorbell and waited. There was no response and no noise from within. After a minute or so I peered nosily through one of the mullioned windows, shading my eyes with my hand to try and cut out my reflection, but I couldn't see anything between the gap in the curtains except the raised lid of a grand piano.

I followed a path around the house, through a wrought iron gate at the side. I called out a couple of times but except for a wood pigeon flapping off in alarm from the branch of a fir tree, there was no sign of life.

Bert's back garden was huge. For a moment I lingered jealously, taking it all in, imagining what I would do with this space if it was mine. Most of it was taken up by a lawn, manicured to within an inch of its life. A lawnmower was abandoned in the middle, halfway along a green stripe it had been shaving on the grass. Someone was about then, either Bert or a gardener, someone called away mid task by the ringing of a phone perhaps, or an urgent call of nature.

I tried a couple of loud hellos, then followed the path to a flight of stone steps, leading down to a second area of garden, dominated by a large pool. As I looked down at the dark water a golden koi carp the size of a torpedo glimmered briefly under the surface. And there was something else. Lying at the edge of the pool was a pair of sandals, truly horrible mauve socks leading to even more horrible skinny white legs knotted with varicose veins, and a bum in a pair of khaki shorts. The rest of the body was only dimly visible, under the water.

I flung myself down the steps on to the path, on my knees, and pulled hard on the waistband of the shorts. 'Mr Evans!' I yelled, as I tugged at his body. 'Bert!' I could tell from the way his arms floated out on the surface that he was dead. The poor old sod must have had a heart attack, pitched forward and landed face down. I sank my arms in the cold water, getting one arm around his waist from underneath and grabbing the collar of his shirt with my other hand. As I hauled desperately, a tiny goldfish darted through the waterweed of his floating hair. I managed to shift his body back, only a few inches, but enough for me to grab his hair and lift his head out of the water. His face was a bluish white, slack-jawed, his pale eyes staring, as dead as any fish on any slab. I lowered his head, grabbed him by the legs, and dragged him ignominiously until his body was beached, his face turned sideways, his cheek resting on the stone kerb of the pond. Water dribbled from his gaping mouth like a gargoyle. It was not the face of a man who'd died peacefully. I knelt and felt at his neck for a pulse, just in case, but found not the faintest flicker.

I ran back to the house. The kitchen door was open and I was halfway across the floor, dripping water on the shiny tiles, heading for a phone I could see mounted on the wall, before I stopped and gazed about me at an upturned table, scattered chairs, a broken vase in glassy diamonds strewn across the floor. Through double glass doors I could see into a sitting room and a similar scene of chaos: ripped sofa cushions flung about and trampled on, books and ornaments swept from their shelves and lying on the carpet, a smashed photo frame, a shattered lamp.

I froze into stillness, rigid. Could whoever had done this still be in the house? I listened, ears straining, but could detect no sound beyond the ticking of the kitchen clock. After a minute I felt safe enough to move, dialled for the police, then picked up a kitchen chair and sat, wet and shaking, waiting for them to arrive.

They seemed to take for ever, but I don't suppose they were long in arriving. Two uniforms came first, one of whom stayed with me and asked me questions, whilst the other went to check out the pond, and returned pretty smartly, speaking into his radio.

Reinforcements arrived quickly after that, and an ambulance, and a concerned neighbour who poked her nose into the kitchen, worried about what was going on. A paramedic wrapped a blanket around me and checked my pulse and a few other things, just in case I was going into shock. By the time he was satisfied I was only suffering from cold, the house and garden seemed to be crawling with police, and the dear lady neighbour, having been sent away rather sharply by a uniformed officer, returned with a determined and slightly martyred expression, bearing a tray of mugs and a pot of tea.

I sat with grateful hands wrapped around a mug, just waiting. A detective would be arriving shortly, I was informed, and would want to ask me some questions. I just nodded. I didn't want to mention that I'd been through this procedure, that I'd found a dead body before; but the inevitable was closing in, and it arrived, shortly afterwards, in the person of Detective Inspector Ford.

His horrible little sidekick was with him, the putty-faced black-haired girl with the smirking mouth who sat beside him at our first interview. Her name, it turned out, was DeVille.

At the sight of me, sitting shivering in the kitchen, her black eyebrows flew upwards and she directed a meaningful glance at her boss. He was looking at me strangely, as if he wasn't sure what to make of my being there. 'Miss Browne?' he asked, frowning.

I nodded. 'Juno,' I reminded him.

He turned to his constable. 'Go next door, will you, and interview that lady who was so anxious to speak to someone.'

Her little mouth twisted but she could only nod and do what she was told.

The inspector picked up an upturned chair, righted it, and sat down opposite me, drawing out a notebook. He sat, studying me for a moment. 'So *you* found Mr Evans?' he said at last. 'I hope you're not going to make a habit of this kind of thing.'

I gave a weak laugh. 'So do I.'

'What are you doing here, Juno? Were you a friend of his?'

'Not really,' I admitted. 'I met him at an auction with Nick. I just wanted to talk to him, really . . .' The doubtful way the inspector was eyeing me told me I'd better come clean. 'I saw him, hanging about outside of Nick's shop a couple of nights ago. I thought he was trying to break in. I wanted to know what he was up to.'

'The correct course of action would have been to inform the police at the time,' he said severely.

'I know,' I responded, nodding. 'I'm sorry.'

'So, tell me what you found,' he added, rather more gently.

I described what had happened. He let me talk, didn't interrupt me with questions, but I had to repeat several times exactly how I had found the body.

'I shouldn't have moved him, should I? I could see he was dead, really. But I thought there might be a chance . . . I felt I had to try,' I finished lamely.

The inspector smiled. 'Of course you did.'

'He was murdered, wasn't he? He didn't just collapse. Whoever did this . . .' I gestured feebly around the ransacked room.

'Well, we won't know until the post-mortem exactly how he died, but there are indications that he didn't go into the water voluntarily.'

'Someone held his head under.' I shuddered, remembering his face.

The inspector was obviously reluctant to say too much, but he didn't have to.

At that moment the detective constable returned and signalled to her boss from the doorway. He excused himself and joined her there. She spoke in a lowered voice but I could hear her well enough. 'The neighbour reports seeing a car parked in the private lane when she went out shopping this morning, and noticed it was still there when she returned – a dark-blue BMW.'

'I don't suppose she noticed its number plate?'

'I'm afraid not, sir. She didn't appreciate its significance.'

'No, they never do, do they?' he sighed. 'All right, thank you, Constable,' he said, and she left.

'A dark-blue BMW?' I repeated. 'That was the car that Vlad—'

The inspector cut me off. 'Miss Browne, later today I shall send an officer to your address to take your statement but in the meantime, I think you should go home.' As I began to protest, he raised a hand, silencing me. 'I'm not happy about you driving at the moment, you've had a shock. I can arrange for my constable to take you, or you can call a friend, if you'd prefer.'

'I'd prefer,' I told him bluntly and phoned Ricky and Morris.

They were only too happy to drive over and gawp at the police cars and the aliens in white suits going about their business. I rode home with Morris in the comfort of their old Saab, heater on full blast, whilst Ricky followed in my van, grumbling all the way.

'That bloody thing's never going to get through another MOT,' he informed me as we got out at the end of our journey, and slammed the door.

We were at their house, not mine. I held out my hand for my keys but Ricky shook his head and put them in his pocket. 'Not on your life, kiddo! You're not going home before you've had a stiff drink and filled me in all the juicy details I missed while you were in the Saab with Morris.'

'Unless you'd rather have a cup of tea, Juno,' Morris offered, as he opened the front door.

'No, a stiff drink will be fine.'

'You sort it out, then,' he told Ricky, 'while I run her a bath.' He gazed at me mournfully. 'We really ought to get you into some dry clothes.'

Morris's presence was always reassuring, and I'd relaxed a little in the car, but it was as I lazed in a deep bath of exotically scented bubbles, my second glass of brandy placed on the corner of the bath, that gradually my physical and mental numbness started to ebb away. I began to feel more myself.

There was a loud knock, the bathroom door opened a few inches and a hand appeared brandishing a coat hanger on which hung a silky, peach-coloured dressing gown. 'There's this one,' Ricky's voice announced from behind the woodwork. 'It's a Dior original. Di Davies wore it in *Present Laughter* or . . .' the dressing gown disappeared momentarily and was replaced by a heavier green one, 'there's this if you'd rather go comfy than glam. It's a bit more Celia Johnson.'

'Who's Celia Johnson?' I asked and he tutted in exasperation. 'I'll have the green one!' I called out hastily. I didn't feel up to a Dior original.

By the time I had bathed and had come downstairs, wrapped in Celia Johnson, the smell of something wonderful was emanating from the kitchen and Morris was laying the table in the breakfast room. 'I thought some comfort food,' he told me, taking my empty brandy glass, 'so I've made a shepherd's pie. Your clothes are in the tumble dryer,' he added, 'they'll be ready by the time we've eaten.'

I felt like bursting into tears. 'You are wonderful,' I gave him a big hug.

Ricky came in with three very large wine glasses. 'Merlot or Shiraz?' he asked, as he set them down. 'Or there's a nice Rioja.'

'I'll never be able to drive home,' I protested.

'No, you won't! Anyway, you're staying the night,' he informed me firmly.

'I can't. The police are coming to take my statement.'

'Don't fuss! I phoned Adam, told him where you are. The police can come round here if they're that anxious to see you.'

I felt I should argue, but the thought of going home to my empty flat suddenly seemed too depressing. So I sat down and ate too much shepherd's pie and drank too much red wine and we talked about poor Albert Evans and his watery demise and the significance of a certain dark-blue BMW; and why Bert had been sneaking about Nick's place, and whether Vlad and Igor – for undoubtedly it was their BMW – were really searching for something in Bert's house, or whether they had trashed it to make it look like burglary gone wrong. In which case, why had they killed him?

The police didn't call till next morning, as it turned out, and I went to bed in Ricky and Morris's spare bedroom, slightly drunk and very full and sure I would sleep like a baby. But sleep eluded me, and as the little bedside clock ticked its way through the small hours, all the things we had talked about that evening went round in my brain until I didn't know what to think. Only one thing I was sure of. If I wanted to know what Bert was after, I was going to have to break into Nick's place to find out.

CHAPTER TWENTY-TWO

I didn't need to as it turned out. Break in. Fortunately, I took a few days to ponder the wisdom of the scheme. After all, I didn't know what Bert might have been looking for. Perhaps he knew about the money Nick kept hidden in the place. Perhaps he wasn't trying to break in at all, he was just being nosy. But I didn't really believe that. He was after something. Was that something the thing that had got him murdered? And was Vlad after the same thing when he had killed Nick?

Anyway, during all these deliberations, I had a phone call from a Mr Young, from the firm of Young, Young, Grantham and Young, Solicitors, based in Exeter. I wondered if Mr Grantham felt outnumbered but I didn't ask.

'It is rather a delicate matter.' Mr Young sounded awkward. 'I understand that you were the late Mr Nickolai's cleaning lady?'

'I worked for him, yes.'

'Well, now that Mr Nickolai's body has been released for burial—'

'Has it? But . . . surely, the case isn't closed?'

'Well, I wouldn't say that any murder case is closed until the perpetrator is apprehended,' Mr Young replied pedantically, 'but the police are satisfied that all . . . er . . . necessary forensic evidence is safely in their possession . . . and nothing more can be got from the crime scene. Therefore, there is no reason why poor Mr Nickolai cannot be laid to rest.'

'I see.' It seemed very odd to me, when his murderers were not only still at large but still murdering, but I suppose poor Nick's body couldn't tell the police any more than they already knew.

'The funeral is next Thursday,' Mr Young went on. 'His family will be coming down before—'

'His family,' I repeated. 'You mean, his children?'

'That's right. His daughter, Mrs Helena Burgoyne and her husband, and his son, Mr Richard . . .'

'Nice of them to turn up for his funeral!' I blurted out. 'Pity they couldn't visit him when he was alive.'

Mr Young made shocked harrumphing noises at the end of the phone. 'I . . . er . . . understand that family relations were strained.'

'They were non-existent as far as I can see.' They hadn't even turned up for the inquest. Their father had been murdered, didn't they care what had happened to him? Weren't they even curious?

'Indeed. However,' he went on hastily, 'we are hardly in a position to judge.'

I didn't agree but didn't argue.

Mr Young coughed uncomfortably. 'I understand they will be putting up at The Dartmoor Lodge, but of course they will wish to visit Mr Nickolai's home. And as his death was in such extremely distressing circumstances, Mr Young – old Mr Young, that is – thought the experience would be less unpleasant for the family if the flat had already been . . . er . . . cleaned up.'

'Cleaned up?' I repeated.

'We have a key to the property and we wondered if you might be prevailed upon to clean up the relevant . . . er . . . for a fee, of course.'

'You mean, clean up the scene of the murder?'

'To spare the family any suffering . . .'

'But surely, the police . . . ?'

'No, no, a common misapprehension, apparently. Once the police have removed the forensic materials that they consider crucial, from an evidence point of view, any . . . er . . . residual . . . cleaning . . . is left to the victim's family, or a neighbour . . . or someone like yourself.'

'Are you – or indeed, old Mr Young – aware that I discovered Mr Nickolai's body?' From the horrified silence at the end of the line I gathered he was not. 'How about sparing me some suffering?' I suggested.

'Miss Browne . . .' When he found his voice it sounded abject. 'I am profoundly sorry. Naturally, I will find someone else to do the job. I can't apologise enough.'

'Wait a second.' I stopped him before he could put the phone down. Outraged as I felt, I didn't intend to pass up the chance to get into Nick's place. 'I'll do it.'

'I really wouldn't feel comfortable . . .' Mr Young began.

'No, it's all right,' I assured him, in as calm a voice as I could muster. 'Really, it's OK.'

'Well, I'm not sure . . .' he began doubtfully.

'I knew Mr Nickolai and I don't like the thought of a stranger doing the job.' It was true, I didn't like the idea. 'It seems like an intrusion on his privacy.'

It took another five minutes to persuade him that I meant what I said, but eventually Mr Young overcame his reservations. If I was sure I was up to the job, then he would be so grateful. I agreed to meet him at Nick's place next morning. At ten o'clock.

Paul phoned that evening. He sounded upbeat. There was a greater quantity of work for a furniture restorer around Nottingham, it seemed. And he was looking into buying a plot of land in a village not far from there; planning restrictions were easier. And if they did decide to build their own house, Carrie and the children could continue to stay with her family until it was ready. Meantime, he asked, how was I?

I told him how I'd found Bert Evans amongst the fishes. 'Tom Smithson told me he liked to dabble in murky waters,' I joked grimly. Paul listened in silence whilst I went on to describe the ransacked house.

'God, Juno! What the hell possessed you to go there?'

he cried, loud enough to make me move the receiver away from my ear. 'What if you'd arrived earlier, when his killers were still there?'

That thought had already occurred. I could only be grateful to Maisie's washing machine for delaying me. 'The neighbour reported seeing a dark-blue BMW parked in the road outside,' I told him.

He gave a low whistle. 'You think it was Vlad and Igor?'

'Well, I know there's more than one dark-blue BMW in the world but—'

'Juno,' he interrupted me, 'that's even more reason to stay away. I know you're upset about Nick, but you must leave things to the police. You're not some kind of amateur sleuth,' he reprimanded me, 'and that pair are dangerous.'

He was beginning to sound like Inspector Ford. I promised I'd behave. I decided not to tell him I was going to clean up Nick's flat, he'd know damn well I was going in there to snoop for clues, but I did tell him about Nick's funeral.

'I don't suppose you'll be coming down for it?' I asked.

There was a brief silence at the end of the phone. 'Probably not,' he said.

'OK.' I tried to say it without reproach.

'Mind you,' he went on quickly, 'I'd like a look at these children of his.'

'I'm gagging to see them myself.'

Paul was quiet a moment. 'Look, I know it's tempting to blame them for ignoring him when he came out of prison, but they were only young kids then. And Nick never spoke

205

about them. He didn't seem lonely or unhappy to me. To be honest, I don't think he was all that bothered.'

I sighed. In my days as a carer I'd come across a lot of families who weren't that bothered. But as young Mr Young had said, I wasn't in a position to judge. Not, I had to admit to myself, that that was likely to stop me trying.

CHAPTER TWENTY-THREE

The clock in Nick's living room had finally stopped. Young Mr Young and I stood together on the pale rectangles where the bloodstained rugs had lain, looking around us. The curtains were drawn and the feeble yellow light added to the pervading sense of sadness.

'Are you all right, Miss Browne?' young Mr Young asked me anxiously. He was a thin, dried-out husk of a man in his fifties. I couldn't imagine what old Mr Young must look like.

'I'm fine,' I assured him. But the atmosphere in the room was getting to me. The flat had been shut up for weeks and the smell was difficult to describe. Not the sharp, metallic tang of blood when it is fresh, but something sweeter, sicklier, more corrupt.

I felt a little nauseous. 'Let's open some windows, shall we?' I asked, in an attempt to sound brisk. Crossing the living room, I swept back the curtains and threw up the sash.

Mr Young hurried into the kitchen to do the same. 'That's better,' he breathed, 'let's get some fresh air circulating.' Then he turned to me. 'You're sure you won't be nervous here, Miss Browne?'

'Perfectly sure.'

'In that case, if you'll forgive me, I must make a phone call to my office . . .'

'You won't get a mobile signal here,' I warned him.

'No, no, I am aware. I have an old colleague working in solicitors on St Lawrence's Lane. I thought I'd make the call from there . . . as long as you're happy to be left alone. I'll come back to lock up in . . . shall we say, an hour?'

'An hour?' I repeated in dismay. I was going to have to work fast. I'd realised as soon as we'd opened the front door that it was going to be a bigger job than I'd anticipated. I'd forgotten the activities of the forensic team. They had brushed the aluminium powder they used to find fingerprints everywhere. It showed as horrible grey smudges on the paintwork, on every door and windowsill, on the walls in the hall, and as a silver dust on dark surfaces like the bannister rail, the mantelpiece, and the backs of wooden chairs. The clutter on the table was still the same, the bottles and jars of cleaning materials still there, but all coated in a fine, silvery dust as if an infinitely fine snow had fallen.

'Will an hour not be sufficient?' Mr Young asked, the

smooth skin of his forehead corrugating into wavy lines as he raised his eyebrows. He looked at his watch. 'Well, I'll pop back around eleven to see how you're getting on.'

I was longing for the fussy man to go, relieved when he went downstairs and I heard the door click shut behind him. I let out a breath and stared at the tiles of the fireplace, where spattered gobbets of blood had dried to a rusty brown. I closed my eyes briefly, and tried to block out the memory of Nick lying dead on the floor. If I allowed myself to remember him, I knew I wouldn't be able to do what was necessary. I had to force myself to think only that this was a cleaning job, like any other. Dithering would only weaken my resolve.

I'd brought my own rubber gloves and bag of cleaning materials. I just needed a bucket and I knew Nick kept one in the cupboard under the kitchen sink. As I walked into the kitchen, I remembered what Inspector Ford had told me. There were no traces of blood in the kitchen, no sign that the killer had been anywhere in the flat but in the living room and on the stairs.

Nick had told me he kept some nasty things under his sink and he wasn't wrong.

I had to move an ancient bottle of ether and a tin of naphtha out of the way before I could extract the bucket. I filled it with cold water from the sink, added some bleach, pulled on my gloves, selected an old cleaning cloth, then carried the bucket back into the living room.

I knelt before the fireplace, feeling like I ought to say a prayer. This was a job that should be carried out with reverence: wiping away the last, sad traces of a friend. I hesitated, then quickly wiped blood from the fender and the tiles, not stopping, not giving myself time to think.

Next I applied myself to the carpet. There was a telltale dark outline where one of the rugs had been removed and blood had seeped beyond the straight edge onto the carpet beneath. I sprayed vigorously with some carpet shampoo, scrubbed hard, and left the foam to do its stuff whilst I turned my attention to the wall. The splatters here were more of a problem. As they had dried, they had seeped into the surface of the thick, old-fashioned paper. I tried wetting one of the splashes with the cloth but all that did was make it spread, leaving a paler but larger, more noticeable stain.

I looked around me for inspiration. On Nick's table lay a scalpel. I picked it up and scraped at the bloodstain, very carefully. I managed to scratch off the stained surface, leaving the clean backing paper behind. I did this several times over, meticulously scraping away at each droplet of blood, frustrated at the time it was taking. When I had finished, the wallpaper looked scarred, as if it had been scraped by furniture. But no one, who didn't know already, would associate those marks with murder.

I returned to the carpet. The foam had turned a horrible pink and I decided to leave it a bit longer and get on with the dusting. Time was running short. The aluminium powder came off the polished surfaces easily. I paused briefly over the mantelpiece: the rectangle where the candlestick had once stood was still visible. I wiped the dust away, then, shoving the duster under my arm, I flipped through the post propped up behind the clock.

Most of it was unopened and it all looked like bills. One torn envelope revealed a receipt for money paid for restoration work, dated two years before. Not likely to be significant.

I peeled back the cuff of my rubber glove enough to see my watch, checked the time, then rushed to the stairs where I did some hasty dusting on the woodwork. The smudges on the wall were more difficult to deal with and required rubbing in vigorous circles with a wet cloth. As I viewed my handiwork I had to admit that it was slovenly. Frankly, I'd have sacked myself if I'd been employing me, but I had to finish work in the living room and time was against me.

The carpet foam had taken most of the stain away, leaving a faint pink mark, made more noticeable because the halo of carpet surrounding the stain was now cleaner and brighter than the rest. I didn't have time to scrub the entire carpet, and I wasn't prepared to do it anyway. It really needed taking up and burning and that wasn't my decision to make. There was only one way to solve the problem for the time being.

I nipped into Nick's bedroom, dragged the rug from beside his bed into the living room, and laid it down over the stain, covering up my handywork.

Finally, I closed the windows and sprayed lots of air freshener around in the room. I'd done as much as I was prepared to do. If his children wanted deeper cleaning done, they could damn well do it themselves.

I checked my watch: hardly any time left for sleuthing. I dusted the top of Nick's bureau and turned the key, pulling down the lid and exposing the wooden pigeonholes inside. They were stuffed, the slots jammed tight with paperwork. It would take hours to search through them. And any connection with Vlad or Bert was unlikely to exist on paper. I doubted if Nick kept written records of his illegal dealings. I wondered where all his account books were. Perhaps the police had taken them.

I closed the lid of the bureau, pulled open the drawers in turn and poked about with a yellow rubber forefinger. I found nothing but old pencil stubs, a couple of odd radio batteries, a few barley sugars, and springs and bits of metal that looked as if they'd come from inside a pocket watch. I sighed hopelessly. I was being an idiot. The police must have already searched through this stuff.

The chimes of St Andrew's Church clock sounded as it prepared to strike the hour. Mr Young would be returning any moment. I'd wanted to search the bedroom but I didn't want him to discover me rummaging through Nick's drawers, and I still had to tidy up my cleaning things.

As I emptied the bucket down the sink, watching the dreadful pink water swirl around the plughole, I congratulated myself on how calmly I had coped with the emotions of the situation. I rinsed the bucket and put it away, stripped off my rubber gloves, collected the rest of my things from the living room and surveyed my handiwork. And suddenly I could see Nick, shuffling about in his carpet slippers. *I am not ready to be ghost.* His words came back to me and I buckled, sank to my knees near the fireplace and wept.

All of a sudden I was rushing for the bathroom. I made it to the toilet just in time and vomited violently. After I'd flushed, I hastily gathered myself together, washed my face, blew my nose and scuttled down the stairs like a frightened spider. Some sleuth I was. I decided I'd wait for Mr Young outside.

CHAPTER TWENTY-FOUR

The atmosphere in the private room in The Dartmoor Lodge was strained to say the least. I sat on one of four upright chairs, facing the table where young Mr Young presided, just me and three other people who wondered who I was and what right I had to be sitting there.

I had to wonder myself. I'd received a phone call from old Mr Young, thanking me on behalf of the family for my efforts in their father's flat. They had visited it, apparently. He also informed me that I should be present at the reading of the will because I was a beneficiary. I couldn't imagine what Nick might have left me, or why, for that matter. I commented that it must be quite a recent will and Mr Young replied that yes, it was, and had only come to light in the last day or two, when the family were in the flat looking for something else. Fortunately, he added, and I didn't really understand the relevance of his words until later, young Mr Young had been present at the time.

I didn't get a good look at the family at the funeral. They'd been down in the pew at the front of St Andrew's Church and I'd stayed with the handful of people at the back: Tom and Vicky Smithson, Mr Singh, Ricky, Morris and me.

Nick's family obviously weren't expecting anyone but themselves to be attending.

There were no refreshments laid on for mourners afterwards, and they didn't even wait at the church door to receive our condolences. They just swept off. Mr Singh had to get back to his shop, but the rest of us made our own little party and raised a few glasses to Nick's memory in the bar at The Exeter Inn.

Now I was close enough to get a good look at the three of them. Helena Burgoyne was in her fifties. She wore an expensively tailored black suit and high heels, but whilst she was certainly not fat, she was too thick through the waist and in the calves to look really elegant. But she was well maintained, her red nails glossy and her blonde hair, cut in a smooth bob, highlighted in shades of caramel that don't exist in nature.

She sat rigidly upright, staring straight ahead, as if trying to pretend I didn't exist.

In contrast, her husband fidgeted constantly, as if he couldn't be comfortable sitting still; a bristly man with bristling, irritable vibrations. Even his breathing was fidgety and impatient. I got the feeling that he'd rather be elsewhere and resented this waste of his time. He looked the kind of man whose time is always more important than anyone else's.

Sitting between Mr Burgoyne and me, was Nick's son, Richard. He was a good ten years younger than his sister and there was nothing about his clothes or his manner that was the least funereal. He wore the same black jeans and trainers he'd worn to the service, with a blue crew-neck sweater and a cream sports jacket slung over the top, the sleeves pushed back to show his tanned forearms. He lounged in his chair with his legs stuck out in front of him, ankles crossed, his hands thrust deep in his pockets. With his wavy brown hair and beard he reminded me of a college lecturer, the sort that first-year students fall in love with. He looked vaguely familiar but I suppose that was because he'd inherited his father's wicked blue eyes. When I sat down in my chair, he did a double take, grinned at me, and, to my amazement, winked.

I was glad that I'd yielded to pressure from Ricky and Morris and not worn the same black sweater, skirt, and slightly scruffy suede boots that I'd worn to the funeral. For the reading of the will I should not look like a poor relation, they told me: they insisted on dressing me up. The classic black wool dress came from a production of *Witness for the Prosecution*, as did the royal blue, edge-to-edge jacket that covered it. I'd resisted the tiny black velvet hat, despite their cries that it looked fabulous perched on my red hair; I thought a hat might be over the top. The burnt-orange silk scarf flung around my shoulders came from *French Without Tears*, along with the black shoes; and the amber earrings were Cordelia's. I was grateful I'd agreed to carry the gorgeous, little royal-blue clutch bag that went with the jacket. It was comforting to have something to clutch.

Young Mr Young cleared his throat several times, the tense atmosphere obviously getting to him. 'Shall we begin?' he asked, smiling nervously.

The reading of the will took much longer than I had anticipated. It seemed that, as well as stowing cash in little bundles around the flat, Nick had invested in stocks and shares. And he'd been pretty canny at it and all. I lost count of what the various investments added up to, but they were bequeathed in their entirety to Helena Burgoyne. I dared a glance at her profile, but her expression didn't flicker. To his son, Richard, he left a much smaller sum of money and also the Riley car, a fact which drew an appreciative chuckle from him and earned him a disapproving glance over the bifocals from Mr Young.

Nick's flat, shop, the contents and stock, were left to Juno Browne.

There was a shocked intake of breath, not just from the Burgoynes, but also from me. Richard didn't seem at all fazed by the news, just eyed me rather quizzically.

There was a codicil contained in the will, Mr Young hurried on before anyone had a chance to object, which stated that anyone who contested it in court would lose what they had received, which would then be awarded to the other parties concerned.

Richard laughed out loud. 'The old devil!' he cried cheerfully.

'This is outrageous!' Helena's husband let out his

breath in a snort of disgust. 'It's a bloody disgrace!'

'Oh, belt up, Harry!' Richard advised him pleasantly. 'You surely weren't expecting the old man to leave you anything? You never even met him.'

'Of course not!' Harry turned slightly pink. 'But Helena's got her rights.'

'And I would say,' Richard responded calmly, 'with investments amounting to close on two hundred thousand, her rights have been very well taken care of.'

Helena, meanwhile, was saying nothing. She sat with eyes downcast, chewing her lip and looking a lot more upset than she had in church.

'What about the property?' Harry demanded.

'Helena doesn't want a grubby old flat and a shop full of tat.'

'Look, we're talking property here.' Harry jabbed an aggressive finger. 'That shop and flat are worth money. The builder down the road has already offered—'

'Has he indeed?' Richard cut him off, obviously nettled. 'And when did this conversation take place?'

Harry did not speak; he huffed in embarrassment and turned a deeper shade of red.

'We should count ourselves lucky that the old man left us anything,' Richard told him frankly. 'None of us have been near him in years. We couldn't blame him if he left it all to a cats' home.'

'But he didn't, did he?' It was the first time that Helena spoke, and her voice quivered with outrage and bitterness. 'He left it to her!'

Everyone turned to stare at me. I rose to my feet. 'Please

don't quarrel,' I said after a moment. 'I'm as shocked by this as you are. I'd only known Nick for a few months and—'

'You must have worked remarkably quickly, young lady!' Helena said spitefully. It was the first time she turned to face me. Apart from her thickset figure, she bore no resemblance to her father.

'Cleaning lady!' Harry snorted contemptuously. 'Look at her! She looks like a . . . a . . . film star!' I didn't realise I looked that good.

'Tart!' he added with devastating emphasis.

Or that bad.

'Mr Burgoyne!' Mr Young protested. 'Really, that kind of language is most uncalled for!'

'I understand that you're angry,' I told Helena. 'But . . . as I said . . . I haven't known Nick long. I wasn't expecting anything from him . . . I feel awful about this.'

I was about to tell her that I renounced any claim to what Nick had left me, that I didn't want it, they could have it all. But I didn't get the chance.

'Oh, I expect you've earned it.' Helena's glare was killing. 'On your back!'

I laughed. 'Are you serious? Nick was old enough to be my grandfather!'

'For all we know,' her husband chipped in, shaking a pointing finger in my direction, 'she was in cahoots with these Russians, or whoever they are! Once she'd worked her wicked wiles on your father, got him to sign the will in her favour – if it's genuine . . .'

'Mr Burgoyne!' Mr Young sprang to his feet. 'I really must insist you withdraw that allegation!' He waved the piece of paper he was holding. 'I can assure you that this document is genuine. It has been witnessed and dated . . .'

Harry began to bluster again but I cut in. 'Has it occurred to you,' I asked, struggling to keep my voice level, 'that if any of you had come down here to see your father now and again, I might not have had the opportunity to work my wicked wiles, as you call them?'

Suddenly Helena sprang forward. For a moment I thought she was going to slap me, but she grabbed my wrists, turning my hands over to look at my fingers. 'Where are my grandmother's rings?'

I tried to pull my hands away, shocked at her sudden strength. 'What rings? I don't know what you're talking about!'

'We searched that flat and they're not there! What have you done with them? They belonged to my mother's mother! They should come to me!'

'Oh for God's sake, Helena!' Richard protested loudly. 'You'll be lucky if the old man didn't sell 'em years ago!'

'I don't know anything about your grandmother's rings!' I protested, jerking my hands away.

Helena pulled out a handkerchief and began to cry. 'Well, *she* shouldn't have them!'

'Be reasonable, love,' Richard spoke to her more gently. 'We never liked the old man and he never liked us. And if his leaving the shop to Miss Browne here is his way of putting two fingers up at us, well that's not her fault. And,' he added smiling, 'it's probably what we deserve.'

I said nothing. I felt ill, physically sick with the certainty that what Richard had said was true. Nick had used me as a weapon of revenge against his nearest and dearest and I could have hated him for it. I didn't want his shop. I didn't want any part of the plot he'd been hatching against his family. He'd made a fool of me. I'd not expected to profit by his death and now everyone would think I had. I was on the verge of tears myself.

Richard put his arms around his sister. 'Come on now, Helena. It's not as if he left you penniless, is it? And old Harry here is as rich as Golden Balls anyway.'

'I want my grandmother's rings,' she insisted tearfully. 'I don't want that trollop to have them.'

'I don't know anything about any rings,' I repeated. Dear God, if it wasn't bad enough Verbena Clarke thinking I'd pinched her earrings, here was another one who thought I'd helped myself to her baubles! I turned to Mr Young. 'Is there anything else, or can I go now?' I just wanted to escape from the room, get away from the sobbing Helena, away from all of them.

'No, no. There are obviously legal formalities, Miss Browne, but nothing that needs your attention today.'

'Then I'll take my leave,' I said with as much dignity as I could muster.

Mr Young hurried to my side. 'I'll show you out.'

'Thank you for acting with such restraint in there,' he said, as soon as he had closed the door behind us.

I deflated like a balloon. 'I don't want any of this.'

'I wouldn't be too quick to refuse it, Miss Browne. It is a considerable bequest. And,' he added kindly, 'I believe that Mr Nickolai left it to you because he had become fond of you – what I'm saying is, don't act in haste. Take your time to think about it. You can always dispose of the property later if you don't wish to keep it.'

I nodded glumly. I could hear voices being raised again behind the door. Richard and the Burgoynes were getting going again. I wanted to go somewhere quiet, somewhere I could think.

'Harry Burgoyne is a very wealthy man in his own right,' Mr Young continued. 'He and his wife certainly don't need the money, and I don't believe they'll contest the will. They won't risk losing what they've been given. And they don't really have a case.'

'But they're his children.'

'If Mr Nickolai had cut them out of the will altogether, given everything to you, they, as his children, would certainly have been able to make a claim. But, in fact, in financial terms, they have been awarded the greater part of the estate.' He smiled dryly. 'And Harry Burgoyne is not a man to let his wife make a fool of him in court.'

I just nodded. I didn't want to talk about it any more. Mr Young shook my hand. We could discuss things another time, he told me, whenever I felt ready. I went home, miserable, and not feeling at all like a woman who'd just been given a considerable bequest.

When I got to my flat, I phoned Paul. I just wanted someone to talk to. He wasn't answering his mobile, so I tried his landline. Carrie answered. She knew of my existence, of course, although not what had taken place between her husband and me in their caravan. She didn't sound pleased to hear my voice. I could hear the baby crying in the background. This was not a good time. Paul wasn't there. What did I want? I invented some story about someone wanting some restoration work done. Nothing urgent, I told her. He could ring me back anytime. Carrie said she'd pass the message on and put the phone down.

I let out a sigh. It wasn't fair of me to ring Paul. He was looking for a new start, a new life elsewhere. I mustn't keep trying to drag him back to the old one.

I kicked off the high heels, massaged my tormented feet and sat with my legs up on the coffee table, wondering what to do next and feeling about as motivated as a stunned slug. I'd put myself through the ordeal of cleaning up Nick's blood to spare his children's feelings. I could have laughed at the irony of it. They weren't exactly prostrate with grief. All Helena seemed to care about was her grandmother's rings.

There was a knock on my living-room door. I opened it to Kate, who gave me a curious look and said there was someone downstairs who wanted to see me. Unwilling to put the torturing heels back on, I padded downstairs in my stockinged feet. Richard Nickolai was standing on the doorstep, hands in pockets. He smiled when he saw me. 'Hello there!'

My response was less than friendly. 'How did you find out where I live?'

I couldn't believe that Mr Young would have given away my address, not after the scene he had witnessed that afternoon.

'Well, I had to do a bit of detective work,' he admitted. 'As luck would have it, I called into the local shop for a packet of fags and I recognised the guy behind the counter, with the turban – he was at the funeral. I thanked him for coming. We got chatting and I asked about you. He showed me your business card, the one you have displayed in his window. It's got your phone number on it and I looked up your address in the phone book. I wanted a chance to apologise for what happened this afternoon, for the way you were treated.'

'You've nothing to apologise for,' I told him. He was the only one who'd been nice to me.

'You'll have to forgive Helena. She's not usually so emotional.'

That I can believe.

'No excuses for Harry,' he went on cheerfully. 'He's always like that, grasping bastard.'

'I'm sorry I caused the upset.' I couldn't think what else to say.

'Anyway, I wanted to apologise for their behaviour,' he went on, 'and I wondered if you'd let me take you out to dinner this evening.'

I hadn't seen that coming.

'It seems the least I can do,' he added.

I really wanted to tell him he could stuff his dinner, but felt I couldn't because, after all, he'd been the one who'd defended me against his horrible sister and her even more horrible husband. But there was something about him I couldn't quite take to. Possibly it was the fact that his jaunty, devil-may-care attitude seemed more studied than natural. I was casting around in my mind for an excuse when I stopped. I looked at him, standing there on the steps, all smiley and twinkly-eyed, and I heard the words 'Yes, that would be lovely, thank you' come out of my mouth.

'Great!' he said. 'I've booked a table at Gidleigh Park. Be a pity to waste it. I'll pick you up at seven.'

He whistled as he jogged off down the steps. I would have been indignant at his supreme self-confidence if my mind had not been fully occupied with the reason I'd agreed to go out with him: it had suddenly occurred to me, as he'd been standing there on the doorstep, where and when I had seen him before.

CHAPTER TWENTY-FIVE

Ricky's phone call forced me out of the bath. He and Morris were agog to know about the reading of the will, and I'd promised I would phone them as soon as I got back. My mind taken up with other matters, I'd forgotten them. They put me on speakerphone so they could both listen. I didn't feel like addressing a conference.

I gave them as brief a summary of events as I felt I could get away with.

'Come on round to us, Princess!' Ricky offered. 'We'll cook you dinner and you can tell us all about it.'

I had to explain then that I already had a dinner date and with whom.

'Where's he taking you?' Morris asked.

'Expensive!' Ricky exclaimed when I told them the name of the restaurant.

'Is it?' I asked.

'It's famous. Michelin star, celebrity chef . . . um, what's-his-name . . .' There was a momentary pause and then they both spoke together. 'What are you wearing?'

'I thought my cream silk dress.'

'You're not wearing that old rag!' Ricky informed me in a voice that brooked no argument. 'What time are you going out?'

'He's picking me up at seven.'

'You go and dry your hair. We'll be round in half an hour.' And he put the phone down before I could protest.

I have to confess that the simple, bias-cut bronze silk with the handkerchief hem, last worn by the character of Amanda in *Private Lives*, did look pretty sensational.

It certainly caused Richard Nickolai to raise appreciative eyebrows.

'You look ravishing!'

My turn to raise an eyebrow: the *dress* was ravishing.

'Why the suspicious glance?' he asked me. 'You're lovely.'

'I've got a suspicious mind.' This much was true. I didn't for a moment believe that he was taking me out to dinner to make up for the events of that afternoon. He had some ulterior motive. But then, so did I.

I had to admit he was attractive. He'd swopped his clothes of earlier in the day for a dark suit, white shirt and tie, which looked great on him and would have been more suitable attire at the funeral. I'd hung on to the orange shawl I'd worn that afternoon and wrapped it around my shoulders as we walked to the car. Any agonies of guilt I might have suffered at the thought of depriving Richard of his inheritance melted away as he guided me towards a gleaming, new, cream-coloured Mercedes. He opened the door, saw me into the front seat, closing the door and walking round to the driver's side with the easy stride of a man who's confident he's making the right impression.

I suppose if you own a powerful car, you drive it, well, fast. But the blind bends are safer in the evening, when headlights light up the solid green walls of the hedgerows and you can see if anything is coming. I forced myself to relax, watching Richard as he changed gear – tanned hands, immaculate nails, shining white cuff with gleaming gold cufflinks, Rolex watch. Rich and expensive from the wrists down; dead, I suspected, from the neck up. But I was probably being unfair.

'You seem to know the area very well,' I commented casually as we took the road to Chagford, 'for someone who doesn't live round here.'

'Not really,' he answered, smiling. 'The receptionist at The Dartmoor Lodge was very helpful with directions. And there's always the satnav if we get desperate.'

'Are you planning on staying here long?'

'Just for a couple more days. You know, you really took us by surprise this afternoon. We knew that the old man had left something to his cleaning lady but, frankly, I was expecting some old girl in an apron and slippers.'

'Curlers under her headscarf?' I suggested.

'Something like that,' he admitted.

'So, what do you do, Richard,' I asked, 'for a living, I mean?'

'I'm in the motor trade,' he volunteered cheerfully, 'in London. We're a private company. Basically, a customer contacts us, telling us what he wants and we find it for him. Strictly the class end of the market, of course.'

'Of course.'

He failed to detect the note of irony in my voice and rattled on. 'We'll go anywhere to find the customer the car he wants. I've just driven a Lamborghini back from Milan for one of our Arab customers.'

'You just deal with new cars?'

'No, no. Vintage models sometimes.'

I had to hide a smile. A second-hand car salesman; it suited him down to the ground.

Gidleigh Park Hotel was up an extremely long and winding lane, which, once it had convinced you that you must have taken a wrong turn miles back, suddenly opened out to reveal a sprawling mock-Tudor pile set in its own grounds.

We had a drink in the bar whilst we debated whether to go à la carte or opt for the seven-course tasting menu. We decided on the à la carte and followed the waiter to a panelled dining room and our candlelit table. After Richard consulted with the sommelier over the extensive wine list, we sat in silence, studying our menus.

I debated over the langoustine ceviche to start, or the coffee-cured sea trout.

I decided on the langoustine, followed by lamb. Richard went for Cornish venison tartare and then Brixham turbot.

'You know, I haven't really thanked you for sticking up for me this afternoon,' I said when the waiter had taken our orders.

'You mustn't think badly of Helena,' he responded cheerfully. 'She's not such a bad old stick. She had a pretty ghastly time of it when we were younger.'

'You didn't seem surprised about the will.'

'Not really. There was never any love lost between us.' He gave a rueful grin. 'We're an unnatural lot, I daresay.'

The waiter brought our wine and Richard was distracted by the ritual of tasting and approving it. Glasses filled, we clinked and drank.

'To Nick,' I said.

He stared at me a moment, but if he found my toast inappropriate he didn't say so. 'To you,' he said. 'You are very lovely by candlelight.'

I started to laugh.

'Now, why are you laughing?' He pretended to be put out. 'You shouldn't make a chap's romantic lines sound ludicrous.'

'Even if they are ludicrous?'

He grinned. 'Sorry. I'm probably not very good at this sort of thing.'

His sudden honesty was a lot more disarming than his glossy charm. I had to remind myself to be on my guard. Fortunately, my langoustine came to the rescue, a welcome distraction.

'You know, it was a real shock to me, what happened this afternoon,' I ventured, after a minute or two of contented eating. 'I don't understand why Nick would leave his shop to someone who . . . well, was a friend, certainly . . . but . . . I suppose what I really want to know is what caused such a terrible break up in your family.'

Richard was thoughtful for a moment. 'Mum always said that the old man loved things more than people.'

I remembered the way Nick's hand would caress the surface of a fine wood veneer, or hold up an old cup so that I could see how delicate the painting was, how translucent the porcelain. 'He loved antiques,' I said, almost as a defence.

'Didn't he, though?' Richard's smile was sardonic.

'Did you all live above the shop?' I asked. Somehow, I couldn't imagine a family squeezed into that small flat.

Richard shook his head. 'No. We had a house at the time, on the edge of town. When he was sent to prison for the second time, Mum decided it was time to get out, to go whilst the going was good. I think she was a little afraid of him. I'm not saying he was ever violent, but I don't know if she would have had the courage to leave if he hadn't been safely put away. She didn't like some of the dodgy characters he associated with, and she didn't want us to spend our childhood visiting him in prison, so we moved out to live with her sister.'

'Is your mum still alive?'

He shook his head.

'And Nick never tried to re-establish contact when he came out of prison?'

Richard shrugged. 'He agreed to a divorce. The house was sold, and he moved in above the shop. We saw him again, of course, in the first few years, but gradually contact slipped away. At Christmas he would send us money. I always felt he was relieved' – he paused to consider – 'relieved of the burden of a wife and two children. Glad to shed the emotional baggage.' He spoke without any bitterness and raised his glass to me. 'But we're getting rather gloomy.'

'That still doesn't explain why he left the shop to me,' I said. 'It wasn't as if I did much for him. If anyone deserves to be rewarded for their kindness to him, it's Mr Singh.'

Richard was silent a moment and then spoke, very quietly. 'If you think the old man rewarded kindness then you really didn't know him very well. He rewarded strength, pragmatism, acumen . . . ruthlessness. If he's rewarded you, it's because he's seen something in you that is like himself.' The mask of foolish affability had slipped, and I could see in that moment that he didn't like me any more than Helena and Harry did. I must have looked taken aback because when he spoke again he was all smiles, his voice returned to its hearty, fruity tones. 'I'm sure Nick left you the shop because he had confidence in you, thought you could make a go of it.'

'Did you ever know a dealer called Bert Evans?' I asked.

He shrugged. 'No, but of course I haven't seen the old man in years. I don't know who he associated with.'

'Well, he knew your father, had dealings with him. And he was murdered too.'

He raised an eyebrow. 'You think their murders are connected?'

'I don't believe it's just coincidence.'

'Unless someone's out there randomly picking off dodgy antiques dealers.' He raised his glass. 'Good luck to him, I say!'

For a moment I was too angry to speak.

'So, you haven't been near him for years?' I asked when I could find my voice.

'Guilty as charged,' he admitted, inclining his head.

'Well, that's really strange,' I told him. He looked uncertain and it was my time to smile. I leant back in my chair. 'You don't remember our first meeting, do you?'

He frowned, his head cocked on one side. 'Have we met before today?'

'Oh yes, we bumped into each other – almost literally. I was forced to drive my van into the hedge because you were coming around the bend so fast – not in the car you're driving today, but another big, swanky job – and I warned you to slow down because of horse riders on the road.' I could see the memory of the event slowly unfold in his mind. 'Surely you remember?' I prompted. 'This was just a mile outside of the town where your father lived – just a few weeks before he was murdered.'

Richard stared at me for what seemed like a long moment, his fingers playing idly with the stem of his glass. 'All right, Juno, it's a fair cop,' he breathed at last. 'I admit I did come down to see him, to tap him for money. The firm had been experiencing cash flow problems and . . . well, it wasn't the first time he'd helped me out.'

'He gave you money?'

'I didn't have to kill him for it, if that's what you're implying. I've never told Helena because . . . well, because she and Nick never got on, not even when she was a child. She hated him. If I'd told her I'd been seeing the old man on and off over the years, she'd have felt I'd betrayed her and Mum. I could do without her reproaches, and I could certainly do without Harry's.'

'I'm surprised that Nick should be so . . . amenable.'

'I am his son. And he always thought the way to gain affection was to buy it, so why not let him carry on?'

I found his cold-bloodedness chilling; he really was a heartless bastard. 'So, that's why you accepted the will so calmly?'

'Certainly, I'd already received most of my share.' He flicked open the dessert menu that the waiter had just brought. 'Now what do you fancy? Dark chocolate fondant with salted caramel and orange compote?'

I said words I never thought I would hear coming out of my mouth. 'I really don't feel like dessert.'

'Oh, come on, Juno, don't let me down! Let's try and work out who really killed him. You can tell me all about these Russians, over the piña colada and coconut mousse.'

I told him all I could about Vlad and Igor, and the murder of Bert Evans, but I could see that none of them meant anything to him. He told me about the rings.

There were three of them, apparently: a small diamond cluster, a square cut emerald and a heavy gold ring set with three rubies. None of them were spectacularly valuable but they had belonged to Helena's grandmother and had sentimental value. Richard's mother had inadvertently left them behind when she had fled the family home, and when he was released from prison, Nick had told her the only way she was going to get them back was if she came to fetch them herself. She never had the courage, and so it was assumed Nick had kept them all this time. Helena had searched for them when she and Richard had visited the flat, but had been unable to find them.

Could they not be in a safety deposit box somewhere, I'd asked. Richard shrugged. There was no record of one. He thought it was more likely that, at some time in the past, Nick had sold them.

It was very late by the time we'd finished our coffee. Richard had insisted on liqueurs but I'd been feeling fretful about going home. It was all right for him, but I had to get up early the next morning and walk the dogs. Eventually I spoke up, and despite his protests that the night was young, he agreed to take me home.

'My carriage is at your service, fair damsel.'

I couldn't help noticing that the drive home from Gidleigh Park was a lot more leisurely and unhurried than the drive there. Possibly because Richard had consumed a fair amount of alcohol and didn't want to arouse interest from patrolling police cars. I couldn't convince him we were very unlikely to meet any on the roads between Chagford and Ashburton. I got the feeling that he was deliberately taking his time.

It was a fine, clear night, and the stars were out in force. 'Wow!' Richard leant forward over the steering wheel to try and get a better view. 'You never see them like this in London. Too much light pollution. Let's just stop a minute.'

Before I could argue he'd pulled over into a lay-by, stopped the car, got out and was standing, gazing up at the Milky Way above him. Muttering, and drawing my shawl tightly round my bare arms and shoulders, I got out and joined him. It was true the sky was a magnificent sight. I'd rarely seen the stars look so bright and clear, glittering, sharp, pricking the velvet black night. Richard began pointing out constellations, whilst at the same time protesting that he didn't know anything about astronomy. My shawl clutched around me I soon began to shiver and reminded him of my need to be up early. Apologising, he got back in the car, but I still couldn't shake off the feeling that he was deliberately wasting time.

I felt profound relief when we drew up outside the house. But whatever I felt about Richard, or he felt about me for that matter, he had treated me to a fabulous and expensive dinner. 'Thank you,' I said, and leant across to kiss him lightly on his bearded cheek. He turned his head, cupping my chin with a swift motion and kissed me on the lips. It was not at all unpleasant and the swift efficiency with which he had accomplished the manoeuvre took me by surprise. 'Well!' I breathed.

He kissed me again, in a rather more leisurely fashion and I let him. Possibly it was the wine I had drunk during the evening, but kissing him suddenly seemed like a very good idea.

He drew back and looked down at me. 'God, but you're beautiful!'

That was it, the brief illusion of romance shattered, split asunder by my loud crack of laughter. 'And impossible!' he added, leaning across me to open the car door. Giggling, I got out. Then I turned to look back at him, serious again. 'I still haven't made up my mind about the shop and the flat . . .'

'Just take it, why not?' Richard shrugged. 'It was what the old man wanted.'

'I'll think about it.'

'I promise you, there won't be any fuss from Helena and Harry. I'll make sure of that.'

I nodded and thanked him, trying to stifle a hippo-sized yawn.

He laughed. 'Get to bed!'

I closed the car door and ran up the steps, waved as I reached the doorstep, and he started the engine. The front door was unlocked. Kate had left it that way in case I'd forgotten my keys. I never have, to my knowledge, but it is a possibility that seems to obsess her.

Inside, the house was in darkness. I guessed she and Adam were already in bed. She must have been making flapjacks during the evening because the smell of apple and cinnamon lingered temptingly in the hallway. I tiptoed up the stairs, trying not to make too much noise. There was no need to switch on the light. Enough orange glow came from the solitary lamp post outside the house, shining in through the landing window, for me to see well enough as I fumbled for my keys.

As it turned out, I hadn't locked my door anyway. Not like me to forget, but I'd had a stressful day. I dumped my bag and keys in the nearest armchair, kicked off my shoes and padded over to the bookcase with the intention of switching on the table lamp that stood on it.

I didn't make it to the switch. I froze with a clutching feeling of horror in the pit of my stomach and the absolute certain knowledge that I wasn't alone. Someone was in the darkness with me, someone breathing softly, someone close.

'Who's there?' My voice sounded sharp with fear. I reached out for the lamp and a sudden violent shove sent me toppling forward. I fell against the bookcase and the lamp crashed to the floor. Swift footsteps crossed the room, I heard the door open.

I struggled to my knees in time to see a figure silhouetted in the doorway, illuminated by the orange lamplight.

'Hey!' I yelled.

It turned to look at me, eyes glittering over a ski mask. I staggered to my feet and scrambled towards the door. I didn't see what the figure was holding until it was too late: a heavy, rubber-covered torch. I saw the glass disc, a blinding circle of white light as the figure raised its arm. I saw it in a sweeping blur as I averted my face and it hit me hard across the side of the head. I didn't see anything after that.

CHAPTER TWENTY-SIX

Three blurred faces were hanging over me. I blinked as Adam, Kate and Richard swam into focus.

'It's all right, Juno,' Kate told me reassuringly. 'You're going to be all right.'

I wondered what in the hell she was talking about, why she was in her dressing gown and why she was holding my hand. 'The ambulance is on its way,' she said brightly, as if she was announcing some special treat. As she leant forward her long, dark plait swung down and brushed my face.

I twitched it away irritably. 'What ambulance?' I had a dull, throbbing ache at the back of my skull and it took me some moments to connect this, and the fact I seemed to be lying on the sofa in the downstairs living room, with the approaching conveyance. 'I don't need an ambulance,' I said, struggling up on to my elbows.

'Oh, be careful!' she squeaked.

'I said she didn't need an ambulance.' Adam spoke with obvious disgust. 'She's only been out for a minute.'

'She was unconscious!' Kate protested dramatically.

'She fainted,' he sneered.

'How are you feeling, Juno?' Richard helped me to sit up, propping sofa cushions behind my back. I moaned, putting a hand to the back of my head. I discovered a very sore place and took it away again. 'Steady now,' he advised, 'I'd keep still if I were you.'

'What are you doing here?' I was still struggling to understand what was going on.

'I had just turned the car around,' he explained, 'was barely halfway down the street, when I looked in the mirror and saw this masked figure rush out of your front door.'

I accepted a cold compress from Kate, a bag of frozen peas wrapped in a towel, and held it to the back of my head. 'Why didn't you go after him?' I asked, wincing.

'I was rather more concerned about you, my girl. I thought you might have had a visit from one of your Russian friends. But by the time I got back here, these two good folks were already to the rescue.'

I thought Adam gave him a rather questioning look, but all he said was, 'Yeah, hell of a racket you made, Juno.'

There was another hell of a racket then, on the front door. 'That'll be the ambulance.' Kate jumped up to answer it. 'And the police!'

'Why didn't you call the sodding fire brigade as well?' Adam demanded gruffly.

'I didn't call the police,' Kate responded in a cross whisper, 'but when I said that Juno had been struck over the head by someone, the lady in the control room said she would be sending them anyway!'

'Well, why didn't you say she'd just fallen?' he whispered back.

'Because she didn't!' Kate whispered fiercely as the knocking on the door continued. 'The police should be here. Richard is right, it could have been one of those Russians!' And she flounced off to open the door.

The girls in green and the boys in blue arrived together; the policemen waiting patiently while a very calm lady paramedic inspected the bump on my head, shone a little pencil torch in each eye and asked me sane and sensible questions. I assured her I didn't feel nauseous or have ringing in my ears and wasn't seeing double. She said I'd been lucky, it could only have been a glancing blow, I didn't have to go to casualty if I didn't want to. Barring a bruise and a headache, I'd probably be fine. On the other hand, if I experienced any blurring of the vision or nausea, that might be a sign of delayed concussion blah-de-blah. I barely listened. I'd picked up enough elderly people who'd bumped their heads and I'd heard it all before. She left fairly promptly.

As luck wouldn't have it, the boys in blue turned out to be the same ones I'd encountered up on the moor. I remembered them distinctly and, unfortunately, they remembered me. Why this should make me feel guilty and uncomfortable, I can't imagine, but it did. They seemed to take ages, taking statements. I told them everything

I'd seen and so did Richard, but I got the feeling they didn't believe me, any more than when they'd questioned me that day on the moor.

'And neither of you saw this person's face?' This was the officer who'd driven the car before.

No, we repeated, neither of us had. 'I just saw this man in dark clothes – it was definitely a man – leave the house in a hurry,' Richard told them. 'I didn't get a look at his face.'

The police turned their attention to Kate, who was bursting to speak, hopping from one foot to another like an excited wallaby. 'Well, we were in bed, you see,' she began, rolling her eyeballs dramatically, 'and we heard this noise – this terrible crash – from upstairs. We sleep in the room underneath. And Juno called out, and then there was this noise on the landing – sort of bumping – and we heard someone run down the stairs and open the front door. And of course we got up, just to check, and the front door was wide open and Juno was lying on the landing. And Adam went to the front door and saw this figure in black scrambling through the hedge.'

The policeman studied Adam. 'And you didn't attempt to follow him, sir?'

Adam looked down at his striped nightshirt, bare, hairy legs and slipperless feet. 'No,' he said acidly.

'And you've nothing else to add?'

'No.' Adam didn't like having police in his house. He wasn't going to add anything that might encourage them to hang around. But if I rolled my own joints from a plant on my kitchen windowsill, neither would I.

Kate babbled on like a little stream. 'The thing

242

is . . . well, the thing is . . . I think I must have heard him – the intruder – coming in. Only I thought it must be Juno, creeping up the stairs so as not to wake us.'

'Coming in through the front door? Are you sure?'

'Oh yes. I'd left it unlocked.'

The policeman paused and gave her what I can only describe as an old-fashioned look.

'I nearly called out goodnight,' she rattled on, 'but I didn't.'

The policeman cleared his throat. 'And what time was this?'

'Well, it couldn't have been long before Juno came in, because I swear I'd only just dozed off when we heard the rumpus . . . perhaps, half an hour?'

Half an hour? For half an hour that man had been lurking in my flat? Doing what? Robbing me, or just waiting? I thought I'd better speak up, 'I didn't get a chance to see what state the flat's in. I don't know if anything's been taken . . . not that there's anything up there worth stealing.'

The police officer taking statements nodded to his colleague who disappeared upstairs to check things out.

'You were just unlucky, Juno,' Richard said. 'You surprised an opportunist thief, that's all.'

'Opportunist?' Kate raised her eyebrows, 'with a torch and in a ski mask?'

'Fairly standard burglar equipment, I would have thought,' he answered.

The police officer came back to report that, apart from the broken lamp, everything in the flat appeared neat and tidy. If there had been a search, it must have been a careful one. But of course, I'd need to go up myself to see if anything was missing.

I didn't want to, my head ached and I was longing for my bed, but I knew I had to come clean. I didn't believe that the person I'd encountered in my flat had been either Vlad or Igor, but I knew I had to tell these officers about them, of my connection to Nick and the investigation into his murder. I also threw in the murder of Bert Evans.

It was as if I'd pressed an alarm bell. Suddenly, everything moved into a different gear. The policeman started speaking into his radio. He was answered by a disembodied alien parked on Mars, but he seemed to understand it well enough.

'A detective will be on the way from headquarters,' he informed us, 'and someone to dust for fingerprints.'

'Now?' Adam asked in disgust. He had to be up early, to start preparing breakfasts at *Sunflowers*, and it was already close on one in the morning.

'I'm afraid so. Now sir, perhaps you could show us where this potential murder suspect disappeared through this hedge?'

'Surely, Richard can leave?' I was sure he was longing to get back to his hotel. After taking his contact details, the officer agreed that he could go, warning him that he might need to go over his statement again in the morning.

'I'll call you tomorrow, Juno,' he promised, squeezing my shoulder. 'Try to get some rest. And don't worry. This was probably just a random burglary. No connection to anything more sinister.'

Shortly after he'd gone, the detective arrived. Not, unfortunately, Inspector Ford, but Constable DeVille. She was accompanied by a uniformed officer, a police dog handler, and another of the white-suited aliens who went upstairs to dust my flat for fingerprints while the police dog and his handler rooted about outside in the hedge.

After briefly talking to the first officers who'd turned up, she dismissed them, read through my statement, and made me repeat it all for her benefit. I got the impression she was enjoying herself. 'And despite the fact you didn't see this man's face, you are confident it was not either of these two foreign gentlemen you encountered on the moor?'

'As confident as I can be. Wrong size, wrong shape . . . just not the same.' Something about that intruder was bothering me, but I couldn't put my finger on what it was. I was convinced of one thing: it wasn't Igor or Vlad.

'You didn't hear him speak?'

I shook my head, then regretted such impetuous movement. 'No, not at all.'

'Are you sure you're all right, Juno?' Kate asked. 'You're looking ever so pale.' She turned to Detective Constable DeVille. 'Is this going to take very much longer?' she demanded. 'Juno should really be in bed.'

Cruella put away her notebook. 'No, that's all my questions for now.' She turned to me. 'Do you have anywhere to stay the night, Miss Browne?'

'Stay the night?' I repeated dumbly.

'Well you can't go back in your flat until forensics have finished and that won't be for a while, I'm afraid.' I suppose she couldn't help the little smirk.

'Don't worry, Juno, you can sleep in our spare room,' Kate told me. 'Now, I really think it's time you went to bed.'

The detective constable didn't argue. Graciously she

agreed to my retiring and left the premises, warning me that she might be back to see me again in the morning.

Kate relieved me of the now soggy bag of peas and fussed over me all the way to the spare room, which lay next to their kitchen. I let myself be fussed over, I didn't have the energy to resist. She brought me tea, aspirins and a T-shirt of Adam's to sleep in.

I lay awake for hours, listening to footsteps tramping up and down the stairs. Once I swear I heard the police dog panting in the hall. When the police left, I could hear Kate was tidying up in the kitchen, talking in a whisper that would have reached the back row of any auditorium.

'So, you don't think,' she was asking Adam, 'that this intruder was the same man who broke into Nick's and killed him and that he was looking for something he didn't find?'

Adam's only reply was a long, drawn-out yawn.

'And that whoever-it-is – the murderer I mean,' Kate prattled on, 'thinks that Juno's got it now, this thing that he was searching for?'

'We don't know Nick's killer was searching for anything,' Adam replied testily. 'He wasn't robbed . . . Christ, I'm going to bed. I've got to get up in two and a half hours.'

'Just because Nick wasn't robbed, doesn't mean the murderer wasn't looking for something.' Kate was babbling on unstoppably as she turned off the kitchen light and followed him to their bedroom.

After the house had quietened down, I listened to my own head throbbing. Had I been wrong all along about Vlad and Igor? Could Richard have killed his father? Had they quarrelled, had Nick refused a request for

246

money? During dinner I had glimpsed a darker nature beneath the amiable idiot that Richard tried so hard to portray, but that didn't mean he was a murderer. There was Helena, of course. She'd hated Nick apparently – could she and Richard have conspired together? Were they lying about the true value of the rings? Could Helena have committed the murder on her own? If she had, she must be a pretty cool customer. And surely, neither she nor Richard had murdered Bert. Perhaps their deaths weren't connected after all, perhaps it was just a grotesque coincidence.

Something rustled in the room and a moment later Bill landed lightly on my stomach, shredding what was left of my nerves. He was overjoyed to have found me, his paws padding up and down on my sternum, and set up a saw-like purr. I stroked his head idly with one hand. After several minutes of delirious padding, he tucked his paws primly under him and slept.

Something about Richard's account of things that evening bothered me. He had turned his car around, he said, and was just driving away up the road when he'd happened to glance in his rear-view mirror and seen a masked man – 'It was definitely a man', those were his words – leaving by the front door.

Something in the timing was off. I'd crept up the stairs, hunted for my keys, found the door unlocked, groped my way into the living room, put down my bag and reached out to switch on the lamp; the intruder had pushed me, then made his escape out of the room and down the stairs, stopping only to wallop me with a torch.

From start to finish, this must have taken a full minute, perhaps two. And during that time, Richard's powerful car hadn't even made it to the bend in the road? And Adam had given Richard a strange glance when he'd said he had come straight back.

I kept turning his words over in my mind. *It was definitely a man*. Why had he said that? Suddenly, something about the attack came back to me with such clarity that I let out a laugh, startling Bill. I didn't know who'd murdered Nick, but I had a pretty good idea who'd been in my flat that night and walloped me with a torch.

CHAPTER TWENTY-SEVEN

Next morning, I asked the receptionist at The Dartmoor Lodge for the room number of Mrs Helena Burgoyne. She and her husband had already checked out, she informed me, and were returning to Bradford. Had they indeed? It was still quite early. The Tribe hadn't had a very long walk that morning. Mr Richard Nickolai, then? I asked.

She gave me the room number. He was expecting me, I lied blithely, no need to ring him. I'd find my own way.

He wasn't expecting me and when he opened the door his expression, just for a moment, was less than welcoming.

'Nightshade,' I said to him, before he had a chance to speak.

'Nightshade?' he repeated blankly.

'It's the name of a perfume. I think we ought to talk about it. Aren't you going to ask me in?'

'Of course! What am I thinking?' He stepped back to let me in. 'How are you, Juno?' he asked, voice suddenly laden with concern. 'How's the head?'

I looked around. The room was comfortable, countrified in a chintzy sort of way, with a large four-poster bed and mullioned windows. There was a smell of scented steam in the room, as if someone had just taken a shower. Richard indicated a chair by the window and I sat.

'I was planning on popping round to see you.' He ran a hand through his hair, a little nervously, I thought. 'That was a ghastly business last night, ghastly business altogether!' He stared at me. 'Are you feeling OK?'

'I'm fine, thanks, apart from a sore head.'

'Now,' he took up a position, leaning against one of the bedposts, his hands in his pockets. 'What's all this about perfume?' As he spoke, with one foot he tried surreptitiously to nudge a red, high-heeled shoe beneath the bed. I pretended I didn't see him.

'Nightshade,' I repeated. 'It's a perfume. Our intruder last night was wearing it.'

He laughed. 'You must be mistaken. Perhaps it was aftershave.'

'No, I'm very familiar with the smell. Helena was wearing it yesterday and my cousin Brian sent me a bottle a couple of Christmases ago – all gone now, sadly. But I smelt it last night, just before someone hit me with the torch. And I'll tell you something else. I can smell it in here as well.' I nodded towards the closed door that led to the en suite. 'Why don't you tell her to come out?'

He laughed. 'Tell who?'

'Helena.'

'Helena?' He was shocked enough to take his hands out of his pockets. 'Helena and Harry have gone back to Bradford.'

'Oh, come on, Richard! It was a woman in my room last night. It was Helena, searching my flat for her bloody rings!'

'You're out of your mind!' Richard laughed. 'Or that bump on the head has affected you.'

'We both know it was her, so why don't you stop playing around?'

'You've got it all wrong!'

'All that money you lavished on dinner, too. And that long, long drive home, stopping to look at the stars – but you still couldn't keep me out of the house long enough for her to burgle my place and get away safely. Of course, she had to wait for Adam and Kate to go to bed before she could creep in, which must have been frustrating for her. Is that why you decided to kiss me? Just in case she was still in there? Give her a few more minutes to get away?'

'Juno, I can assure you—'

'It must have given you quite a scare to see her running out of the house, even more so when she told you she'd bonked me on the head. You must have been worried sick, in case she'd killed me. You picked her up and brought her back here before you returned to the house. That's why the poor police doggie couldn't find any trail leading from the hedge.'

Richard rubbed a hand over his face. 'Juno, I swear to you, Helena had nothing to do with this.'

I stood up. 'Tell that to the police.'

He hastily stepped in front of me, barring my way. 'Look . . . all right, I admit I did take you out last evening to get you out of your flat.'

I sat down again. 'Go on.'

He flicked an undecided glance towards the door of the bathroom, then strode across and opened it. 'You'd better come in here,' he called sourly.

The woman who walked out of the bathroom was not Helena Burgoyne. She was a Mediterranean-looking creature with polished dark hair, high cheekbones and a deep golden tan accentuated by the white towelling bathrobe she wore. It was her black eyes I had seen glittering at me through the slits in the ski mask. They glittered now, with a kind of sulky defiance.

'You bungled it, dearie,' I said pleasantly, and she flung me a look of scorching detestation. Between her and Richard there was, to say the least, an atmosphere.

'Who is this?' I asked him.

'I'm Richard's wife,' she answered, with a toss of her shiny dark head.

'Are you?' I raised my brows at Richard. 'You've been keeping her quiet.'

'There was no need for Tamara to be involved until . . . until yesterday. I phoned her and told her to come down from London. I knew Nick hadn't sold the rings because he told me so the last time I saw him. He said that if Helena wanted them she'd have to come and visit him. When we couldn't find them in the flat, we thought that . . . well, I realised the old man might have been lying. But then I thought—'

252

'You thought that I had them.'

'Well, when you refused to give them to Helena . . .'

'I didn't refuse. I've never laid eyes on the bloody things. Helena is welcome to them.'

'We thought . . . well I thought, that if you did have them, you wouldn't have left them at the old man's. You'd have hidden them somewhere.' He looked guilty and miserable, like a schoolboy caught cheating in an exam. 'Helena deserves those rings,' he went on defensively, 'she had a hell of a time when . . . She'd never have married a shit like Harry if—' He broke off.

I turned my attention to Tamara, who was now lounging on the bed like a petulant puma. 'Are you a professional burglar by any chance?'

'I'm a professional model,' she snapped.

'How did you get into my flat?'

'With a credit card.' She hunched a shoulder and sneered. 'It's easy with those old locks.'

'I see.' I tried not to sound impressed.

'Juno,' Richard said. 'I swear we had nothing to do with the old man's murder.'

'I didn't imagine you had.' Not quite true; during the night I'd imagined all sorts. But despite Tamara's prowess with the torch, I sensed that she didn't have the bottle for murder. And, for the time being at least, I decided that Richard didn't either. He was looking pale beneath his tan, and if he'd seen what I'd seen – his father's murdered body – he'd have looked a good deal paler.

'So what will you do?' he asked anxiously, as I got to my feet.

'If she wants revenge,' Tamara eyed me with loathing, 'she'll go to the police.'

'If she wanted revenge,' I replied, gingerly touching the bump on my head, 'she'd have brought her own torch.' I turned to Richard. 'You know, I should really thank you for helping me to make up my mind. I've decided I'm going to keep what Nick left me, the flat and the shop, if for no other reason than because you bastards don't deserve it. And because I liked him.'

Richard smiled bitterly. 'He never gave you cause to hate him.'

'No,' I agreed vehemently, 'he didn't! As far as the rings are concerned, if I ever find them, Helena is welcome to them. I don't care. All I want to know is that this is the last time I am ever going to lay eyes on you, any of you. Take my advice and go back to London today, because if I ever see you here again, Richard, I will call the police and tell them how you used to come down and tap him for money.'

'Juno, you have my solemn word . . .' Sensing that he was getting back on safe ground, he smiled, switched on the sincere charm. 'I swear to you—'

'Save it, Richard. The only word I want to hear from you is goodbye.'

He shrugged. 'Goodbye, Juno,' he said, and opened the door for me.

I turned to look back at Tamara. 'I should watch it, dear,' I advised her, jerking my head in Richard's direction. 'He's a second-hand car salesman. He trades-in old models.'

She bit her lip angrily and then flounced back into the bathroom, slamming the door.

'You can tell Helena I meant what I said about the rings,' I told Richard. 'If I ever find them, I promise I will return them to her.'

Richard smiled. 'That's more than we deserve, I fear.'

'Yes,' I agreed as I marched away down the hotel corridor, 'it most certainly is.'

CHAPTER TWENTY-EIGHT

There was a visitor waiting for me when I got back to the house. As soon as I opened the front door, Kate called to me from her kitchen. I went in reluctantly.

I'd had enough dramatics for one morning, my head ached and I wanted to lie down.

Sitting at her scrubbed pine table, a mobile of glass dolphins revolving slowly over his head, sat Inspector Ford, in soulful contemplation of Bill, who was sitting upright on his lap, gazing up at him intently like a little Cyclops. Kate was standing with her back against the sink, very obviously blocking the inspector's view of the windowsill and of one pot plant in particular. She might as well have hung a sign.

'Good morning, Inspector,' I said. 'No, please, don't get up.' He'd begun to rise, inconveniencing Bill who dropped, grumbling, to the floor. I sat at the table on his left, so that the inspector would have to turn away from the windowsill to look at me.

'Good morning, Miss Browne,' he answered pleasantly, 'an unfortunate coincidence, this.'

'Yes, isn't it?' I responded, trying to sound bright. The inspector was being very formal. Whatever had happened to 'May I call you Juno?'

'Kate, be a love and make me a cup of tea.'

Kate rolled her eyes meaningfully, as if to convey silently that she couldn't leave her post. I ignored her. Unable to think of a reason why not to, she reluctantly moved away and filled the kettle. 'Camomile?' she asked.

'What a disgusting suggestion,' I shuddered. 'Ordinary tea, please, and a couple of aspirins, if you've got them. Proper ones.'

'Your head is troubling you?' the inspector asked.

'It's a bit tiresome.'

'Then I won't keep you any longer than I need. Have you discovered if anything from your flat is missing?'

'I looked first thing this morning. No, there isn't.'

'Detective Constable DeVille reports that you're convinced your attacker was not one of the Russians that we are searching for following Mr Nickolai's murder.'

'I'm sure I would have recognised either of them, even in a mask. I don't suppose there's been any progress in finding them?'

'Sadly not.' Inspector Ford shook his head. 'So, as things stand, there's no evidence to suggest that there's any link between the incident last night and the murder of Mr Nickolai.'

'You don't subscribe to Kate's theory, then?'

He looked blank. 'I didn't know that . . . er . . . Kate . . . had a theory.'

'She thinks that Mr Nickolai's murderer was searching for something,' I explained, 'and having failed to find it on the night of the murder – whatever it is – has pursued it here.'

Kate was nodding enthusiastically as she put down a mug of tea and a bottle of aspirins. 'That's what I said.'

He surveyed Kate thoughtfully for a moment and then turned to me. 'But you don't think so, Miss Browne?'

I shook my head and then wished I hadn't. I tried to open the bottle of aspirins but my fingers were trembling and the childproof cap clicked irritatingly round and round. 'No, I don't. Why would Nick's killer think that I had what he was looking for?'

Inspector Ford didn't answer. Instead he gave me one of his long, steady stares and then took the bottle of aspirin out of my hand. 'On the whole, you don't seem to be as upset about this incident as I thought you would be.' He opened the bottle with an ease that made me feel foolish.

'Really?' I stared back innocently. He knew I was holding out on him, that I knew more than I was saying.

He held my gaze for a fraction longer, then gave a soft laugh and handed me back the bottle. 'I understand congratulations are in order.'

I frowned. 'I'm sorry, I don't understand.'

'I hear that you have come into a nice little inheritance, Miss Browne.'

A horrible thought occurred to me. 'Does that make me a suspect?'

'Should it?' he answered blandly.

'Well, I . . . I don't know,' I admitted.

'Of course, in the investigation of any murder, one has to ask the question – who benefits?' He laughed at my horrified face. 'Just my little joke,' he assured me, standing up. 'I won't keep you any longer, Miss Browne, you really do look shockingly pale.'

'Before you go, Inspector, tell me, do you believe that Nick's murder and the murder of Bert Evans are connected?'

He turned to look at me. The long, steady stare was working overtime. 'At the moment we are treating them as separate investigations, Miss Browne.'

He pushed in his chair and then wandered over to the kitchen windowsill, where he stood considering the pot plant for a moment, before poking his finger into the compost. 'A little more water,' he told a gaping Kate with a pleasant smile, 'and a little less sun.'

I had to bite my lip to stop myself giggling hysterically.

He went to the kitchen door. 'Don't worry, ladies, I can find my own way out.'

We waited until we heard the front door slam before we dared to look at one another.

'Bloody hell!' Kate squeaked, flopping down on a chair.

I gulped down my aspirin. 'I'm going to bed. And I don't care who calls, don't wake me. I've already had far too much excitement for one day.'

CHAPTER TWENTY-NINE

It took me several minutes of just standing, staring at the scratched black paintwork, before I got up the courage to open Nick's door – my door now. At the first attempt the key wouldn't turn, although it was the right key, placed into my hand only the day before by young Mr Young. The weeks of legal wrangling had lasted through Christmas and the new year, passed my birthday, through all of February and into March.

During that time, although I did not speak with her personally, Helena Burgoyne had continued to restate her conviction that I had kept her rings, that I'd been given them for services rendered. I would have laughed if it wasn't so tragic.

But now everything was sorted. Nick's place was legally

mine. I tried the key a second time, and this time I didn't fumble it. The door opened and showed me the stairs. This time there was no Mr Young to accompany me. I was on my own. I took a deep breath and ran up, stopping on the threshold of the living room.

I hadn't been there since the day I'd come in to clean it. I wondered if the Burgoynes might have disturbed anything on their pre-funeral visit, but nothing seemed to have changed since the last time I was there. Something glinted on the table, the light catching the edge of Nick's spectacles, still lying next to the dusty bottles, where he had last placed them. I picked them up, folded them neatly and put them back where they were. I didn't know what else to do with them.

Any delusion I might have had that Helena wanted a keepsake from her father's possessions was dashed as soon as I walked into the bedroom. Nothing seemed to have been taken. His suits and coat still hung in the wardrobe, his folded shirts, vests and socks still occupied the chest of drawers. Despite her desperation, her search for the rings must have been a tidy one. Then I remembered that Mr Young had been present. If she'd been left on her own, she might have torn the place apart.

The only sign that she had been there at all was a small wooden jewellery box, upturned on Nick's bed, its contents scattered across his pale-green eiderdown. I sat on the bed and picked up a pair of gold cufflinks, a watch and chain: not a bad watch, either – a decent half-hunter; of no interest to Helena, obviously. I picked up the box, lying open with its hinged lid, and lifted it out of the way. Beneath it I found photographs, tiny black and white prints of a young woman and two children, a girl with pigtails holding her little brother's hand – clearly Helena and Richard. Memories of a happier past, surely – how could she bear to leave them? And one of Nick himself as a young man, hair neatly parted in the middle, but with the same bristling moustache, the same wicked eyes twinkling at the camera.

I took the photo of him and stood it up on the chest of drawers, leaning it up against a little clock. I would find a frame for it later. The other photos, together with the cufflinks and the watch, I would pack up, give to Mr Young, and ask him to send them to Richard. Perhaps one day, if not now, he might be glad to have some mementos of his father.

The only other thing I touched was Nick's chess set, still set out on a table in the living room, ready for the next game. I packed the set away in its handsome box.

I would give it to Mr Singh.

I went down into the shop, switched on the dreadful fluorescent light and surveyed the scene of chaos: the walls partly painted, the shelves and heavy furniture shoved into the middle of the room and draped with old sheets. I threaded a route through the furniture to the door at the front of the shop, a door I had never seen open, and sorted through a handful of keys until I found the right one, an old iron key that fitted into the large keyhole. I tried it but, despite all my rattling about, it was too stiff to turn. The bolts wouldn't move either. I'd have to return with a can of WD40. Another day.

I was due at a client's in a few minutes to tackle a load

of ironing. Once a fortnight I worked my way through a basketful for an accountant who was very particular about his shirts.

I switched off the light, tucked the chess set under my arm and prepared to go out the way I had come in. When I opened the door, I shrieked and almost dropped the box. Paul was standing right outside, his hand raised as if he was about to press the bell.

'Juno!' He laughed. 'Sorry, I didn't mean to scare you!'

We both laughed then, and after a moment's hesitation, we hugged each other. Although we'd spoken on the phone, we hadn't seen each other since before Nick's murder, hadn't touched. He knew all about my inheritance of course, after one long, long phone call. 'I was driving by and I saw your van parked across the road. I noticed the light was on in the shop, so I thought I'd stop and say hello.'

'I'm glad you did. It's good to see you. Are you here for long?'

'Just for a few days, whilst I'm sorting things out. I'll be up and down quite a bit from now on.'

'How's your family?' I asked.

'Great. They're all great.'

'Good.' He looked great himself.

There was a slight pause while we both stood smiling and shuffling our feet.

'How's it going in there?' Paul nodded in the direction of the shop.

I sighed. 'To be honest, I don't know what I'm going to do with it all.'

'Can I help?'

'That's kind of you, but I'm sure you've got enough to do.'

'I can find time to give you a hand.'

'Look, Paul . . . I've got to go now,' I said, checking my watch. 'I've got a client in a little while.'

'Still working, then?'

I made a face. 'I can't afford to stop.'

'What about this evening?' he suggested. 'We can grab a pint and a bite to eat and you can tell me all about it.'

'That would be wonderful.'

We agreed to meet at seven.

After an hour in Paul's company I began to feel whole lot better. I filled him in on the details he didn't already know – mostly my adventures with Richard and Helena and all the tussles over the will.

'But they didn't contest it?'

'Not in court, no,' I admitted, 'but Helena and her husband put up obstacles every step of the way – delayed things, refused to answer emails – all very petty, really. In the end the solicitors had to get heavy.' I sighed. 'I wish Nick hadn't done it, named me in his will.'

'Well, I don't blame him. His kids never gave him the time of day, and he'd grown fond of you. He certainly wouldn't have wanted you to agonise over it.'

'I suppose not,' I admitted reluctantly.

'What are you going to do?'

I shook my head. 'I don't know if I can bear to live there . . .'

'Creepy?' he asked.

'No, not that so much,' I told him, 'just sad. There are all his things . . . I'll have to get rid of them. And there's a lot of stock in the shop that I haven't got a clue what to do with . . .'

'Don't look so worried.' He put an arm around my shoulders, giving me a friendly hug. 'It'll all work out.'

'I suppose. But at the moment, I find it unnerving, just going in there.'

'Well, that's understandable, especially with all Nick's things still there.'

'His children didn't take any of it. There are his clothes . . .'

'You need to clear the place out, make a fresh start. Look, I'm busy tomorrow morning, but I could be free in the afternoon. Why don't I help you? We'll go in and clear all his clothes. That'll be a start.' He picked up his beer glass and clinked it against mine. 'You never know, we might find these rings.'

'I wish we could,' I told him devoutly. 'At least then I could prove I hadn't taken the bloody things.'

He frowned thoughtfully into his pint, his dark brows drawing together in a manner I was trying hard not to find adorable. 'You don't think that Helena or her husband might have hired someone to look for these rings before? That maybe that's why Nick was murdered?'

'The thought has crossed my mind,' I admitted, 'but it doesn't make sense, does it? I mean, if Nick had them all this time, or Helena thought he had, then why would she suddenly make a move to grab them? She'd already been waiting for years. As far as she knew, she was going to inherit everything when Nick died anyway, why not just wait a little longer?'

Paul nodded reluctantly. 'And there's been no sign of our Russian friends, I take it?'

'No,' I told him gloomily. 'Sometimes I think that we'll never find out what happened.' Suddenly I found I had to dash tears away. 'What was the old fool up to?' I asked angrily, groping in my pocket for a tissue. 'What did he do to get himself killed?'

Paul presented me with a handkerchief. 'I don't suppose we'll ever know that either.'

CHAPTER THIRTY

Next morning, after I had walked the Tribe and called in on Maisie, I went to Nick's place and began a systematic search. I was looking for the rings and anything that might throw light on Nick's murder. I started in the bedroom where I stripped the bed and turned the mattress, inspecting it for holes, tears, or any places where stuffing might have been removed to create a hiding place. Then I took out every sock, shirt and item of underwear from the chest of drawers, shook it out, folded it and replaced it. A small round tin, stuffed between layers of clothes, rattled in a promising manner, but only contained collar studs. I searched the pockets of all the coats and suits hanging in the wardrobe, probed the linings, felt down the length of all his ties and shook out every one of his shoes. I found nothing.

The cabinet in the bathroom revealed nothing but a shaving brush, soap and denture fixative. I'd probably been watching too many movies, but I decided to take the lid off the cistern. It seemed to be a common hiding place for drugs, guns, and other potentially lethal things wrapped in plastic. The lid weighed a ton. It took me a minute or two of grunting, trying to heave the wretched thing aside enough for me to look underneath, and then the only object confronting me was the ballcock.

Disgusted, I turned to the airing cupboard, removing every sheet, blanket, towel and pillowcase before shaking it and refolding it, as I had with the clothes.

I was about to begin in the living room when the sickly rattle of the doorbell announced Paul's arrival. I gave a silent cheer. I felt as if I'd been alone there for hours. It was a relief to see another human being.

Together we got a lot done. We bagged up Nick's clothes, curtains and bedding, loaded them into Paul's van and drove them to Ashburton's only charity shop. Paul tore up the carpet in the living room, and, along with the mattress, took it to his field to burn. I scrubbed the floorboards until my knuckles were raw and felt a lot better.

Finally, we went down into the shop. After a struggle we managed to get the door of the shop open, and with the jangling of a little iron bell, let in fresh air for the first time in years.

'There you are, open for business!' Paul declared.

'Well hardly.' I looked around me at the shrouded furniture, the still unfinished walls. I had a long way to go before I reached that point.

And progress was about to slow down again. Paul was returning to Nottingham next day. He'd shut up his unit in the bazaar and put his plot of land up for sale. He'd be back in a few weeks, he promised, to sort out his workshop. He would give me another hand then, if I still needed it.

He gave me a little present before he left, wrapped in tissue paper. 'Saw this in a market in Nottingham,' he told me, 'and I thought of you.'

Inside the tissue paper I found a gleaming silver hatpin ending in a carved knob of black stone. 'Whitby jet,' he informed me.

I thanked him with a hug, reminding myself I must try and find a netsuke for his collection some time. I was relieved he was going away, to be honest. It was altogether too comfortable having him around. No point in getting cosy. He wasn't mine to keep.

I went back to the shop later and let myself in. It still felt very strange to me, letting myself in with my own keys. I wondered if I'd ever be able to climb those stairs without thinking of Nick, of the morning I had found him dead.

Walking across the bare boards of the living room, my footsteps sounded like thunder. When Paul and I had removed the carpet we had pushed all the furniture up to one end of the living room. It was still there, the dining chairs stacked on the table. I squeezed my way around them to the bureau, opened it and collected every scrap of paper from the pigeonholes and drawers, put them in a cardboard box I'd brought for the purpose and brought it home.

I spent the evening going through it, my feet up on the coffee table, Bill sleeping on my lap. Most of it was correspondence, and most of that told the story of a long and increasingly acrimonious dispute between Nick and the Inland Revenue. He had settled before they took him to court, but only just. I kept the document showing his proof of payment and threw the rest in the bin. It was junk. I doubt if the taxman had murdered Nick, however much he might have felt like it.

CHAPTER THIRTY-ONE

The phone rang as I was getting breakfast.

'Good news, Miss Browne.' It was the inspector's voice. 'We think we've found one of your Russians.'

I put down the bowl of breakfast cereal I'd been about to tuck into. 'Where?'

'In London. His name is Ilya Pietrov, Ukrainian by birth and known to the EU police, but judging from your description of him, I think you probably know him as Igor. Unfortunately, he's dead. I'll be sending an officer down to you with a photograph to see if you can identify him. I'm afraid it's not pretty to look at.'

'What happened?' I asked. Bill came to sit on my lap as if he wanted to know too.

'He was picked up on CCTV, a few days ago, getting out

of a taxi opposite St Thomas Hospital. As he was crossing the road towards Accident and Emergency, he was mown down by a hit-and-run driver in a dark-coloured BMW, which was later found abandoned.'

'Was he killed outright?' I asked.

'More or less. But he wasn't well to begin with. He was suffering from sepsis, probably a result of dog bites for which he had never received proper medical attention. Anyway, the good news is, forensics have matched his prints to some found in the house of Mr Albert Evans, definitely placing him at the scene on the day of the murder.'

'But nothing that links him to Nick?' I asked.

'Not so far. I'm sorry.'

I thanked the inspector for telling me, promised to look at the photograph, and put the phone down. I dialled Paul's number straight away, to tell him the news, but there was no reply from his mobile, so I left a message. I was reluctant to try his landline in case Carrie picked up the phone. I didn't want to make any more waves in that department.

Later that morning I went round to Ricky and Morris. I'd agreed to help with an urgent order for costumes for *Twelfth Night*, but was delayed by the arrival of two female police officers – the same two who'd interviewed me about Verbena's jewellery – with the photograph.

'And was it him?' Ricky's voice floated from behind a clothes rail jammed tight with costumes, his precise whereabouts undetectable save for the occasional rustle as he searched for the one he wanted. 'Was it Igor?'

'It certainly was. It was a head and shoulders shot taken in the mortuary. He looked horrible. Mind you,' I conceded, brushing at the velvet collar of a cloak with a stiff brush, trying to remove traces of old stage make-up, 'he didn't look too pretty when he was alive.'

'He must have been suffering.' Morris spoke with a pin pressed between his lips as he worked on a repair. 'I mean,' he added, removing the pin, 'to have reached a point where he was prepared to risk getting caught in order to seek medical treatment.'

'A risk Vlad wasn't prepared to let him take,' I added. 'He killed him to shut him up.'

Morris tutted, over the tear in the costumes rather than Igor's demise. 'At least now the police know who murdered Bert Evans.'

'Apparently,' I went on, 'the police pathologist thinks that microbes in the water in the fish pool may have been the real cause of Igor's sepsis.'

Ricky's head appeared, parting the costumes on the rail. 'What comes around, goes around,' he grinned.

'Don't be callous,' Morris protested mildly.

'Oh, *Maurice*, try not to be such an old woman! He got what he deserved.'

He turned to look at me. 'And you can stop having nightmares about him.'

I smiled but didn't say anything. I wish I could have felt reassured but somehow the thought that Vlad was on his own, operating out there somewhere as a lone wolf, was scarier than the thought of him and Igor together.

* * *

There's a sign on the door of the Ashburton Art and Antiques Bazaar, which clearly states that dogs are welcome in the cafe. I suppose taking the entire Tribe in all at once is stretching a point, but they were very well behaved. EB, the miniature Schnauzer, sat upright on my lap, being a very good boy. Schnitzel disappeared under the cafe table, nosing for scraps, Sally, the elderly Labrador, flopped down on the floor, glad of a rest after our walk, and Nookie and Boog sat quietly by my chair, Boog leaning the warm weight of her body against my thigh.

Across the table sat Sophie Child, staring at EB. 'I don't do that kind of thing,' she told me, pulling a face. 'Pet portraits,' she added disdainfully, 'not my thing at all.' She pointed at the easel on her unit, a delicate watercolour in progress. 'That's my sort of thing.'

I had to admit that her sort of thing was exquisite: a painting of a rusty garden gate, its slim iron rails entwined by bindweed, the stone pillar to which it was attached encrusted with lichen and half smothered by ivy. Dead leaves had swept in under the gate and scattered across the broken paving of a pathway, leading through an overgrown garden, an ocean of weeds and wildflowers, an abandoned cottage just visible in the distance.

'I don't do pet portraits,' she repeated, batting her long lashes and sliding her glasses back up her titchy nose.

'But EB's mum would like his portrait painted and so I thought of you.' This wasn't quite true. EB's mum had decided to take him to a professional photographer; it had taken some persuasion on my part to convince her that a painting would be better.

'Lots of other artists do pet portraits,' Sophie told me, shrugging her thin shoulders. 'Why don't you ask one of them?'

'Yes, lots of other artists paint pets,' I agreed, annoyed that my efforts on her behalf were being met with such ingratitude, 'and because they do, they can afford to buy food and pay rent.' I nodded in the direction of the painting on her easel.

'When was the last time you sold something like that?'

Sophie didn't answer. 'Why's he called Ebee?' she asked.

'EB,' I corrected. 'It's short for his name.'

'Which is what?'

'It's a secret. You have to guess.' I have strict instructions from EB's mum to play this game whenever anyone asks.

EB, sensing he was the subject of our conversation, sat up very straight, his fluffy forelegs thrust out in front of him, his bushy eyebrows twitching anxiously.

'Edward Bear?' Sophie suggested vaguely.

'Wrong. Look, he's gorgeous, how can you *not* want to paint him?'

'Edward Bone?'

'It isn't Edward anything. Stop changing the subject.'

'What's this one called?' she asked, pointing.

Champion Boxer, Bollywood Boogaloo Boogie Nights of Bognor – known to all who love her as Boog – was excited at being pointed at, as this usually meant she was about to receive a rosette. She snuffled, and licked herself on the nose.

'She's sweet!' Sophie exclaimed, clicking her fingers. Boog bounded to her feet. With no tail to wag, her whole rear end went into a ridiculous calypso of welcome. Nookie, who up until this point had been sitting aloof, staring into the distance as if gazing at snowy arctic wastes, also stood. Leads began to tangle, and the cafe table, to whose leg most of them were hitched, was dragged two feet across the floor before I got control of it. I could see the cafe owner looking at me askance. It was time for the Tribe and me to depart.

'Look Sophie, if you make a good job of EB then other dog owners will want their portraits painted too. Boog's a champion. Her mum is a breeder, she knows loads of others and they're all besotted with their animals. You can't afford to turn it down.'

'Well, I suppose . . .' Sophie began reluctantly. I thrust a piece of paper at her, with EB's phone number written on it. 'At least give it some thought.'

'I will,' she promised, as if she were doing me a favour. 'Oh . . . and . . . thanks,' she ended weakly.

By then I'd gathered up the various leads and my escalating temper and was hauling my charges off in the direction of the door.

I left the bazaar and turned down Sun Street, ready to take the various members of the Tribe to their respective homes. As I walked them along, trying to keep them up together, the long, low shape of Verbena Clarke's Porsche swept by me. I watched it drive to the end of the street and turn left. The last time I had seen her was in the alley that linked Sun Street with Shadow Lane. Understanding hit me like a brick. What an idiot I was, not to have realised at the time. Verbena hadn't simply been trying to avoid me. She didn't want anyone who knew her to see her in that alley, because she'd been coming from Nick's.

CHAPTER THIRTY-TWO

I parked my van in Verbena's courtyard, right next to her Porsche. The Range Rover was parked there too, which meant she was certainly at home. The kitchen door was locked; perhaps, post-robbery, she had become more security conscious.

I crossed the courtyard to her studio.

She was sitting at a drawing board, pencil in hand, surrounded by drawings and swatches of furnishing fabrics. 'Shades of grey, eh?' I asked, surveying the swatches as she looked up, startled. 'That's a bit last year, isn't it?'

'What do you want?' she demanded, suddenly pale.

'You and I need to talk,' I set my bum down on a swivelling stool on the other side of her desk and perched there, arms folded.

'We have nothing to talk about.'

'Yes we do,' I said, swivelling slightly. 'You accused me of theft.'

She blushed to the roots of her hair. 'I never accused you!'

'You sent the police round to me.'

'I didn't send them.' Her schoolgirl voice was petulant. 'I simply said you were the last person to go up into the bedroom. It was obvious that they should want to interview you.'

'But they told me you weren't certain when the theft had taken place. So you can't be sure I was the last person, can you?'

She closed her eyes, holding up the palm of her hand as if mentally pushing me away. 'Look, I never accused you. Now, please leave!'

'Then why did you sack me?'

She didn't answer. She began doodling on the paper in front of her, her eyes downcast, her black mascara lashes spidery against her cheeks. For a moment I watched her pencil making circles.

'I had been working for you for two years,' I reminded her. 'I think I have a right to know.'

The pressure on the pencil increased, the circles growing blacker. I waited. Suddenly the point broke, Verbena gave a furious sigh and threw the pencil across the room. 'God, this is so humiliating!' She put her head in her hands, slender fingers lacing through her blonde curls.

'Just tell me, Verbena!'

'It's none of your business,' she cried fiercely, glaring up at me.

'Certainly it is. In case you've forgotten, Nick was murdered. I found his body. And if I ring the police now, and tell them that I've remembered seeing you coming out of his place shortly before the murder, they are going to wonder why, after the appeals they put out in the media for anyone who knew him to come forward, you kept silent.'

It had only been a hunch really, that Verbena had been to visit Nick, that she wasn't using the alley as a shortcut, like everyone else. But the look of horror frozen on her face as she slowly gazed at me confirmed that I was right.

'Oh, God!' she moaned.

'Just tell me, Verbena,' I repeated, this time more gently. When she didn't speak, I prompted her. 'Was it something to do with the earrings?'

Her blue eyes filled with tears. 'They were never stolen,' she admitted in a tiny voice. 'I thought they were, I really did! And the cash was taken. I put in a claim on the insurance but the company wouldn't pay out because there'd been no break-in. I'd left the door unlocked so they said it was down to my own negligence.' She shrugged. 'Well, they were right about that, I suppose, but they made me feel as if I'd made the whole thing up just to claim the insurance money.'

'Were the earrings very valuable, then?'

'Neil had them made especially for me. They were insured for fifteen grand.'

She hesitated. 'And then, a few days later, more cash went missing. And this time I knew no one had been in the house, except' – she stared fixedly down at her hands, her slender fingers knotted together – 'except the girls.'

'Your daughters?'

She nodded, her head hung low. 'Then the earrings mysteriously reappeared in the dish they had been taken from. Amelia tried to claim that she'd only borrowed them to wear to a party, that she'd even asked my permission. But I knew she'd taken them, and then got scared when I called in the police and the insurers.'

'And the money?' I asked.

'Oh, that was just spite.' She gnawed at her lower lip. 'Apparently, their father encourages the girls to steal from me. He tells them the money is really his and they're doing him a favour.' She returned her gaze to my face. 'Now you're wondering why I sacked you.'

I waited.

'God, Juno, it was all so embarrassing!' she burst out. 'I couldn't bear the thought of having to admit to you what had really happened.'

'But you didn't have to,' I protested. 'I'd have accepted that you'd found your earrings, that they weren't stolen after all. Anyone can make a mistake.'

She eyed me dubiously. 'What about the money?'

'Well, it wouldn't surprise me if you did get cash stolen,' I told her frankly. 'You will leave your wallet lying around . . .' I shook my head. 'I just find it incredible that you'd rather sack me than tell me the truth.' Actually, I did understand. The fear of humiliation, the avoidance of embarrassment, is a far stronger force than most of us are prepared to admit.

Verbena's eyes swam with tears again. She heaved a truly tragic sigh. 'I felt so ashamed, about the girls . . .'

I'd been trying hard not to feel sorry for her, but now I did. She wiped her eyes with a tissue, making black smudges beneath her lower lashes. 'I don't care about the bloody earrings . . . or the money. It's the fact that they were prepared to steal from me to please their father . . . The truth is, not even my own children like me . . .' She blew her nose and subsided into sniffling sobs.

'I'm sure that's not true,' I told her gently. It was a lie. I'd never met her daughters and I wasn't sure at all. They were always at school when I came to clean. I only knew the kind of mess they left lying around. But it must be a horrible thing not to be able to trust your own kids.

'I didn't want to wear the earrings again,' she sniffed. 'I couldn't bear the sight of them. I wanted to sell them, but I didn't want anyone to know. I was frightened Neil might find out.' She gave a bitter little laugh. 'They'd been made for a famous rock star to give to his dolly chick. Their provenance was more interesting than the earrings themselves. I knew if I put them on the open market they'd arouse a lot of interest, that he'd find out . . .'

'But I don't understand. Why did it matter if he found out you were selling them? You're divorced, the earrings were yours.'

'Well, that's just it . . .' she said awkwardly. 'The divorce was so bloody . . . In the turmoil, somehow . . . when everything was being declared for the settlement – and I mean, everything – they got missed out. I realised Neil had forgotten them.' She gave a nervous giggle like a schoolgirl caught cheating in an exam. 'He'd bought me so much jewellery over the years. He liked to make extravagant gestures, especially public ones . . .'

'So he forgot about these earrings and you didn't want to remind him.'

'Exactly. I needed someone to sell them for me, someone who'd be discreet . . .'

'So you went to Nick?' I finished for her.

She nodded. 'I knew what he was like, that I wouldn't get the price from him that I'd get from a jeweller. He sold them privately. I got less than half their value but I didn't care.' She hunched a shoulder. 'At least I was rid of the things.'

'Did you kill him?'

She gazed at me, blue eyes wide with shock. 'Of course not! Why would I?'

'So why didn't you tell the police that you'd been in contact with him?' I asked. 'You weren't doing anything illegal, if the earrings were yours to sell.'

She hesitated, her hands fidgeting with a tissue. 'I didn't want the police to take my fingerprints . . .'

'Well, what if they did? They can only match up prints they already have on file . . .'

I stopped. Verbena's whole body was rigid, her mouth set in a line.

'It was when I was very young,' she muttered. 'I was at a club in London. The police raided it for drugs. They arrested everyone. We all had our fingerprints taken. I got off with a fine.'

'So you didn't want the police to know that you were a teenage drugs fiend?' I mocked her gently.

'I didn't want the girls to find out!' she cried, suddenly passionate. 'You don't know what they're like. They'd be vile if . . . And I didn't want the whole of bloody Ashburton to know,' she added defiantly. 'Things get around.'

I wasn't sure she'd told me the truth, or at least, that she'd told me all of it. Supposing the little earring deal had gone wrong, supposing she and Nick had quarrelled?

'You don't happen to know who bought the earrings,' I asked her, 'who Nick sold them to?'

She gave an impatient shrug of her shoulders. 'I kept out of it. I think it was somebody foreign.'

'I see. Thank you.'

She began chewing her lip anxiously. 'Are you going to tell the police that I visited Nick?'

'Not if you promise me that you will.'

She hesitated and then nodded reluctantly.

As I drove back down the hill, I wondered whether, armed with that heavy candlestick, she could have delivered the crushing blow that had killed Nick. She was only a slender creature. But fuelled with rage, determined to protect her reputation at all costs, I wasn't convinced that she couldn't.

CHAPTER THIRTY-THREE

Whatever my thoughts about Verbena Clarke, I had promised myself that the following day I was going to put in some much needed work on the shop. Ricky and Morris had come in to lend a hand with the decorating, but frankly they were more of a hindrance than a help. Morris was meticulous but deadly slow and Ricky's work was so cavalier and slapdash that the only task he could be trusted with was rubbing down the woodwork. And they kept arguing with me about colour. I'd painted the walls a soft white to make the shop look lighter. Morris suggested that it needed a little more warmth and Ricky said it looked like a bleeding hospital mortuary and why didn't I slap some colour on the walls? Still, having them around was more fun than working on my own.

In the absence of Paul, I'd asked Adam to come in to help me shift the heavy bookcases back against the walls, and I'd cleaned the inside of the windows, removed all the dust and dead flies from the windowsills, taken down the wire mesh grilling and washed the exterior paintwork. The outside really needed a new paint job and a freshly painted sign over the door, but I didn't have the cash to pay for a professional signwriter. It was going to have to wait.

Meantime, I'd come in to paint the ceiling. There was a recurring stain right in the middle, a rusty brown cloud, and no matter how many times I dabbed at it with a roller, it kept on bleeding through.

As soon as I'd prised the lid off the paint tin with a screwdriver, I realised I wasn't going to get another coat out of it. Reluctantly, I stripped off the paint-freckled overalls I'd just put on, grabbed my bag and headed for Church's, hoping they hadn't just run out of the last tin of brilliant white. Church's Ironmonger's is set in a medieval building that used to be the Mermaid Inn. It's a low-ceilinged, mind-your-head, sort of place. But when I got there the door was closed and there was a sign that said BACK IN TEN MINUTES.

I cursed mightily, but if I wanted my paint I had no option but to wait outside on the pavement and try and find something interesting about a display of garden rakes, yard brooms and galvanised buckets. Ten minutes was more like twenty, but an old fella turned up, who'd only come out for a couple of screws, so at least I had someone to grumble and moan with until the custodian of the hardware returned, flushed and apologetic, and let us in. Sorry, she said, she'd had to go to the bank. I understood. The high street banks have deserted Ashburton, leaving the town with a solitary cash machine outside the post office; two of them still visit the town once a week in big mobile vans, but they don't stay long. It's not what I'd call a service. Anyway, the old fella got in ahead of me and I had to wait whilst she tried to sort out his obscure screw requirements, which took ages, before I could buy my paint.

By the time I got back to the shop I'd been gone nearly an hour. I climbed back into my painting togs, ready to start work. But it seemed that the last time I had used them I hadn't cleaned the brushes as thoroughly as I might and the bristles had dried stiff. It was clear that no amount of bending them back and forth was going to unglue them. They needed a good soak in white spirit and there was only a dribble left in the bottle. For a moment I resigned myself to another trip to the hardware shop. But I was willing to bet Nick had a bottle, amongst all that paraphernalia in the cupboard under his sink, so I trotted up the stairs.

I went into the kitchen and froze. Someone had been here, I could tell at once. I'd been up there on my last visit to fill the kettle and I knew I hadn't left the doors of the under-sink cupboard open, the contents emptied out on to the floor. I stared around me. A kitchen drawer was open. I hadn't left it like that either.

The floorboard creaked a moment too late. An arm came round my neck from behind, a smelly rag squashed over my nose and mouth. It was too late to scream. I struggled, fought to pull the arm away, scrabbled to tear off the acrid-smelling cloth. Strange smell. Not perfume this time; not Nightshade. Not a woman's smell. A smell that reminded me of hospitals.

The world began to spin. I struggled, both hands tugging uselessly at the arm that held me, a man's arm, so strong. My hands felt heavy, fell away. The fight within me dissolved. And as the world began to darken, I remember thinking that this couldn't possibly be happening to me. Not really.

CHAPTER THIRTY-FOUR

Inspector Ford was in no mood to be fobbed off, and anyway I was too scared for fobbing. He was polite, sympathetic even, but across Nick's kitchen table the penetrating stare was boring into me.

'Do you have any idea who attacked you, Miss Browne?'

'No, I don't,' I responded, more or less truthfully. I didn't know who it was. I knew who it wasn't. It wasn't Vlad because Vlad would have killed me. The only other possible suspect was Richard searching for the rings, and I didn't believe he'd be barmy enough to try that again. But I thought I'd better mention him, and Tamara. I threw in Verbena Clarke for good measure.

'You should have told me about Mr and Mrs Nickolai and these rings at the time,' he admonished me sternly.

Next to him Detective Constable DeVille tried to look equally severe but could hardly keep the smirk off her nasty little mouth.

'So, just to be clear,' he went on, 'you are now telling me that it was Mr and Mrs Nickolai who broke into your flat and coshed you with a torch?'

'Well, it was only Tamara – Mrs Nickolai, but I think it was Richard's idea.'

He sighed heavily. 'And you didn't see fit to inform us?'

'I didn't want to press charges,' I admitted unhappily.

'Breaking and entering and assault are serious offences,' Constable DeVille informed me smugly, 'it wasn't up to you.'

'It certainly wasn't Tamara who attacked me this morning,' I added.

'Possibly not, but if the recovery of those rings is so important,' the inspector went on, 'then the Nickolais may have employed the services of someone less queasy about using violence. In any event, Mr Nickolai has lied to the police – he said he hadn't seen his father in years.'

'You don't think Richard murdered his father, do you?'

'He has an alibi for the time of the murder, which puts him in the clear. So does Mrs Burgoyne. But if either of them is responsible for this latest piece of mischief they are going to find themselves in serious trouble.' He stopped and for a moment a faint suggestion of a smile crossed his lips. 'Incidentally, they do have their own theory about who murdered their father.'

'They do?'

'You.' It was Constable DeVille who spoke, only one word but she managed to fit an arpeggio of malice into it.

I flopped back in my chair. 'You're joking?'

'His altering the will in your favour would naturally make you a suspect, Miss Browne,' the inspector said lightly, 'in their eyes.'

'Actually, there are a few people in Ashburton who think . . .' Ricky's voice trailed off as the inspector turned his gaze upon him.

It was Morris and Ricky who'd found me. They'd called in at the shop to see how I was getting on, discovered me collapsed in a groggy heap on the kitchen floor and phoned for police and ambulance. We'd already been through the whole farrago of flashing blue lights and screaming sirens before the inspector had arrived.

'Are you telling me,' I asked Ricky, aghast, 'that everyone in Ashburton thinks I murdered Nick?'

'Well, not everyone,' he replied, looking uncomfortable.

'Not anyone who knows you, obviously,' Morris assured me, blushing slightly.

I glared at the pair of them. I could just imagine the gossip they'd been indulging in. 'Fantastic,' I muttered.

The inspector cleared his throat, returning us to the matter in hand. 'We shall also be interviewing Mrs Verbena Clarke.'

I folded my arms and grunted. I bet her tongue had been wagging too. So, she hadn't come forward voluntarily? That wasn't going to look good, I thought with satisfaction.

Inspector Ford took his stare off me and gazed at the horrid rag that had been squashed over my face, now screwed up on Nick's kitchen table. It was one of his old polishing rags.

'We'll get this analysed, but it's undoubtedly ether.' He slipped it into a plastic bag and handed it to DeVille. 'That would have rendered you unconscious very quickly.'

'There's a bottle on the table in the living room,' I told him. 'Nick used it as a solvent.'

The inspector shook his head in despair. 'It's a highly volatile and flammable substance. It shouldn't be stored in the home, and certainly not with other cleaning and chemical substances. You should get any bottles like that properly disposed of, Miss Browne.'

'But where's the bottle now, Inspector?' Morris piped up.

'It seems that whoever attacked Miss Browne took it with him, probably because his fingerprints were on it,' the inspector answered. 'However, his methods do reveal certain things about him.'

'Like what?' Ricky asked.

The inspector hesitated. I'd asked, when he'd arrived, if Ricky and Morris could stay, but it was clear that whilst he tolerated their presence, he would have preferred not to have them in the room. 'If he was the sort of thug who'd wanted to do you serious harm, he could have done so. But his use of ether indicates his objective was escape.'

'Which seems to bring us back to Richard,' I said gloomily.

'Or an opportunist thief,' the inspector said. A smile glimmered briefly. 'That is the most likely culprit, you know – a passing opportunist.'

'But there's nothing in here to steal,' Ricky objected, 'except a lot of crappy second-hand furniture.'

'Thieves will steal anything, anything they can sell, especially if they're desperate for drugs money,' he answered.

'And even Ashburton is not immune from these problems.'

'Do we know how he got in?' Morris asked.

'There's no sign of forced entry, so presumably he just walked in, as you did yourselves.' The inspector looked at me more kindly. 'You really must remember to lock your shop door when you leave it, Miss Browne.'

'I thought I had,' I responded miserably, 'but I was so pissed off about the paint.'

'Most likely, someone saw you go out and decided to snoop around. He found himself trapped upstairs when you returned and took desperate action. If he was in the living room, then the cloth and the ether were conveniently to hand.'

'So you don't believe that this is anything to do with Nick's murder?' Ricky demanded.

'If Miss Browne had been a target in any way, then I fear she would not have escaped so lightly.' He smiled at me again. 'I'm sorry. I know this has been a horrible experience for you, but unfortunate coincidences do happen. However, if anything else should occur, Miss Browne, you won't be tempted to keep it to yourself, will you?'

'Cross my heart, Inspector,' I promised devoutly. 'You'll be the first to know.'

As soon as the inspector and Cruella DeVille had gone, we put on the kettle for a cup of tea. Morris suggested going to a cafe but Ricky wanted to stay where we were so he could smoke a fag.

'Just be careful where you light up,' Morris advised him, looking around.

'Watch out for hazardous chemicals.'

Ricky ignored him and flicked his lighter. 'We were going to drop in for a cuppa anyway, weren't we Morris,' he said, drawing deeply, 'before we found her ladyship here laid out in a swoon.'

It seems they'd brought fresh milk with them, because they didn't think I'd have any, and three new mugs, because they didn't fancy using Old Nick's. I was prepared to swallow my indignation because they'd also brought three Danish pastries. Their shopping had been dropped and forgotten when they'd found me on the floor, but turned out to be only slightly squashed.

'But first things first,' I said, as I busied myself with the kettle, 'tell me who you've been talking to. Who have you been discussing me with who thinks I murdered Nick?'

But this time they already had their minds on something else.

'He's nice, isn't he, your inspector?' Ricky opened the window so he could blow his smoke outside.

'I think he likes you,' Morris smiled coyly.

'He's not *my* inspector!' I said firmly. I knew immediately where this was leading.

Morris wagged a finger. 'I reckon he's got a soft spot for you.'

'Pity he's wearing a wedding ring,' Ricky sniffed and flicked ash over the windowsill.

'Oh, eff off,' I advised them affably. I wasn't going to let them wind me up.

'That's why she don't like you,' Ricky went on, 'that dark-haired one. Cruella! She's got a thing about her boss.'

'Has she?' I was astonished. For one thing, the inspector was probably old enough to be her father.

'Haven't you noticed the way she looks at him?'

'Well, no,' I admitted. I hadn't noticed how she looked at the inspector. I'd only noticed how she looked at me – with varying degrees of smug malevolence. I must pay more attention if there was ever a next time.

'Pretty girl,' Morris ventured, putting a paper bag on the table and carefully tearing it open to reveal the three Danish.

'Pity about the mouth.' Ricky took a deep drag and then squashed his cigarette out in the sink.

'It is, isn't it?' I agreed spitefully, sitting at the table.

'Well, not everyone can have a bleeding great gobhole like yours, Juno,' he told me pleasantly. 'Now, choose your weapon – lemon curd, apricot or custard?'

CHAPTER THIRTY-FIVE

Next morning, I took the Tribe across the fields and sat on a stile while they raced around joyfully, tails wagging, ears flapping in the wind. It had rained in the night, and the grass glistened, the ferns in the hedgerows dripped, the wooden stile on which I sat was damp. I didn't care. I'd been awake most of the night, trying to decide what to do. The day before, after we'd devoured the Danish pastries, Ricky and Morris had stopped talking nonsense and spent a long time trying to persuade me to the sell the shop. I would be getting rid of a big problem and liberating myself from poverty at the same time.

I had to agree it was the sensible option. But I wanted to try to make a go of it, for Nick's sake as much as my own. Although, how I was going to run it and keep my existing business going, I didn't know. I wasn't prepared to abandon Maisie and my other clients, and couldn't afford to anyway, until the shop started bringing in some money – if it ever did. And nagging at me all the time was the thought that somewhere in that place was the clue to Nick's murder and if I sold the place that clue would be lost for ever. Sally the Labrador flopped down at my feet, panting. She looked up at me from wise brown eyes and I asked her what she thought, but whatever it was she was keeping to herself.

Despite a promise to Ricky and Morris to let them know when I was next going to the shop so they could keep me company, I slipped in at the end of my day's work, just for an hour. The ceiling was not going to paint itself and I needed some quiet time when I could concentrate. I didn't get it. I hadn't even levered the lid off the paint before a light tap on the shop door made me squawk like a startled chicken.

The figure grinning through the glass at me was Paul.

'C'mon, open up! It's starting to rain out here.'

'I didn't know you were back,' I cried, letting him in. 'What a nice surprise!'

I let myself be kissed on the cheek.

'How are you?' he asked cheerfully. 'I hear you had a bit of bother yesterday.'

'You could call it that. God, news travels fast in this place! Mind you, I suppose the ambulance and police car parked outside were a dead giveaway.'

'The girls in the bazaar were buzzing with it all. But you weren't hurt?' he asked, more seriously.

'Only my pride.'

He looked about him at the newly painted shelves, the sparkling white walls. 'You're making progress.'

I gazed up at the splodged ceiling. 'Not enough.'

'Leave it! I've come to take you away from all this. The choice of pub is yours.'

My resolve to get the ceiling painted held sway for an entire moment. Ten minutes later we were cosily ensconced in a hostelry that is a bit spit-and-sawdust but has the advantage of a roaring fire, spring temperatures not being quite what they could be. It also sold real ale, which was another advantage, according to Paul. I stuck to cider, refusing his tempting offer of a pint of Badger's Bum.

'So, when did you get down here?' I asked.

'Last night, I just missed the excitement. Tell me all.'

I did. When I finished, Paul was looking askance at me, his hands linked behind his head, his brows drawn together in a frown. 'You haven't been doing any more sleuthing, have you?'

'No, I swear to God!' I assured him, holding up both hands. 'Well, if you don't count my going to see Verbena.'

'You haven't irritated any dangerous thugs lately?'

'Not knowingly.'

He took a pull of his pint thoughtfully and licked a smear of foam from his top lip. 'Well, I'm sure your police inspector is right. It was probably an opportunist thief yesterday, just snooping around. You were lucky you didn't come off worse, though.'

I nodded gloomily.

'As a matter of fact,' he added, 'someone has been

snooping around my place while I've been away, they tried to break in to the caravan.'

'Really?'

'The lock on the door has been tampered with. They must have been pretty stupid. It would have been much easier to break a window and get in that way. It was probably kids, messing about in the field.'

'Was anything stolen?'

'They didn't manage to get in. Anyway, there's sod all in there to steal.'

'There's your netsuke collection,' I reminded him.

For a moment he stared blankly as if he didn't know what I was talking about.

'Oh that!' He dismissed it airily. 'I took that away with me the last time I came.' He gave a grim smile. 'I suppose I'm lucky they didn't torch the place.'

'Did you report it to the police?'

He shrugged. 'Not much point. But I do need to improve my security arrangements. The workshop is vulnerable with me being away most of the time. That's one of the reasons I'm down here, to take my tools back with me. I don't want them getting nicked.'

'So, you've had no luck with selling the place?'

'Not so far. I'll bully the agents while I'm here. But,' he added, triumphantly drumming his fingers on the tabletop, 'I think I've got a buyer for the stripping tank – my mate with the architectural salvage business. He says if I'm not around to strip his doors, he might as well do it himself. But he's got some work he wants me to do first, that's the other reason I've come down here.

When I've done that, I can finally drain the tank.'

'And how are things in Nottingham?' I ventured. 'Henry Wain and Arnold Bishop doing well?'

'Thriving!'

'You must have discovered another pot of Darkolene.'

'No such luck! Actually,' he said, giving a shy grin, 'I've started selling paintings under my own name.'

'Good for you.' I picked up his empty glass. 'That deserves another pint.'

'No, no! My round.' He took it from me as he stood up and jerked his head at the chalkboard menu on the pub wall. 'I'll even stand you to supper. I've got to deliver a very expensive repair to a lady in Truro tomorrow, so I'm feeling flush.' He raised his eyebrows at me. 'Pie and chips?'

I thought he'd never ask.

CHAPTER THIRTY-SIX

Next day being Thursday I went around to Brook Lane in the afternoon to see Maisie. I was much later than usual; I really felt I'd done enough for the day, but if I didn't sort out her recycling before the rubbish was collected the following morning, she'd put everything in the wrong boxes and the refuse collectors wouldn't take them.

A curiously unpleasant smell emanated from her kitchen. A clue came from Jacko, who was staring transfixed at a point on the kitchen counter and making yearning, whining noises deep in his throat. I lifted up a teacloth on the worktop and found a packet of pudgy sausages the colour of dead fingers.

'How long have these been here?' I called to Maisie, trying to squint at the best-before label without getting my nostrils too close.

'Oh, I've been looking for them,' she informed me cheerfully, shuffling up beside me. 'I was going to have them for me tea the other day. I got them out the fridge and then I lost 'em.'

'It's a good job you didn't find them,' I told her firmly. 'You can't have them now.'

She sniffed. 'Jacko can have them.'

'No, he can't.' Jacko with an upset stomach was an idea that didn't bear thinking about.

Maisie wandered away, no longer interested. 'Put 'em out for the birds.'

'What, vultures? No, Maisie, they're going in the bin.'

She tutted as if I was making a fuss about nothing, but didn't argue. I inspected the rest of her fridge contents, disposed of anything life-threatening, sorted her recycling into the correct receptacles and put it all outside for collection next morning.

I left the van parked outside and walked the abominable Jacko into town. He was as badly behaved as ever and it was a relief to tie him up outside the chemist's while I fetched Maisie's prescription. I left him there while I did the rest of her shopping. He was looking forlorn by the time I got back, and feeling guilty at abandoning him, I let him have some of the doggie chocs I'd just bought him in Mr Singh's. 'Just don't be sick,' I warned him.

Maisie was fast asleep in her armchair when we got back. There was no need for me to tiptoe about; I knew nothing short of an earthquake would wake her. I stowed away her shopping, checked she had no laundry imprisoned in the washing machine, made her a ham sandwich for her supper and put the plate, together with her change and her prescription, on the table by her elbow. I let myself out.

Jacko had jumped up on to the sofa and from there to his favourite spot on the windowsill where he settled down for a doze. As I turned to close the garden gate behind me, he abruptly sat up, poked his snout through the lace curtain and began growling at me, showing his teeth, the curtain draped around his head like the veil of some ghastly bride.

'What's up with you?' I mouthed at him. I crossed the lane to the van, coming around to the passenger door so that I could dump a bag of groceries I'd bought for myself on the front seat.

Late afternoon had turned to evening. The sun was already low in the sky, a glowing red ball netted in branches. Time for me to go home and get some supper.

I put my right hand in my pocket for my keys. By now, Jacko was really going for it, snarling and barking his nasty little head off.

Too late I realised he wasn't barking at me. Something clobbered me in the back, knocking the breath out of me, slamming my body hard up against the side of the van, trapping my arm against the door. An iron fist gripped my wrist and forced my free arm behind my back. I yelped, shopping falling to the ground, tins rolling in the gutter.

'Hello, girlfriend,' a voice hissed in my ear.

I could turn my head just enough to see the reflection in the wing mirror: Vlad, his body close against mine, his lips pressed to my ear.

He chuckled as Jacko's barking reached a frenzy. 'Your

little friend over there can't help you. No big black dog to save you now, eh?'

Once more it seems my van had led him straight to me. I tried to push away from him, but he gave my arm a warning twist, making me cry out. 'What do you want?'

He grabbed a handful of my hair and pulled savagely. 'I want it back. I want what is mine. They say the old man left you everything, girlfriend. You must have it.'

My voice came out in a broken whisper. 'I don't know what you're talking about.'

'Like our friend with the fish. He didn't know either.'

'Murderer!' I kicked back hard with one foot, catching him on the shin. He cursed, but didn't loosen his hold.

'I'm just a businessman,' he told me softly and laughed.

I couldn't shift my right arm, trapped against the van door but I could just wriggle my fingers. Deep in my pocket they found my keys. I let them slide into my palm and then closed my fingers in a fist.

'We go for nice ride in car,' Vlad's voice was silky with menace, 'up on moor. Maybe then you remember.' He started to pull me away. The lane was deserted except for a red car parked a few yards down. If he got me into that vehicle, I knew I was dead.

I let him drag me away from the van, pretending to resist. He still had my left arm bent behind my back, his fingers knotted in my hair. Slowly I drew my right fist from my pocket, keys projecting between my fingers in a spiky knuckleduster, then swung my arm back fast, as I pivoted on one foot, turned and hit him hard in the face. If the blow had connected squarely, he'd have lost an eye. As it was, I misjudged a little, but the keys scraped across his forehead, leaving bloody tramlines over his brow and across the bridge of his nose.

He leapt back, cursing. I hit him again and this time the keys made a soft, sickening connection. The impact shuddered through my fist sending agonising pain up my arm. Vlad screamed, staggering, reeling like a drunk, shielding his eye with his palm. I tried to unlock the van but my shaking fingers wouldn't work. I dropped the keys as he launched himself towards me. There was no time to pick them up, to get in the van, no time to do anything. All I could do was run.

Ahead of me the lane was lost in darkness, the masses of the hedgerows blocking out the evening sky. I saw the flickering swoop of a bat hunting in the dusk.

I hurtled down the track, praying that no rut or stone would trip me, send me flying. As I reached a bend, I risked a glance over my shoulder. Vlad was getting into the red car. He could catch up with me in seconds, run me down. I had to get off the lane and there was only one place I could go.

As Paul's gate came into view I swerved and more or less threw myself over it into the field. I landed hard, slipping on mud and cursing, and raced off towards the caravan. No friendly light shone out from its windows, no promise of safety. I banged on the door with clenched fists and yelled his name. No answer. He wasn't at home. Of course he wasn't, I remembered, as I stood there, heaving air into my lungs, nursing my throbbing hand: he had told me. He was in bloody Truro.

I glimpsed a flash of red through the branches of the hedge as Vlad's car passed. Then I heard tyres crunch to a gravelly halt. The car backed slowly into view and drew to a stop beyond the gate. I cursed softly.

As I heard the car door open I ducked down out of sight behind the workshop. The safety of home was only two fields away. But if I made a break for it, I'd be out in the open. Vlad would see me and I wasn't sure I could outrun him the full distance. Better to find a hiding place.

I dodged down the side of the old barn, hunting for a way in. Halfway down, almost hidden by a clump of nettles and ragwort, was a low wooden door, frail and rickety-looking with gaps between its shrunken planks and a space at the bottom where the wind whistled through. A kid might have wriggled through that gap, but not me. I tried the rusty doorknob and it rattled loosely. I shoved the door with my shoulder, once, twice, and it gave, pitching me forwards into the murky interior. Slamming it shut it behind me, I collapsed against it, relief flooding over me like cold water. My heart was thumping, trying to burst out of my chest. I took in a deep breath.

It was almost dark inside the workshop. I stood, breathing hard, waiting for my eyes to adjust to the gloom. Where was Vlad now? The big metal door in the adjacent shed rattled and I swore softly. He was closer than I thought. I felt for the lock on the little door behind me. My fingers found the cold metal of a lock-plate and the draught through the keyhole. There was no key. I slid my hand up and down the wood, my fingers searching, but there were no bolts either, no way of securing the door against outside. And soon Vlad would find it, as I had.

I grabbed the nearest chair from a stack of old furniture and rammed it under the door handle; it wouldn't hold out against an assault for long, but it might buy me a few minutes.

Crossing the workshop on tiptoe, I opened the door of the tank room. I could just make out the shape of the big caustic tank. Above it hung the grid for lowering furniture, and above that, the skylight, one window open to the sky. If I could get up on to that grid, I might be able to squirm out through the skylight and on to the roof. The lid of the tank was shut and if I stood on it, I could probably reach the grid, haul myself up.

I closed the tank-room door, lifted a chair and set it down quietly next to the tank. As I stood on it, I heard a banging against the wooden door in the workshop. Vlad was trying to get in, throwing his body against it. I stepped up on the lid, feeling it flex slightly with my weight. Inside the tank I sensed the slightest movement as the body of lethal liquid shifted, and prayed that the lid would hold. I reached up with both arms. There was a crash as the little door to the workshop shattered, the scrape of the chair as it slid across the stone floor. I stretched up for the bars of the grid, standing on tiptoe, and my fingers closed around the cold metal bars. It rocked and the chains that supported it jangled.

There was a sudden *flick-flick* of strip lights from inside the workshop and brightness flooded in under the tank-room door. Footsteps crossed the workshop and stopped. I stayed still. If I moved, the rattling chains would give me away. I held my breath.

Vlad was searching around, stopping now and then. I heard him walk around the saw-bench, stop, circle a stack of furniture. He moved to the foot of the ladder that led to the hayloft. 'Are you up here, girlfriend?' he laughed, his voice mocking, and began to climb.

Now was my chance. Gritting my teeth, I locked my fingers around the bars and jumped up, pulling with both arms, straining to heave my body on to the flat surface of the swaying grid. It was like trying to climb on to a floating raft. Not easy.

The grid swung backwards with me clinging to it and for a dreadful moment I lost my grip. I cried out before I could stop myself, scrabbling at the bars with my fingers and clung on, hanging by my arms as it swung back and came to rest once more above the lid of the tank. Footsteps pounded down the ladder and a few moments later the light in the tank room flicked on.

Vlad stood in the doorway. His eye was horrible, bulging, a blood-red golf ball, the bruised lid barely able to close over it. But it was the other eye, the ice-blue, cold stare glittering with hate, that was more frightening to look at. He surveyed me, hanging by my arms, toes barely touching the lid of the tank, and he laughed.

'You know what is in tank, girlfriend?' he asked casually.

I didn't answer. The bars of the grid were digging into my palms and my arms were starting to tremble. I could feel sweat running through my hair.

'So, where is it?' he asked, advancing towards me. 'You get it from the old man, eh? You get him to leave you everything. Clever girl!'

'I don't know what you're talking about,' I told him. 'What is it you want?'

He picked up a long piece of wood from a pile of odd timbers resting against the wall and banged the side of the tank with it. The metal clanged and the liquid sloshed inside. 'Pretty full in there.' He inspected the controls of the machinery and grabbed a lever. 'What does this do?' He pulled it towards him and I felt the grid move. I let out a scream. Suddenly my feet left the lid, and I was dangling helplessly, the grid biting into my fingers.

'Ah!' he nodded. 'This one makes you go up and down.' He let go of the lever, leaving me dangling. The muscles in my arms were tearing, screaming for relief.

'If you kill me,' I cried desperately, 'you'll never find out where it is.' I didn't know what 'it' was but I reckoned bluffing was my only chance.

He gave an evil grin. 'I don't need to kill you, girlfriend. I dangle your toes in that tank and you'll soon be begging to tell me where it is.' He surveyed the controls again, studying the two remaining levers, touching first one, then the other, as if trying to choose between them. I watched him, transfixed. Then he smiled up at me. 'Now, which one opens lid?'

He reached for the middle lever and I screamed. 'Not that one!'

He raised his eyebrows questioningly. 'No?' he asked, grinning, and pulled it towards him.

I knew he would.

He wasn't prepared for the sideways movement of the grid, the sudden swing out. I'd operated the machinery and

I was. I braced myself and clung on, bending my knees and then thrusting my legs out straight. Both boots kicked him in the throat before he realised I was swinging in his direction. He sprawled backwards, hitting the floor. I let go of the grid, dropping to the concrete, yelling at the impact as I landed on my feet.

Vlad staggered upright, laughing, breathless. 'Now I think I kill you,' he said, and the knife flickered in his hand.

He was between me and the door. I dodged right, but so did he. I began to back away, behind the tank, but I was backing my way into a corner and searched around desperately for a weapon. There was nothing except the coiled hose mounted on the wall. I grabbed the end of it and pulled, unreeling a length of hose whilst with the other hand I struggled with the tap. It was stiff and unyielding, squeaking as it began to turn.

Vlad laughed when he saw what I was trying to do. 'You drown me now, girlfriend?' he asked. 'I don't think so.'

I aimed the nozzle. Nothing happened. There was no powerful jet of water to force him back, not even a trickle. He came towards me, blade gripped in his fist. Suddenly the hose became a writhing snake as the pressure surged through it. I struggled to keep hold as water gushed from its mouth, but the hose was a sinuous, coiling monster, drenching us both in an avalanche of cold water. Cursing, Vlad dodged back. Water poured across the concrete floor and I almost lost my grip. I grappled with the hose, gripping it hard, about three feet from its end, my wet hands choking off the water. As Vlad surged towards me, blade in hand, I swung it like a club and the brass nozzle caught the side of his head. It knocked him out cold.

I stared at him lying on the floor, the water gushing over his body. When I was sure he wasn't moving, I went to the wall and turned off the tap. The outpouring dwindled to a trickle and then stopped.

I stood, breathless, dripping, wondering if I'd killed him. I wasn't prepared to get close enough to find out if he was faking it. I kicked him savagely in the balls. Not a flicker. Slamming the door of the tank room behind me, I ran through into the workshop and dragged a heavy Victorian dressing table across the floor, shoving it against the tank-room door. It took me a while. It was a hefty beast and I had to stop twice to draw breath. I didn't think Vlad would be coming round any time soon, but when he did, I wanted to be bloody sure he couldn't break out.

The little wooden door into the workshop was broken, hanging off its hinge. There was nothing I could do to secure it. I had to move fast. I stumbled down the lane until Maisie's cottage came into view. My keys were still in the gutter where I dropped them. I selected Maisie's key and let myself into her cottage. She was still fast asleep. Jacko jumped down from his windowsill, and for once, failed to bark, but circled my ankles, wagging his tail. I patted him briefly. 'Thanks for trying,' I whispered.

As I picked up Maisie's phone and dialled, she began to stir.

'Police,' I said breathlessly as a voice asked which service I required. I was dripping wet, trembling, and my right hand was bruised and puffing up nicely. Maisie, finally waking, noticed none of this. She just blinked at me as I stood there, holding her phone.

'You still 'ere?' she said.

CHAPTER THIRTY-SEVEN

'It's like *The Adventures of Robin Hood*,' Ricky said, grinning. 'I wish I could have seen you, swinging about on that thing like Errol Flynn on a chandelier.'

'Errol who?' I asked sweetly. He poked out his tongue.

'How's your hand, Juno?' Morris asked anxiously. 'Is it still hurting?'

'A bit,' I admitted. It was barely twenty-four hours since my encounter with Vlad and actually, it was hurting a lot. I gazed ruefully at my bruised knuckles, at the bandage around my palm.

'Well, I think you deserve a medal,' he told me proudly, slicing up a Victoria sponge.

'That'll be the day! I don't think Inspector Ford approves of me at all.' He had interviewed me that morning, asking me lots of questions. I'd told him all about my fight with Vlad. I didn't mention the kick in the balls.

I had no idea what it was that Vlad thought I had in my possession, but I wasn't sure the inspector believed me. 'And poor old Paul!' I went on. 'When he got back from Truro, there were police crawling all over his place, his door's broken, half his workshop had been flooded and he got a ticking off for not securing it properly.'

Morris tutted and passed me a slice of cake. 'Well, the police would never have caught Vlad without you.'

'Except his name's not Vlad,' I pointed out. 'It's Sergei Zhotahyehski,' although he would always be Vlad to me.

'And do we know what he was after?' Ricky asked, taking out a cigarette and tapping the end of it on the breakfast table.

'No. He's being very tight-lipped about that. In fact, according to Inspector Ford, he's being tight-lipped about everything, refuses to co-operate.'

'What I don't understand,' Morris began, stirring his tea thoughtfully, 'is how this Vlad found out that Nick had left the shop to you. I mean, that's why he came after you, wasn't it? Because he thought Nick had left you something that he thought belonged to him?'

Ricky paused in the act of lighting his fag. 'Oh, come on! You've only got to hang around Ashburton for five minutes and you can pick up gossip on just about anybody.'

'Especially if they've been talking to either of you two,' I put in sweetly.

'But he hasn't been hanging around Ashburton, has he?' Morris objected. 'Not recently.'

'Well, not that we know about,' I conceded.

'Of course!' Ricky clicked his fingers, hit by sudden inspiration. 'Bert Evans told him.' He turned to me. 'Didn't Vlad say to you yesterday that Bert didn't have this thing he was after, whatever it was?'

Morris's brow crumpled in confusion. 'But why would Bert Evans tell Vlad Juno had it?'

'To save his rotten skin, of course!' Ricky puffed out smoke and dropped his lighter on the table. 'Keep up, *Maurice*! If two blokes kept stuffing your head in a fish pond, wouldn't you tell them that someone else had got it?'

'There's just one problem with this theory,' I pointed out, before the conversation could get more heated. 'Bert was already dead, long before the reading of the will.'

Ricky's shoulders sagged as his theory imploded. 'So he was,' he muttered.

For a moment the three of us were silent.

'He might have seen it, though,' Morris glanced from Ricky to me. 'The will, I mean. Nick might have showed it to him. Somebody had to witness it, didn't they?'

'That's true,' Ricky admitted, nodding thoughtfully.

'I suppose Mr Young would know who witnessed it,' I said. 'I could ring him.'

Ricky jerked his head at the clock on the wall. 'I don't think you're going to find a solicitor in his office at half past five on a Friday afternoon.'

'Probably not,' I sighed, but I tried his number anyway. The answer machine kicked in after several rings and I put the receiver down. There was no point in leaving a message. It would have to wait until Monday. I drained my teacup.

'Thanks for the tea,' I said, getting up. 'I'm going home.'

'Well, at least you can stop worrying about Vlad,' Morris told me, catching my arm. 'He's safely under lock and key.'

'You look after yourself, Juno,' Ricky advised, pointing his fag hand at me. 'Take it easy over the weekend.'

'I will,' I promised, lying. Bloody ceilings do not paint themselves.

Stupidly, I decided to get the job out of the way that evening. I was already knackered, but I argued to myself that a quick coat of paint with the roller couldn't take long and if that didn't do the trick it could dry overnight, ready for another coat next morning.

But when I let myself inside the shop, I found it was raining. There was a large shiny puddle on the floor, a steady dripping from above. I looked up and swore. The stain on the ceiling was a dirty cloud; I held my hand out beneath it and felt a cold droplet of water on my palm. I stared as another droplet bounced off my skin.

The nearest bucket was upstairs, so I fetched a willow-pattern chamber pot from the corner and placed it on the floor to catch the drips. Then I ran up the stairs into the living room.

I surveyed the bare floorboards, looking for one I could lift. I found one right in the middle of the floor, in front of the fireplace, lifted it out with a bit of heaving and groaning, slid it aside and knelt, peered down into the black void beneath.

I grabbed the torch from my bag and shone the light into the hole. I didn't know what little critters might be lurking underneath the floorboards and I didn't fancy putting my hand down into the dark. The beam illuminated dust, cobwebs and a rusty-looking pipe. I lay on the floor and reached my arm through the hole, stretching to the ends of my fingers. The pipe was wet to the touch. I knelt up, aimed the torch and took another look. Judging from the dark patch on the surface beneath the pipe, it had been dripping for some time, slowly. It probably wasn't going to cause a major flood. Not until around two in the morning, I thought grimly, when the ceiling of the shop collapses. I was going to need a plumber and I didn't know where I was going to get one. When the sun goes down in Ashburton, all tradesmen, like little furry animals, go home to hide in their holes. I scowled into the space beneath the floorboards. I would have to leave it till the morning and hope for the best.

Before I replaced the floorboard I shone the torch around once more. The light picked up a dark lump, lying a foot or so from where the pipe was dripping. I couldn't make out what it was. It seemed to be some sort of package. I put the torch down, lay on the floor and began groping around, my arm at full stretch. I couldn't reach it. Unless I could find something to help me get at it, I'd have to prise up another floorboard. I suddenly thought of Nick's walking stick and fetched it from the hall.

Lying down once more I slid it beneath the floorboards, holding it by the rubber ferrule using the curved handle to hook the package towards me. After a few moments' fishing, the handle made contact. I heard something slide beneath the floor. 'Gotcha!' I cried triumphantly and pulled the stick back towards me.

I thrust my arm back down into the darkness and came up with the package. It was about the size of a paperback book, wrapped in black plastic and bound with tape. I sat up and wiped the dust off the surface. Inside I felt a flickering of excitement.

Too impatient to unwrap the tape, I pulled the plastic apart with my fingers, making a hole wide enough to ease the contents out. I was holding something bundled up in soft woollen cloth which turned out to be an old grey scarf. As I unrolled it, I found I was holding my breath. Was this what Vlad had been after? Or perhaps, at last, I had found those damn rings.

But the object I unwrapped was too shallow to be a ring-box. It was less than an inch deep, made of some glossy, dark wood and hinged down both long edges. I realised I was looking at the back of it and turned it over. It didn't open like a book. The lid was divided into two halves, held together in the middle by an ornate clasp of yellow metal. I gently pressed the clasp and the two halves of the lid opened. I stared. An exquisite, sloe-eyed Madonna stared back at me, her radiant face framed by a blue veil, her virgin head haloed in gold.

I gazed in stunned silence. I was holding an icon, very beautiful, very old. For a moment I wondered if it was Greek. Then I smiled, as I realised with absolute certainty, that it wasn't Greek. It was Russian.

CHAPTER THIRTY-EIGHT

On the phone Inspector Ford sounded almost impressed. 'Well done, Miss Browne, on finding the icon. It has some interesting prints on it . . .'

I'd taken the icon over to police headquarters the next morning, feeling very proud of myself, but the inspector hadn't been around and I'd been forced to hand it over to Cruella DeVille. Her little mini-mouth had worked furiously.

'Oh?' I said, trying not to sound excited. I let Bill make himself comfy on my lap.

'The prints of Albert Evans, for one,' the inspector went on, 'and also your friend Sergei Zhotahyehski. In fact, Mr Zhotahyehski has been occupying my attention for most of the weekend.' The inspector sounded weary.

'He's confessed?'

'Well, he's talking,' he went on with a sigh. 'He knows he's going to serve time and he's concerned about where he's going to serve it. He thinks if he co-operates, it might give him some bargaining power. We've enough evidence from the abandoned car to convict him of the murder of Ilya Pietrov, and he's admitted to his part in the manslaughter of Albert Evans.'

'Manslaughter?' I echoed.

'He claims Evans died of a heart attack, they didn't intend to kill him, only meant to frighten him.'

'And Nick?' I persisted. 'Has he confessed to killing Nick?' I felt impatient, wanted to wind the inspector up, like a watch that was ticking too slowly.

He paused before he spoke again. 'Let me tell you what we've been able to piece together so far. It seems that the icon first came into the possession of Mr Evans, possibly legally, although it had certainly been stolen from Mother Russia at some point, maybe as far back as the Second World War. Anyway, knowing that Nick had Russian connections, Evans offered him a share of the proceeds if he could sell it for him.'

'And he tried to sell it to Vlad? I mean . . . Zhotahyehski?'

'Shall we agree to call him Vlad?' the inspector suggested. 'It's a lot easier. According to Vlad, Nick approached his employer, who we have to assume is a Russian national, probably living in London.'

'Don't we . . . I mean, you . . . know who he is?'

'I could make an educated guess, several, but Vlad is not prepared to identify him; he's worried about who might be able to get at him while he's inside. But whoever this man is, he was very interested in the icon and sent Vlad down to look at it and report back. But Nick wasn't prepared to let him see it without a down payment. He claimed there were others interested in the icon and Vlad's boss would have to secure his own interest with cash, as it were. This is not uncommon practice, apparently. The down payment was agreed and handed over, photographs of the object taken, our friend returns to London and reports back to his boss who puts in an offer for the icon, which is accepted. All fine so far.'

'But?' I asked as the inspector drew breath.

'But then it seems that Nickolai and Evans claimed they'd had a better offer from someone else. We have no idea whether this was true or just an attempt to force the price up, but Vlad's boss was furious. The price had been agreed and he was not prepared to get into a bidding war. He sends Vlad and Pietrov down to Ashburton to get his deposit back . . . and I think this is where you enter the story, Miss Browne.'

'That's why they were going to beat Nick up that day,' I said quickly, 'because he didn't want to return the money.' I could just imagine Nick trying to tell Vlad and Igor that the deposit was non-returnable. 'And that must have been the money that Nick gave back to them in front of Paul. But if the money was returned, surely that should have been the end of it?'

'Ah, but Vlad had lost face,' the inspector went on. 'The whole episode was viewed as a humiliation, a failure. The only way he thought he could salvage his reputation in the eyes of his boss was to obtain the icon himself, preferably without having to pay for it.'

'But at this point, surely, he wouldn't know if Nick still had the icon,' I objected, 'or if he'd sold it to one of these other interested parties.'

'He claims that since their encounter with you, Nick had contacted him, privately, told him the icon was still in his possession, and he was still prepared to do a deal.'

I couldn't believe it. I could have wept at Nick's stupidity, at his greed. For the first time I felt he deserved what had happened to him. But when it came to money, Nick just couldn't help himself. 'The old fool!' I cried bitterly.

'Quite!' the inspector agreed. 'Unfortunately for Vlad, his boss decides to send him back to Russia on some dirty work, so he has to wait his time.'

'And then he came back and murdered Nick,' I completed for him.

The inspector gave one of his long, thoughtful pauses. 'Well, now that is the really interesting thing, Miss Browne. Vlad claims that when he and Pietrov returned to England, several weeks later, and came down to Ashburton, Mr Nickolai was already dead and his property was a crime scene.'

'But that can't be true,' I protested.

'They decided this was not a good place for them to hang around and they . . . er . . . persuaded Mr Evans that it was in his best interest to break in to Nick's and steal the icon for them.'

'But he didn't.'

'No, he didn't, and that's how he ended up floating among the fishes.'

I chewed this over for a few moments. 'But we know that Vlad killed Nick.'

'There's no forensic evidence connecting him to the murder scene.'

'But his prints are on the icon,' I insisted.

'So are yours.'

'Meaning what?' I asked.

'Meaning that, like you, he once handled the icon. So what? It's circumstantial. It doesn't put him in Nick's living room on the night of the murder.'

'Shit,' I muttered angrily.

'My sentiments exactly, Miss Browne.'

When I thought about it later, what the inspector had said made perfect sense. If Vlad and Igor had murdered Nick, why wouldn't they have searched for the icon at the time, torn the place apart, as they had Albert Evans's place? The police had also been able to confirm that Vlad and Igor had flown back from Russia on the date he said they had, after Nick was murdered.

So that was that. For so long I had nurtured my conviction that Vlad was Nick's murderer, that now I was at a loss. I didn't know what to think. Richard and Helena were the only other suspects and they both had alibis. I felt a terrible sense of anti-climax. And my mood wasn't improved by the fact that I had attracted the attention of the local press. A spotty youth from the *Dartmoor Gazette* had been round to the house to interview me about my exploits in Paul's workshop. I made it to the front page of the next edition: LOCAL HEROINE CATCHES KILLER. It was so bloody embarrassing. I'd caught a killer all right. He just turned out to be the wrong killer.

Needless to say, Ricky and Morris found all this hilarious. Unfortunately, I was booked to work for them the day after the newspaper came out, so there was no dodging the issue, if you'll forgive the pun. After an hour or so of remorseless roasting, I threatened to go home if they didn't shut up. They promised to be good and I sorted out returned *School for Scandal* costumes, unmolested, until it was time for tea, when the subject of the murder inevitably came up again.

'Did you ring your solicitor,' Morris called out to me, as I dumped an armful of frilly shirts that needed washing into the laundry hamper, 'about who witnessed Nick's will?'

'Yes,' I replied, sitting at the breakfast-room table. 'I tried Mr Young again on Monday. It was Albert Evans.' It seemed quite weird to me, that Bert Evans had known that Nick had left his property to me long before I did. Perhaps that's why he had wanted to find out about me from the Smithsons: he fancied pursuing a woman of property. The thought made my stomach churn.

'And who else, did he say?' Morris asked, passing a cup to me. 'There must have been a second witness.'

'Ooh. I hadn't thought of that!' Ricky declared, excited. 'You mean another suspect, someone who didn't like the fact that Nick was leaving the place to Juno.'

'Well, who was it?' Morris asked, a biscuit poised halfway to his parted lips.

I beckoned them closer, lowering my voice to a confidential whisper. 'Mr Singh.'

They both burst out laughing.

'Can you imagine it?' Ricky demanded. 'Nick, ringing

poor old Mr Singh, asking him to pop round with a packet of biscuits and would he mind witnessing a signature while he was there.'

I could. Poor, dear Mr Singh. I imagined that is exactly what happened.

'Well, there you are,' Ricky went on, eyes dancing. 'Mr Singh, he's obviously the murderer.'

'Never!'

'When you have eliminated the impossible,' Ricky quoted Conan Doyle, miming having a pipe to his mouth, 'whatever remains, however improbable, must be the—'

'Oh, belt up, Sherlock!' Morris advised him.

'Mr Young did mention one thing I found interesting.'

They both looked at me.

'He told me the date the will was witnessed. I worked out it wasn't long after Richard had last visited his father, which made me wonder if they had quarrelled. If that was the reason Nick had decided to alter his will in my favour.'

'Which made you wonder if Richard killed his father,' Ricky said. 'Except that Richard has an alibi.'

'I know,' I sighed. 'I just keep going round in circles.'

'You know, darling,' Morris took my hand, his round face serious. 'Sometimes we never find out the answer to things. Sometimes we just have to accept that we'll never know.'

Ricky nodded in agreement. 'You should stop tormenting yourself about the murder, sweetheart. Let it go.'

Morris patted my hand anxiously. 'He's right, Juno. You know he's right. Let it go.'

I knew they were right, of course, just as I knew it was impossible.

I told Paul as much that evening, when I took him out for a pint. It was the least I could do after the havoc I had wrought in his workshop. He listened, but he agreed with Morris and Ricky. 'Nick had been in business a long time. You can bet that Vlad wasn't the first person he tried to cross. Over the years there may well have been other people who had a motive.'

'For killing him?'

'For quarrelling with him, perhaps,' he said unhappily. 'All I'm saying is, I expect he's made enemies.'

'Well, there's Verbena Clarke . . .' I began.

Paul groaned and put his face in his hands. He gave a muffled cry. 'Juno, please, enough!' After a moment he looked up and gave me that dark, direct stare of his. 'Enough. OK?'

'I'm sorry.'

There was a moment's silence then he changed the subject. 'I got on with draining the tank today,' he told me, leaning back in his chair and picking up his pint, 'and I've put new locks on the doors. I don't want anyone else poking around in there. When I think what might have happened to you' – he flashed a grin – 'famous local heroine.'

'Oh, don't you start!'

'Actually,' he added, serious again, 'now that I've done that, I won't be coming down here again.' He looked down into his glass for a moment, hesitated. 'This is my last visit.'

I hope I didn't look as shocked as I felt. My head told me this was a good thing, but my heart still sank. 'So this is goodbye, then?'

'I've still got some work to finish and some packing up to do, but in a day or two I'll be heading back.'

'I see.'

'We'll get together again,' he promised, 'before I go.'

I summoned up a smile and held up my glass in a toast. 'Here's to Henry Wain and Arnold Bishop,' I said. 'May they never run out of Darkolene.'

CHAPTER THIRTY-NINE

I finally got around to clearing out Nick's kitchen. I'd been putting it off. I didn't know what to do about Nick's flat, knew I wouldn't feel comfortable living there, so I'd put off giving the place the thorough blitzing that it needed. I should have done it weeks ago. Now, it had become part-therapy, a way to get through the weekend, and part-penance. I scraped away at the tiny, frosted-up icebox of Nick's ancient fridge, which had been chugging away valiantly for months because no one – not me, nor the solicitor, nor Nick's family – had thought to turn it off. The contents, in various stages of decomposition, were resting in black plastic refuse sacks en route to the bins outside, along with well-wrapped bottles of various nasty substances cleared from the cupboard under the sink.

After hacking away with a knife, struggling to unjam a packet of fish fingers set solidly into a block of ice, I decided to abandon the fridge, let it get on by itself, leave the ice to defrost naturally, although the polar ice caps would probably have melted before it released its hold on the fish fingers. I spread newspaper on the floor to sop up any wetness and turned my attention to the kitchen cupboards. They were packed with such a weight of tins, jars and bottles I was surprised they'd stayed up on the walls.

Nick had either never heard of sell-by dates or he collected antique food. I threw away ancient tins of tongue and corned beef, packets of dried peas and pudding rice, jars of old pickle and congealing Worcester sauce, bottles of Camp Coffee Essence and tins of mustard powder. I junked the lot.

As I cleared my way to the back of the shelves, I came across an enamelled tin flour shaker and a sugar sifter, old-fashioned kitchenware, quite collectable now. I decided to ditch the contents, wash them out, and put them downstairs with the stock for the shop. As I reached for them, the fridge let drop a chunk of ice, startling me into dropping the flour shaker. The lid came off in a puff of flour and the contents spilt across the worktop. I let out a suitable expletive and grabbed a dustpan and brush.

As I was about to sweep the whole lot up, I saw something glisten. There were lumpy objects in the white powder. I picked one up, blew on it, and a little red eye shone up at me through a dusty coating. I picked up the two other objects, holding them in my cupped palm, and ran them under the kitchen tap, washing the flour away. They came up shining. Three rings: a cluster of tiny diamonds, a row of three rubies, and a square cut emerald.

'You sly old toad,' I said aloud to Nick.

I had to admit it was a good hiding place. I would take the greatest of pleasure in returning the rings to Mrs Helena Burgoyne. I tried them on. I quite liked the emerald, but it was made for daintier fingers than mine and so, reluctantly, I dried the rings off, wrapped them carefully in kitchen paper and stowed them in my bag.

'I don't suppose there are any more in here,' I said aloud to myself as I rattled the sugar sifter. I heard the clunk of a solid object. There was more in there than sugar.

Unlike the flour shaker, the lid of the sugar sifter was stiff, rusty around the rim, and I had to bang it on the edge of the table to force it off. It was about two-thirds full of sugar. As I tipped out the sparkly little granules I could see the top of a pale, rounded object breaking through the surface. I poured the sugar down the sink, watching the object in the bottom slowly reveal itself. Then I slid it out from the sifter and held it in my hand.

I knew now why Old Nick had been murdered. And I knew who had killed him. A cold feeling of dread settled inside me. I knew who the murderer was now. And I wished I didn't.

CHAPTER FORTY

'Hello, Juno.' He looked up from his work, surprised. 'I wasn't expecting to see you today.'

'Hello, Paul. I wasn't sure if you'd be here.'

He had an upturned table on the workbench and was delicately gluing a sliver of thin veneer on to one of its legs. He smiled. 'Just let me get a clamp fixed on this and I'll be with you.'

I watched him silently, watched his strong, clever hands. Why didn't I just walk out again, forget the weighty little object in my pocket, walk away, let Paul go back to his family unchallenged, live his life? Because Nick, lying dead on the rug, wouldn't let me.

He wiped his hands down over the hips of his jeans. 'There.' He looked at me, brows raised enquiringly, and his smile faded. 'Are you all right?'

I swallowed. There was a lump in my throat, hard as a boiled sweet. 'I think this belongs to you.' I pulled the object from my pocket and placed it on my palm, holding my arm outstretched. For a moment his eyes widened, lighting up with relief and joy. He reached out as if to take it and then faltered. His eyes looked into mine, all the colour in his face draining away. Even his lips looked bloodless. He knew that I knew.

'Where did you find it?' he asked softly.

'In the kitchen,' I answered. 'He'd hidden it in a sugar sifter.' We both gazed at the object on my palm: the figure of an old Japanese man, exquisitely carved, carrying a staff, his bald head slightly elongated, a rippling beard flowing down his front. 'Ivory netsuke, eighteenth century, signed by Shugetsu,' I said slowly, 'current value at auction between fifty and fifty-five thousand pounds. I've been doing my homework.' I smiled sadly. 'I never asked you if you'd found the one you lost. It is yours, isn't it?'

Paul couldn't take his eyes off the little figure, but he nodded, slowly picking it up in his fingers and holding it reverently. 'I bought it in an auction, in a box of bric-a-brac.' He shook his head with the irony of it. 'The whole box cost me five pounds. I only bought it because there were a few brass drawer handles that I thought might be useful. I didn't realise this was in there, left the box lying around for months before I sorted through it.'

'Did you realise how valuable it was?' I asked.

'Not then. I hadn't heard of Shugetsu, I thought it might be worth about fifty quid.'

'So what happened?'

He rolled the netsuke gently in his palm. It was a few moments before he spoke. 'I'd told Nick about my netsuke collection. He said he'd like to see it – just out of interest. So, one evening I took them around to him, all wrapped in tissue paper, in my shoebox. We spent an hour or so, looking at them, studying the marks, trying to put a value on each one. I don't remember what he said about this one, he certainly didn't say it was valuable. But when I got home, I found it was missing.'

He smiled bitterly. 'I thought I'd left it behind accidentally. Next time I saw Nick I asked him for it, but he swore we'd put all the netsuke back in the box. I described it to him and . . .' He stopped, drew a long, deep breath, and when he went on his voice had hardened. 'He gave me that look, you know . . . that sly, sideways glance he used to give when he was trying to get one over on you, when he thought he was being clever . . .' He glanced up at me, as if to check that I understood what he meant. I nodded. I knew exactly. 'He denied ever having seen it,' he went on, 'said that I had never shown it to him.' He was gripping the netsuke fiercely in his fist, his voice growing more strident. 'Or perhaps, he said, I *did* show it to him, but he couldn't remember it. Perhaps I had lost it on the way home . . .' He opened his fingers and gazed at the netsuke again. 'And I knew then, from the way he looked at me, that he had taken it, that he was going to keep it. I knew it must be valuable.'

'What did you do?'

'Searched the Internet, found some oriental specialists and contacted them. They got very excited when I described it. They all wanted to see it.' He sighed deep within his chest, his shoulders slumping, and leant heavily on the edge of the workbench. 'Even then, I gave Nick the benefit of the doubt, I searched for it, turned the caravan upside down—'

'I remember,' I interrupted him. 'I came, that day, with the dogs.'

'So you did.' He smiled sadly, remembering. 'But all the time I knew he had it.' His voice trailed off, staring, not seeing me, but gazing into some private hell of his own.

'What happened?' I prompted, bringing him back to the present.

He gazed at me blankly for a moment before he spoke again. 'I went back to see him, told him I knew that he'd kept it, demanded it back. I told him we'd say no more about it if he just returned it to me. He kept on protesting his innocence. He almost convinced me. I left. I was going to Nottingham that night to see Carrie. I drove all the way to Bristol, but I couldn't forget it. That money would make such a difference to our lives. I couldn't just leave it. But . . . if I hadn't needed to stop at the services, to get petrol, perhaps I . . . I don't think I'd have turned around . . . driven back . . .' He trailed off into silence.

I sat next to him on the edge of the workbench. 'You drove back?' I kept my voice very quiet, very calm, trying to coax the story out of him. 'And you saw him again?'

'Oh, yes. It was late by then. I'm surprised he let me in, but he did. Only this time, I lost my temper. I told him I wouldn't be cheated, I threatened him with the police. He laughed. He said I couldn't prove it. I couldn't prove that the netsuke was mine . . .' He shook his head. 'If there had been any doubt in my mind up until that moment, now I knew he had stolen it deliberately. And he dismissed me . . . in that way he had . . . as if I was nothing, and turned his back on me. We were standing by the fireplace and—Dear God, Juno,' he stared at me wretchedly. 'I don't even remember picking up the damn candlestick.'

I took his hand and squeezed it. 'Go on.'

'I must have hit him. Just once, that's all it took. I stood there, clutching the thing, looking down at him, at his skull. I knew that I'd killed him. It was as if I'd turned to stone, standing there watching blood spreading out from under his head. Then I took a step back, before it could touch my shoes.

'I backed out of the room, tried to remember what I'd touched. There was a handkerchief in my pocket. I began rubbing at the bannister, and at the door and then I realised, I'd been in the flat so often that my fingerprints couldn't incriminate me, unless . . .'

'Unless they were covered in blood.' I had to look away.

'I had to be careful.' He smiled, almost innocently. 'I used the handkerchief on the lock when I opened the front door and let myself out. It wasn't till later I realised I'd no memory of the door clicking closed behind me. But it was too late then. I couldn't risk going back.'

'What happened to the candlestick?'

'There was a plastic bag in the car and I wrapped it up. I had some wipes in the glove compartment. I wiped my hands before I touched the keys, the steering wheel. I didn't want any traces of blood in the car. I stopped at one of the motorway service stations . . . I don't remember which one . . . took the bag into the toilet. It was late by then, there was no one around. I washed it in the sink and rubbed it dry, polished off all the prints and wrapped it up again. Later on in the journey, I stopped on a bridge over a stream and threw the thing in the water, watched it sink. There'd been a pile-up on the motorway, long queues, people had been stuck in traffic for hours. It had all cleared by the time I drove back, but it meant that no one questioned why it took me so long to reach Nottingham . . . not Carrie, not the police. Carrie had been in bed for hours. As soon as I got in, I stripped off and put everything I'd been wearing in the washing machine. Next day I ditched my shoes.' He let out his breath in a deep sigh. 'I didn't mean to kill him.'

A tear glistened on his cheek and I wiped it gently with my thumb. 'Of course you didn't.' I was near to tears myself.

'I'm sorry that you had to find him like that,' he whispered hoarsely. 'It must have been terrible for you.'

I didn't say anything. Just at that moment I couldn't speak.

'I never wanted to hurt you, Juno,' he went on. 'That morning in Nick's kitchen . . . I was coming to see you in the shop. You were just leaving – you went to get your paint, remember? I called out but you didn't hear me. I saw you didn't lock the door. So I let myself in and had a good look around. I thought it was my last chance to find the netsuke. Then, you came back . . .'

'You decided to creep up on me with ether.'

'I panicked.' He hung his head like a guilty schoolboy. 'I'm sorry.'

'It's all right,' I enfolded him in a hug and we clung together for a while. He made no noise but I could feel sobs racking his body, deep in his chest. I let him sob. After a few minutes, he found his voice again.

'It feels good,' he whispered into my hair, 'to have told someone at last.'

'Do you want me to come with you, to the police?' I asked.

He drew back his head to look at me. In his dark eyes there was a blank stare of utter incomprehension. 'What?' he asked softly.

'We can talk to Inspector Ford.'

He gazed at me, mystified. 'I can't go to prison. Juno . . . surely you understand? Carrie . . . the children . . .'

'Carrie will stand by you, Paul, if you go to the police now . . . tell them what you told me . . .' He was shaking his head and I took his face between my hands. 'Look at me,' I urged him softly. 'You didn't mean to kill him.'

He shook his head. 'I can't take the risk.'

'Paul, you must!'

He gazed at me sorrowfully for a moment, then raised a hand to caress my cheek. 'I'm sorry, Juno, I can't.' For a moment his lips touched mine. 'I'm sorry, Juno,' he whispered devoutly, 'so, so sorry.'

And it was only then, as he slid his strong, clever fingers down to my neck, that I realised what he was going to do. 'Paul!' I breathed. But it was too late. He choked the word off short. His hands were around my throat.

'I'm sorry,' he repeated miserably. 'I'm sorry.'

He was crushing my windpipe. I clutched at his wrists, trying to break his hold but his hands fitted round my neck like an iron collar. I couldn't breathe. He was forcing me back, my body bent over the workbench. I swept my arms out in a wide arc around me, groping for any tools that might be lying there. Nothing. I drew my arms in between his and chopped at the inside of his elbows. His hold faltered for a moment, but didn't weaken. I scrabbled at his fingers, trying to tear them away, but he only closed them around my throat more tightly.

'I'm sorry,' he murmured, over and over.

I didn't care how fucking sorry he was. My brain was bursting, a dazzling fog of bright, pinprick lights crowding in from the edges of my vision. I let go of his fingers, stopped struggling, let my whole body go limp. His own momentum brought him forward, his face closer to mine. I thrust my hand between his arms, my fingers hooked like claws and jabbed him hard in the eye. He released me with a curse and I collapsed against the workbench, gasping for breath.

I staggered round behind it, my chest heaving, and grabbed a long, pointed chisel from the rack on the wall. As he lunged for me again, I thrust it towards him and he sprang back. He hesitated.

'Paul...' I croaked. It was an effort to speak, my strangled voice raw and husky. 'Listen to me. This ... won't ... do any good ...'

But he wasn't listening, his attention fixed on the chisel in my hand. He tried to grab my wrist, but I dodged away, backing round in a circle, desperate to reach the door. He lunged again and I jumped back, crashing into a stack of furniture piled up behind me. It rocked and tottered and a stool came clattering down, hitting me on the wrist. I dropped the chisel with a yelp of pain and it went skittering across the floor, stopping by Paul's feet. As he stooped to pick it up, I grabbed the stool by one of its legs and hurled it at him. He sidestepped just in time, and began to advance on me, the chisel gripped in one fist. His dark eyes seemed almost unfocussed, as if he was sleepwalking. I backed away, and trod on something small and hard: the netsuke.

Keeping my eyes on Paul's, I bent to scoop it up. I held it out to him, my hand shaking. 'You want this?' I demanded roughly.

He faltered, as if he'd woken from his dream.

I closed my fist over it. 'No wonder you were so keen to help me clear out Nick's clothes,' I accused him bitterly, 'it gave you a chance to search his pockets.'

I flung the netsuke from me, hard. It bounced into a corner, and as he spun around to see where it had landed, I gave the stack of furniture behind me an almighty shove, ramming it hard with my shoulder. A heavy wooden chair tumbled from the top. It fell across Paul's shoulders, breaking across his back, and knocked him to the floor.

I didn't look behind me to see if he was getting up. I fled, through the open door, heading for the field: quickest way home. I raced across the grass, over the uneven ground, tripping on sudden small bumps and clumps of weeds and thistles. I skidded on mud, fell heavily, landing on all fours. As I hauled myself up, my heart hammering, I dared a glance behind me. I could see Paul, on his feet, framed in the doorway of the workshop, watching me. I ran on, the air scorching my lungs as I laboured for breath.

A thick hedge formed a solid barrier before me. I waded through a mass of stinging nettles that grew waist-high, and scrambled through the bushes of the ancient hedgerow, squeezing between branches, breaking off twigs that caught at my hair and tearing my hands on brambles.

As I squeezed through it, I could see the rough ground at the end of my lane. If I could reach the house, find someone, anyone, before Paul caught up with me, I would be safe. I glimpsed a sudden flash of acid yellow. Someone was moving around at the end of the lane. I stumbled onward. I could see clearly then. Two council workmen in high-visibility jackets and hard hats were finally clearing away the fly-tipping from the space where I parked the van, lobbing an abandoned mattress into the back of a flatbed truck. I waved to attract their attention. I managed a hoarse yell. 'Hey!' I waved both arms.

One of them saw me and nudged his mate. As I limped towards them, too breathless for another shout, arms waving, they grinned at one another, then waved back.

CHAPTER FORTY-ONE

'So, Monday, then?' Morris asked, as the waiter poured tea into dainty china cups from an ornate silver pot. A plate of finger sandwiches lay on the immaculate white tablecloth. Taylor's serves a serious afternoon tea.

'*Old Nick's* finally opens its doors,' I confirmed. 'It's official.'

'Official, is it?' Ricky frowned at Morris. 'I don't remember receiving an invitation to cut the ribbon, do you?'

'We'll be there, Juno,' Morris promised, beaming. 'We'll bring champagne.'

'That'll be lovely! Adam and Kate are supplying trays of canapés,' I told him. 'First fifty customers get free nosh.'

'Fifty!' Ricky scoffed. 'Blimey! You're optimistic.'

'I don't know if anyone's going to buy anything, but I

expect there will be a few people coming to have a look at the shop. I caught one of the antiques dealers from the bazaar peering in the window yesterday, trying to see inside.' I knew Tom and Vicky Smithson were coming along for the grand opening. I'd even invited Inspector Ford. He'd given me a severe reprimand after Paul's arrest, for putting myself in danger instead of taking the netsuke straight to him, but I reckoned by now he'd forgiven me. After all, I had caught Nick's murderer.

As for Paul, he had not pursued me. When the police cars arrived at the barn, he was waiting there for them. He confessed to everything, which should count in his favour.

'All of Ashburton's gagging to see what you've done with the place,' Ricky admitted, 'after the murder and all.'

Morris tutted. 'There's no need to bring that up,' he told him primly. He held out a plate of finger sandwiches. 'I must say, the new shopfront looks splendid.'

It should do. In the end, I'd borrowed money from my cousin Brian in South Korea for a newly painted frontage and a complete internal overhaul, as well as the hanging sign, *Old Nick's*, above the front door. Inside, the shop has been divided into units for rent, so I can get several sellers under one roof. Sophie Child and Pat of Honeysuckle Farm have a unit with a shop window each, where they can create and display their wares. Sophie has already set up her easels with beautiful watercolours. But EB's portrait sits in pride of place, a sign proclaiming *Pet Portraits* displayed underneath.

She and Pat have both been evicted from the market, Pat because the coven at the Art and Antiques Bazaar managed to persuade the management that she didn't belong there; Sophie because she could no longer afford the rent. She won't pay me any rent either, neither will Pat, an exchange for taking it in turns to open and close the shop each day and making sure one of them is always there to deal with customers. It also means that I can still carry on with my regular clients, fitting my time in the shop around being a Domestic Goddess. It should work.

Pat has taken the idea of the Victorian panorama I showed her and made it her own. The interiors she has painted are not of Victorian sitting rooms, but of blue skies, green fields and little farmhouses. Her peg dolls are dressed as shepherds with woolly beards. She's knitted hedges, she's knitted gorgeous little sheep, she's even knitted trees. More than one of the craft shops in Ashburton have offered to sell them for her, but these country panoramas remain exclusive to *Old Nick's*.

I've taken over the old storeroom for my stuff: small items of furniture, collectables and bric-a-brac. The other units are currently empty, but I've had enquiries, so I'm hopeful. I'm never going to make any money out of *Old Nick's*, but I'll be happy if, eventually, it doesn't cost me any.

I haven't decided what to do about the flat yet, but I certainly won't be living in it, not in the foreseeable, anyway. I'd been quietly thinking about this and realised that Morris was still proffering the plate of sandwiches. 'Are you all right, Juno?' he asked.

'Oh, yes thanks.' I selected a salmon and cucumber.

'No,' he said, peering at me anxiously over his specs. 'I mean, are you really all right, after everything that's happened?'

I smiled at him. 'Yes, I'm fine.'

Over the weeks, I have stopped feeling conflicted about Paul. In the beginning I felt as if I had betrayed him horribly. But now I feel I can't forgive him. Not because he lost control of his temper and killed poor Nick, not even because he tried to save himself by attempting to murder me, but because of all those solicitous phone calls after Nick's death, those anxious visits to check up on how I was. They reveal a cold, calculating side of his nature, somehow more shocking to me than the exploding heat of his violence.

I sent the rings I found back to Richard. He passed them on to Helena Burgoyne, from whom I have heard not a single word of thanks. Possibly, the humble pie has choked her.

Mrs Verbena Clarke had her interview with the police, which cleared the air. She then had the grace to apologise to me and to offer me back my job. I savoured the moment, but decided to decline.

'So, now you're in antiques do you think you can stay out of trouble?' Ricky demanded. 'Keep away from murder and other sorts of mayhem?'

'I shouldn't think so,' I replied, eyeing up the delicacies on the three-tier cake stand that the waiter had just placed on our table. I selected a raspberry meringue, wincing as I bit through the fragile shell. 'After all,' I continued, when I could speak, 'it was getting into antiques that got me into trouble in the first place.'

Ricky sighed and rolled an eye at me. 'Well, promise us you'll try.'

They both looked at me, expectantly. Morris giggled.

I nodded at them, licking the corner of my mouth for escaping cream. 'I'll do my best,' I said.

ACKNOWLEDGEMENTS

I want to thank Martin, whose support for me never falters, Mum and Rose for their encouragement, and Di Davies, my dear book-swopping buddy, and her sister, Jill – their praise for my early efforts encouraged me to keep trying. I'd like to thank the team at Allison & Busby and my wonderful agent, Teresa Chris, for her skill, guidance and her extraordinary patience.

DON'T MISS THE NEXT
JUNO BROWNE MYSTERY

DEAD
ON
DARTMOOR
STEPHANIE AUSTIN

Juno Browne has a lot on her plate. When her trusty van goes up in flames and nearly cooks a dog it is just the disaster she can't afford – literally. Fortunately, she meets the owner of a large family estate, James Westershall, who invites Juno and her friends from Old Nick's to bring their goods for sale at an upcoming garden fete.

But what should have been a joyous occasion is soon mired in tragedy when one of Juno's friends is discovered dead in nearby woodland ...

STEPHANIE AUSTIN graduated from Bristol University with a degree in English and Education and has enjoyed a varied career as an artist, astrologer, and trader in antiques and crafts. More respectable professions include teaching and working for Devon Schools Library Service. When not writing, she is involved in local amateur theatre as an actor and director. She lives on the English Riviera in Devon where she attempts to be a competent gardener and cook.

stephanieaustin.co.uk